Masters

and Voodoo Death

TWO CLASSIC ADVENTURES OF

by Walter B. Gibson
writing as Maxwell Grant

plus The Shadow Challenged
a radio classic by Jerry Devine

with new historical essays by
Will Murray and Anthony Tollin

SANCTUM BOOKS

This Sanctum Books edition is an unabridged republication of the text and illustrations of two stories from *The Shadow Magazine,* as originally published by Street & Smith Publications, Inc., N.Y.: *Masters of Death* from the May 15, 1940 issue and *Voodoo Death* from the June 1944 issue. "The Shadow Challenged" was broadcast January 19, 1941 on *The Shadow* radio series.These stories are works of their time. Consequently, the text is reprinted intact in its original historical form, including occasional out-of-date ethnic and cultural stereotyping. Typographical errors have been tacitly corrected in this edition.

International Standard Book Number:
978-1-60877-146-2

First printing: May 2014

Series editor/publisher: Anthony Tollin
anthonytollin@shadowsanctum.com

Consulting editor: Will Murray

Copy editor: Joseph Wrzos

Cover restoration: Michael Piper

The editors gratefully acknowledge the assistance of Daniel Zimmer, editor of *Illustration* (www.illustration-magazine.com) and Matthew Schoonover in the preparation of this volume.

Published by Sanctum Books
P.O. Box 761474, San Antonio, TX 78245-1474

Visit The Shadow at www.shadowsanctum.com.

Volume 85

CONTENTS

Thrilling Tales and Features

Cover art by Graves Gladney
Back cover art by Graves Gladney and Modest Stein
Interior illustrations by Edd Cartier and Paul Orban

CHAPTER I
THE SILVER COFFIN

THE Oriental Museum looked like a morgue, inside as well as out. The customs inspector noted the resemblance as he ascended the darkened steps of the squatty brick building and entered the gloomy entrance hall.

Great bronze idols glowered from their pedestals; fearful things, that looked like the creations of a Chinese pipe dream. There were effigies of mandarins in silken robes; of Japanese shoguns clad in half-armor.

Dummy figures, those. Still, the customs man didn't like them. The Chinese mandarins did not matter much; their glass eyes were stern, but their colorful garments made the effigies look harmless. The shoguns, though, were a different matter. Each figure had a mailed fist, gripping an ornamental *tsuba*, or handle of a long, curved sword.

The customs man gave those warriors a suspicious look, as he quickened his step. When he reached a side passage, he let his face relax. He had reached the open door of the curator's office; he was beyond the danger zone.

Not that the curator's office was a modern place. Contrarily, its antiquated furnishings made it something of an exhibit in itself. Perched upon old-fashioned desks and rickety wooden filing cabinets were Hindu idols of various sorts and sizes; from Buddhas with glimmering gems in their foreheads, to three-headed Siva statues that set the visitor blinking.

As for the curator, Isaac Newboldt, he looked like something that the room had hatched. He was a middle-aged man, but he seemed to carry the weight of centuries upon his stooped shoulders, while his roundish face was as solemn as those of the surrounding idols.

At least Newboldt wasn't stuffed. He arose slowly from his chair, extended his hand in methodical fashion. Surveying the customs man in owlish fashion, Newboldt nodded and gave a dryish greeting:

"Good evening, Mr. Matthew."

The customs inspector was pleased. He had been here before, but that was five years ago, when he had held a subordinate position. It was nice to know that Newboldt remembered him. It struck Matthew, however, that the curator was the sort who would remember everything.

"The truck ought to be here by this time," announced Matthew, producing a batch of papers. "If you'll look over that casket with me, Mr. Newboldt, I think we'll be able to clear it without much bother."

"A mummy case is not a casket," corrected Newboldt, as he took the papers. "Such misnomers cause difficulties, Mr. Matthew."

The customs inspector gave a hopeless shrug.

"We'd have labeled it a mummy case," he said, "coming in from Egypt, the way it did. Only, it's made of metal—"

"Of metal?"

"Yes. That's why we tagged it as a casket. Maybe you'd better take a look at the thing, Mr. Newboldt."

The curator's interest was aroused. His stride became rapid as he led the way from the office, through a gallery of mummy cases that loomed like sentinels in the dark, to a stairway illuminated by a single light. The steps went downward; at the bottom was an open door, where a drab man in grayish uniform stood waiting.

The drab man was Kent, the museum's chief attendant. He announced that the truckmen were waiting in the alley. At Newboldt's order, Kent stepped outside. There were scraping sounds from the truck; six men appeared, lugging a burden that was actually too heavy for them.

Though the long box was crated, Newboldt could see the dull glimmer of metal, which he took for lead. Kent was pointing the truckmen up to the mummy room, but Newboldt shook his head.

"Have them put it in the little exhibit room," ordered the curator. "The one we are reserving for the Polynesian collection. This is not a mummy case, Kent."

Then, turning to Matthew, Newboldt added:

"There is a mystery about this matter. I expected a mummy case, not a leaden casket."

"Maybe the mummy case is inside," suggested Matthew. "The lead box may be a"—he hesitated—"a sar—a sar what do you call the thing?"

"A sarcophagus," replied Newboldt. "No. An Egyptian sarcophagus would be made of stone, not of metal. Besides, this casket is longer than would be required for a mummy case, and too flat to contain one. It may be a wrong shipment."

"Then I'd better keep the truck around?"

"Yes," decided Newboldt. "Until we have solved the riddle."

THEY went up to the little exhibit room, where the truckers had set the crated casket on the floor. Newboldt ordered the men to remove the crating, which they did, except for the cross braces on which the casket rested.

All the while, Newboldt's eyes were becoming wider, rounder. Plucking at Matthew's sleeve, the curator whispered tensely:

"Send them downstairs."

The customs man dismissed the truckers, telling them to wait out back. Turning about, he saw Newboldt making the rounds of the room, testing its barred windows. Newboldt's actions seemed jerky; his hand trembled as he pointed to the door; his voice was hoarse as he ordered Kent to stand guard there.

Then, stepping to the low, flattish casket, Newboldt shakily drew a handkerchief from his pocket and massaged the dark metal. Under the rubbing process, the metal took on a luster which brought a surprised exclamation from Matthew:

"Silver!"

"Silver," repeated Newboldt. Then, in an awed tone: "A silver coffin. The coffin of Temujin!"

Matthew didn't understand.

"Temujin!" repeated Newboldt, with a shudder. "The true name of Genghis Khan, the great war lord of the Middle Ages, who ruled half the world with his powerful Mongol hordes!"

The reference struck home to Matthew.

"Say!" exclaimed the customs inspector. "If you're right, Mr. Newboldt, this thing should have come from Asia, not from Africa."

"It *did* come from Asia," insisted Newboldt, as he polished the decorations on the coffin's lid. "Observe these engraved designs; the curve of the coffin's lid. They match the description given by the Belgian missionaries who saw the coffin of Temujin in the region of the Ordos Desert, half a century ago."

Matthew had stooped to examine fastenings of the coffin, which reminded him of a low, elongated trunk. The casket appeared to be hermetically sealed.

"What's in the thing?" he inquired. "Bones?"

"The remains of Temujin," replied Newboldt, solemnly. "Whether they are bones, or ashes, inspection alone can prove. When last reported, the coffin of Temujin was on the move. Its guardians, descendants of Mongols appointed centuries ago, were anxious to prevent its capture by invading Japanese."

"Why so?"

"Because they feared that ownership of the coffin would allow the Japanese to appoint a puppet emperor for Mongolia; a man who could claim himself the legitimate successor of Temujin, the Kha Khan, or great ruler—"

Newboldt stopped himself with a gulp. His stooped frame shivered. Gripping Matthew by the shoulders, he drew the astonished fellow to the door, where Kent stepped back, inspired with the same alarm.

"This is beyond us, Matthew!" voiced Newboldt, in tremolo. "I have just remembered that there *is* a man who calls himself Kha Khan. His name is Shiwan Khan; he seeks to rule all the world."

"You mean he must have grabbed this coffin?" queried Matthew. "That he shipped it here by way of Egypt?"

"Undoubtedly," quavered Newboldt. "From his hidden kingdom of Xanadu, somewhere in Sinkiang, which is west of Mongolia, and therefore on the route that the coffin must have followed."

Pointing to the door of the exhibit room, Newboldt told Kent to lock it and bring the keys to the office. Gripping Matthew by the arm, Newboldt started for the office, dragging the customs inspector along.

As they went through the mummy room, the curator was babbling incoherently; tiled walls echoed his words, voicing them back, as though the dried tongues of long-dead mummies were joining in the chatter.

By the time they reached the office, Matthew was convinced that Newboldt was crazy, but he wasn't sure enough of his own sanity to do anything about it. Then, Newboldt was fumbling with the telephone dial, saying that if he could reach a man named Lamont Cranston, everything would be all right. Matthew decided to let him go ahead.

Both had forgotten Kent.

BACK at the door of the little exhibit room, the drab attendant was locking up, as Newboldt had ordered. But Kent's hand was shaky. He couldn't find the right key on his ring.

Kent remembered Shiwan Khan, the being who styled himself the Golden Master, and the recollection was not a pleasing one. To Kent, the name of Shiwan Khan meant murder.

He was thinking of Shiwan Khan in terms of the silver coffin; and had Kent been gifted with the ability to see through a door, he would have known that his thought was more than coincidence.

Inside the barred room there was motion. Slowly, the lid of the sealed coffin had begun to rise!

Up from the strange casket came a gold-clad form. Above the collar of the decorated robe was a saffron face, the exact hue of the room lights. From its wide forehead the face tapered to a pointed chin. Green, catlike eyes glistened from beneath thin, wide-curved brows. Long mustaches drooped beside lips that were streaks of brown. A dab of beard gave Shiwan Khan an expression that was truly satanic.

Green eyes stared at the glowing lights; their fixed gaze took on a gleam. Brown lips dripped the single word:

"Return!"

Though subdued, the word was heard. It came, like a mental command, to Kent just as the attendant was inserting the right key in the lock. Kent did not connect the thought with Shiwan Khan. The drab man merely recalled that he had forgotten to turn off the lights.

Opening the door, Kent stepped in to press the light switch. Centered on that action, he didn't look toward the silver coffin until he had started pressure. In the last, brief instant that the light remained, Kent saw the gold robed figure, met the demoniac gaze of Shiwan Khan.

Then, darkness, as Kent's hand finished its downward tug. Similarly, the hand of Shiwan Khan had completed a fling from the end of its gold-sleeved arm. Kent did not shriek; his lips were petrified. The sound that disturbed the darkness was a *whir*.

Silence hovered; it ended with the thud of a body that sagged heavily against the door, shutting it with a sharp *click*. Through the totally thickened blackness came the fiendish chortle of the Golden Master, Shiwan Khan!

CHAPTER II
HAND OF DEATH

ISAAC NEWBOLDT was pacing his office, wringing his hands with every stride. The curator was in such a dither that he gave Matthew the jitters. Observing a half-filled whiskey bottle on a corner shelf, the customs man reached for it.

"What you need is a drink," he told Newboldt. Then, when the curator made no reply: "Mind if

In the last brief instant that the light remained, Kent met the demonic gaze of Shiwan Khan.

I take one?"

Newboldt offered no objection. Matthew found a glass and poured himself a brace. Hearing the trickle, Newboldt stopped his pacing, made a wild grab for bottle and glass.

"Don't drink that!" he exclaimed. "It's a sample of an Egyptian embalming fluid!"

Then, as Matthew recoiled, Newboldt calmed himself and stated:

"We shall not have long to wait. I have called the Cobalt Club and talked with Police Commissioner Weston. He is a friend of Lamont Cranston, and is sure that he can find him."

Matthew couldn't understand why Cranston was so important in the matter. The curator explained that Cranston was a worldwide traveler, acquainted with the mystic doctrines of Tibet. Shiwan Khan was also a master of those doctrines; it took a mind like Cranston's to fathom the deep purposes that marked the moves of Shiwan Khan.

In putting it that way, Newboldt was trying to control his own alarm. Actually, the museum curator knew full well the menace of Shiwan Khan. Three times, the Golden Master had come to America, each visit the result of insidious plans for conquest. Unquestionably, Shiwan Khan still termed himself invincible, though on each of those occasions, he had met with defeat.*

Shiwan Khan had met his match in The Shadow.

To Newboldt, The Shadow was quite as much a mystery as Shiwan Khan. A black-cloaked fighter, who seemed to dwell in night itself, The Shadow had uncanny abilities that enabled him to combat the most formidable of foes. In some fashion—Newboldt did not know just how—Lamont Cranston was linked to The Shadow.

It had never occurred to Newboldt that the guise of Cranston might be one that The Shadow, himself, had adopted.

Such an idea would be ridiculous; as preposterous as supposing that Shiwan Khan had come to America again, in the silver coffin of Temujin!

Dismissing such absurd notions, Newboldt tried to impress Matthew with his new-gained calm.

"The police commissioner is sending a man here from headquarters," Newboldt recalled. "Why don't you go out front and meet him, Mr. Matthew? His name is Cardona—Inspector Cardona."

Welcoming the opportunity to leave the spooky confines of the museum, Matthew went out. Seating himself at the desk, Newboldt rested his roundish face in both hands.

Staring at the door, he began to wonder what was keeping Kent. He couldn't go to find out, because there would be no one in the office to answer the telephone, should the commissioner call. His nervousness returning, Newboldt decided to call the Cobalt Club again.

He had just dialed the number and was getting a response, when an odd thing occurred. Newboldt felt a shock that seemed to pass from the hand that touched the dial, to the other, which was holding the receiver. He managed to jerk his hand from the dial; the sharpness ended, but a numbing sensation remained.

Then, as the curator was managing to gasp a hello, something clanked on the desk beside him. While he was listening to a voice on the telephone, he heard another tone, close to his numbed elbow. It was Kent's voice:

"You wanted the keys. Here they are, sir."

"Very well, Kent," began Newboldt. Then, speaking into the telephone: "No, no. I wasn't asking for a Mr. Kent. I would like to speak to Commissioner Weston... Gone out, you say?... Did he leave a message?"

Learning that the commissioner had left no message, Newboldt inquired if he had gone out with Mr. Cranston. The man at the Cobalt Club did not know. Ending the phone call, Newboldt looked at his numbed right hand, found that the fingers worked.

"That was odd, Kent," he said. "I received a shock from the telephone. It reminds me of—"

HALTING, the curator looked for Kent. The attendant was gone. Picking up the keys, Newboldt jingled them, while his face showed a troubled expression.

He had been about to say that the shock had reminded him of an Oriental superstition relating to *naljorpas*, strange mystics from Tibet, who had the reputed power of numbing persons who approached them.

But Newboldt wasn't in a mood to talk about *naljorpas*; they were too closely associated with Shiwan Khan who had all their powers, and more.

In fact, Newboldt was becoming quite nervous. He decided that he needed fresh air, like Matthew. Figuring that Weston had started for the museum, Newboldt saw no reason to wait further for a call. He left the office and went out through the entrance hall. As he neared the front steps, a man sprang in to meet him.

It was Matthew. The customs officer gave a gratified gulp at seeing Newboldt. He made a worried gesture toward an armored dummy representing a Japanese shogun.

"I thought one of those guys was creeping up on me," confided Matthew. "Only about five minutes

---

*Note: See *The Golden Master* in *The Shadow* Volume 75 and *Shiwan Khan Returns* and *The Invincible Shiwan Khan* in *The Shadow* Volume 80.

ago, when I was sitting on the steps, I got to feeling woozy—"

The screech of brakes interrupted. A police car had pulled up outside; from it came a stocky man, whose face was swarthy and stolid of expression. Newboldt introduced Inspector Joe Cardona, of the New York police.

As soon as the curator began to talk in terms of Shiwan Khan, Cardona beckoned for a pair of detectives to come from the police car.

As they started toward the locked exhibit room, Cardona voiced what he considered to be a profound opinion.

"If this has got anything to do with Shiwan Khan," he declared grimly, "it's poison! Bones or ashes, I'm going to see what's inside that silver coffin."

"We'd better wait for Mr. Cranston," advised Newboldt. "We had trouble here once before, Inspector."

Cardona remembered the time. He had made a mistake, on that occasion, when he unwarily handled a dagger called a *phurba*, which had a mystic spell attached to it. But that was different from a silver coffin that had been shipped, tightly shut and crated, from Egypt or somewhere farther.

When Newboldt unlocked the door and turned on the light, Cardona saw the closed coffin in the center of the little room. He approached and examined it; then nodded, when Newboldt repeated his advice to wait. The curator went out to call Kent; they could hear his shouts echo through the museum. Finally, Newboldt returned.

"I can't find Kent anywhere," he declared, soberly. "He didn't go out by the front door, and the truckmen have not seen him. He came to my office and left the keys there; but I can't imagine where he went afterward."

A sudden idea struck Cardona. He pointed to the silver coffin.

"Do you think Kent took a look inside this thing?" inquired Joe. "You left him here, didn't you?"

"Yes," admitted Newboldt, "but I told him to lock up, and he did so."

"But he could have opened the coffin first," argued the police inspector. "You didn't say anything to the contrary."

"No. I didn't. But I don't see why Kent—"

Cardona didn't listen to the rest of it. His hunch was that Kent had opened the coffin and found something valuable inside. If Kent had slipped away with all that he could carry, there still would be come contents left. The way to test that double theory was to look in the coffin.

Stationing a detective at each end of the long silver box, Cardona took a central position in front and gripped two curved ornamentations that served as handles for the lid. As he started to lift, he found that the lid wasn't clamped at all, which bore out his opinion that Kent had pried it loose.

The lid started heavily at first, but under Cardona's increasing heave it shifted back on its crude hinges. Straining upward, Joe twisted his hands to push from beneath. Half crouched, he lunged into a hard shove. As he did, the room echoed to a chorus of yells.

BOTH Newboldt and Matthew had seen something; so had the detectives at the ends of the coffin. But none of those four had time to act. The person who came to Cardona's immediate rescue was a new arrival, a tall man with hawkish, masklike face, who had just entered the exhibit room.

The newcomer was Lamont Cranston; though noted for his leisurely manner, on this occasion he showed a remarkable speed.

As the big lid lurched backward on its hinges, Cranston reached Cardona with a single bound, caught him around the neck and yanked his stocky form sideways.

The two were twisting as the lid jounced wide; from within the coffin came a flashing blade of steel that whizzed straight for the spot where Cardona's head had been!

Skimming the police inspector's dropping shoulder, the knife *zimmed* between Newboldt and Matthew. It reached the wall beside the door and buried itself there with a quiver.

As the whole blade seemed to whine, another man side-stepped from the doorway, to get as far from the weapon as possible. The second arrival was Commissioner Weston.

The knife thrust wasn't all. With the skimming blade came a hand that flung across the edge of the coffin. Its gray-sleeved arm seemed to relax with the hurl it made. The man's gray figure dropped back into the coffin, as though seeking refuge after making the murderous thrust.

Yanking their guns, the detectives aimed for the coiling assassin. But the shots they fired were wide. Disentangled from Cardona, Cranston made a grab for the first detective and hauled his gun hand to one side. Seeing his friend's move, Commissioner Weston grabbed the second detective and disturbed his fire, also.

It was Cardona who came to his feet and pointed a revolver into the coffin, yelling for the thwarted killer to surrender. Newboldt, drawing close, recognized the gray uniform and exclaimed:

"It's Kent!"

The huddled attendant did not stir. Reaching into the coffin, Cardona clamped him by the shoulder and tried to haul him out. He could scarcely budge the fellow, until Cranston rendered assistance. Together, they pulled Kent upward, over the front edge of the coffin, where the form slipped from their grasp and logged weightily upon the floor.

Amazed eyes saw the reason for Kent's inert behavior. The front of the attendant's uniform was covered with blood from a gory wound. Kent had taken a knife thrust previously; a stroke exactly like the one that Cardona had escaped through Cranston's intervention!

Strange, indeed, was the murderous attack that had come from within the silver coffin: so strange, as to be incredible, even to those who had witnessed it.

For the hand of death that came with that stroke belonged not to a living man but to a dead one!

CHAPTER III
THE VOICE FROM THE PAST

KEEN eyes were viewing the figure on the floor: burning eyes that peered from the maskish face of Cranston. The Shadow was analyzing the motive behind strange crimes: the death of Kent; the mysterious attack upon Cardona.

He heard the excited voices of those about him. Newboldt was telling how Kent had placed the keys upon his desk; instead of clearing the mystery, the testimony added to it. Then came a calm, even-toned interruption: the voice of Cranston, spoken by The Shadow.

"You saw Kent when he left those keys?"

"Why, no," admitted Newboldt. "I was speaking on the telephone at the time. But I heard Kent—"

"It was not Kent," interposed The Shadow, calmly. "It was Shiwan Khan."

Newboldt's roundish face became a starchy-white. Remembering the numbing sensation, he realized the truth of Cranston's statement. It was plain that Shiwan Khan had murdered Kent, and taken crafty measures to cover up the crime. Matthew was putting in excited testimony; he was sure that someone must have gone past him on the outer steps.

It was Weston who asked a pointed question.

"Why should Shiwan Khan attempt to cover up?" demanded the commissioner. "He has always been ruthless in his crimes."

"He is quite as ruthless as ever," assured The Shadow. "Shiwan Khan merely preferred to keep his presence in America unknown."

Stepping to the wall beside the door, The Shadow pulled the knife from the woodwork. In Cranston's leisurely style, he moved back to the coffin. Cardona was looking at the interior, puzzled because he found it entirely empty. There wasn't a visible explanation of how the knife had been hurled.

Cardona saw the knife, as Cranston weighed it. It was a long, light-bladed dagger, with an ornamental handle of carved ivory.

"A *phurba*," he heard Cranston say. "An enchanted blade, that can supposedly fling itself from any hand—even a dead one. But we can find a simpler explanation."

He thrust the knife blade between the hinged lid and the solid back of the coffin. It remained there, clamped in the narrow space. Carefully, The Shadow drew the heavy lid upward and forward, finally bringing it down to a shut position.

Pointing to the back, he showed that the tip of the dagger projected through the crack. Moving everyone from in front of the coffin, The Shadow told Cardona to grip one end of the cover, while he took the other.

Then, while the witnesses watched tensely, The Shadow spoke the quiet order:

"Lift."

Together he and Cardona flung the lid up and over, as Cardona had handled it before: but on this occasion, no one was lifting from the front. As the lid went wide, its *clang* muffled the *click* of the pliable knife blade.

Levered by the great weight of the shifting lid, the deadly dagger snapped from its place; flashing, it flipped point first and drove like a winged arrow, straight for the opposite wall. Its *whir* was evidence of the speed that the levering poundage gave it; so was the force with which the *phurba* burrowed into the wall.

Cardona pointed to Kent's body.

"Then Shiwan Khan must have got him first!" exclaimed the police inspector. "He propped him in the coffin, and stuck the knife between the hinges. So it would look like Kent had chucked the knife—"

"Exactly," took up The Shadow as Cardona paused. "In addition, Shiwan Khan expected gunshots to riddle Kent's body, making death appear to be a matter of bullets."

"Then Shiwan Khan must have guessed a lot," decided Cardona. "He must have figured that I would bring a couple of men with me."

"Not necessarily, Inspector," was Cranston's calm reply. "He expected you to fire the shots, when *I* opened the coffin."

WITH those words, The Shadow cleared the remnants of the mystery. Once before, Shiwan Khan had tried to dispose of Lamont Cranston by means of a dagger thrust.

Weston and Newboldt were recalling the occasion; they agreed that Cranston, with his knowledge of Tibetan ways, was a natural obstacle to the plans of Shiwan Khan.

In itself, that was a logical reason. But there was a deeper motive behind the attempted murder that Shiwan Khan had tried to pin upon a dead man. Shiwan Khan knew the real identity of the person who posed as Lamont Cranston.

The death thrust had been meant for The Shadow!

Such a detail was one that The Shadow naturally reserved for himself. Still playing the part of Cranston, he questioned Newboldt about the silver coffin; learned how it had been shipped to New York instead of an expected mummy case.

Obviously, the substitution must have taken place in Egypt, a few weeks before. But it was quite as apparent that Shiwan Khan had used the coffin as a unique means of not only entering the United States, but reaching the man whose life he wanted. As a means of entry, the system had worked; as a scheme of assassination, it had failed.

Kent's death, incidental to the general purpose, had neither enabled Shiwan Khan to conceal his own presence in New York, nor to eliminate his superfoe, The Shadow. It was simply another heinous deed to be charged to the evil account of the monstrous Golden Master.

But the return of Shiwan Khan was, in itself, a menace. It meant that every law enforcement agency in the country would have to prepare for a relentless struggle.

Behind the inflexible calm of Cranston, The Shadow listened to Weston's summary of former outrages committed by Shiwan Khan. The Golden Master had made three previous trips to America.

First, he had sought planes and munitions for use in worldwide conquest. Again, he had tried to acquire important inventions, useful in warfare. Thwarted in such efforts, Shiwan Khan had influenced persons of genius to return with him to Xanadu, there to form the nucleus of a future race that would dominate the world through sheer intelligence.

Until tonight, nothing had been heard of Shiwan Khan since that experiment began. But The Shadow had evidence to prove that the great dream of the future had not worked as the Golden Master anticipated. Again in America, Shiwan Khan was to be dreaded more than ever before. His arrival could mean but one thing: that he meant this visit to be permanent.

The attempt upon The Shadow's life was proof. In seeking to rid the scene of his archfoe, Shiwan Khan unquestionably had schemes of supercrime within his golden sleeve. Knowing The Shadow to be crime's greatest enemy, Shiwan Khan had tried to pave the way to sure success by means of one swift opening stroke.

A distant jangle mingled with The Shadow's reflections. It was the telephone bell in Newboldt's office. The curator heard it and interrupted Weston's discourse. Supposing that the call might be for him, the commissioner followed the curator to the office.

After answering the phone, Newboldt gave a relieved sigh.

"It's only the Cobalt Club calling," he said. "Not for you, commissioner. For Mr. Cranston."

Looking about, Weston saw that Cranston had followed them to the office. Receiving the telephone, The Shadow spoke a calm "Hello." His face was imperturbable, as though he really believed that the call came from the Cobalt Club.

But the voice that The Shadow heard was not that of a club attendant. In answering the call, Newboldt had been tricked again by the same person who had imitated Kent's style of speech. The voice that spoke to The Shadow was brittle, icy, yet with the clear ring of a bell, that made each word an indelible utterance.

It was a voice from the past, brought to the present; a tone delivering an ultimatum that concerned the future.

The voice of Shiwan Khan!

CHAPTER IV
THE SHADOW DEPARTS

LIKE the notes of a discordant chime, Shiwan Khan's chortle trickled across the wire. Recognizing Cranston's voice, the Golden Master knew that his second murder had failed; he was free, therefore, to make his presence known.

For the evil brain of Shiwan Khan had a skill at analysis that sometimes matched The Shadow's. The Golden Master could picture much that had occurred since his departure from the Oriental Museum; enough, certainly, to know that The Shadow had laid bare the game.

This call was his test.

Had Cranston failed to answer, Shiwan Khan would have let the call go for what it seemed to be: a mere message from the Cobalt Club. The thing would have passed forgotten in the horror over Cranston's death.

But Cranston's response was an opportunity for Shiwan Khan to deliver another stroke; one which offered The Shadow life instead of death, yet which was in keeping with the scheming ways of the Golden Master.

There was no anger in the tone; emotions were absent from the makeup of Shiwan Khan. He called himself the Unfathomable, and could live up to the title. From his chortle, it seemed that he relished the fact that The Shadow was still alive.

"Good evening, Mr. Cranston," spoke Shiwan Khan. His emphasis upon the name "Cranston" carried a trace of sarcasm. "I am informed that you contemplate a journey from New York."

"Yes," replied The Shadow, calmly. "I was leaving—"

"For the new city airport at North Beach," inserted Shiwan Khan. "To take passage for Miami, then on the airliner *Panamania*, bound for Buenos Aires."

"Quite so!" agreed The Shadow, in Cranston's style. "But before I left—"

"You called at the Cobalt Club," chimed Shiwan Khan. "Your friend the police commissioner told you of an urgent matter at the Oriental Museum. So you went there, instead."

The Shadow offered no response. He had learned the fact he sought; namely, that Shiwan Khan's spy service had preceded the Golden Master to New York.

Though the conversation, so far, seemed to favor Shiwan Khan, The Shadow had actually baited the Golden Master into certain statements. His present policy was to let Shiwan Khan resume the talk.

"There is still time to catch the plane," spoke the voice across the wire. "If you take the journey, I guarantee that it will be a safe one. But I advise against an immediate return, as you intended. A long sojourn would be preferable. The climate in Buenos Aires could prove very healthful"—there was a pause; in concluding, the voice showed its first trace of venom—"for The Shadow!"

Shiwan Khan waited, to hear the effect of his ultimatum. He had proven conclusively that he held The Shadow surrounded by a ring of deadly spies, who had refrained from murderous thrusts only until Shiwan Khan attempted his own.

His offer of life was bona fide. When Shiwan Khan made a guarantee, he kept it; in a sense, that policy was the basis of the Golden Master's power. Again, by his very guarantee, Shiwan Khan had given The Shadow vital information; perhaps purposely.

It was evident that Shiwan Khan considered the temporary elimination of The Shadow to be quite as satisfactory as a permanent obliteration. It followed, therefore, that Shiwan Khan was planning crime of such swift and comprehensive nature that his position would be impregnable by the time The Shadow had completed a "long sojourn" in foreign parts.

Once away, The Shadow could never return in safety. Such was the burden of the ultimatum. To pretend acceptance of the terms, without abiding by them, would seemingly be useless on The Shadow's part, for Shiwan Khan would have spies on board the plane, to make sure that his defeated foe went south.

But Shiwan Khan's informants, competent though they were, had failed to learn why Lamont Cranston had booked passage on the plane. Inasmuch as they were due for a surprise anyway, it was quite as well to include Shiwan Khan.

"I shall leave here shortly," declared The Shadow. "Until I reach the airport—"

"My guarantee is good," interposed Shiwan Khan, "until the plane departs. If you are on board, the proviso will continue. If you are not—"

THE tone ended in a melodious chuckle that struck a final off-key note, which made the whole tone bitter. There was a sharp *click*, as a telephone receiver settled on its hook. Hanging up at his end, The Shadow turned to the police commissioner.

"Rather unusual," said The Shadow, "to hear from a man so soon after he has tried to murder you."

"What!" exclaimed Weston. "Do you mean that you were talking to Shiwan Khan?"

"I was. As a result, I shall take the journey that I intended."

"But we may want you here, Cranston—"

"So may Shiwan Khan. No, Commissioner, you won't need me. I have given you all the information that I can."

The Shadow was strolling toward the door, when Weston overtook him.

"But where can I reach you?" queried the commissioner, anxiously. "In South America?"

"No," returned The Shadow. "I think my next address will be Tibet."

"Tibet! Surely, Cranston, you are joking? Why, Shiwan Khan is from Tibet."

"Precisely. That is why I prefer Tibet. Anywhere that Shiwan Khan is from is the best place for me to be."

Glancing at his watch as he strolled from the museum, The Shadow noted that he had fifteen minutes to spare in his trip to North Beach. Considering that there were double motives in everything that Shiwan Khan did, The Shadow decided that the Golden Master had made the call just a quarter hour too early.

Not by Shiwan Khan's own calculations. The Golden Master had wanted to impress The Shadow with the fact that there was ample time.

So there was; but The Shadow figured it in reverse. He preferred his present locality during the extra minute of grace that Shiwan Khan had so generously allowed him. It might prove better to be here, than at the airport.

Still, considering the probable proximity of the Golden Master's spies, it would be wise to play a subtle game. In approaching a limousine parked outside the museum, The Shadow showed no quickening of pace. He played the part of Cranston to perfection, even pausing to light a cigarette before entering the big car.

Such action, plus the slowness with which the limousine pulled away, was sufficient proof that Lamont Cranston was going directly to his destination. So he was, but he had chosen an earlier and closer objective than the North Beach airport.

Within the distance of a single block, The Shadow dropped his guise of Cranston. Working with smooth speed, he pulled out a drawer beneath the limousine's rear seat. From it he brought garments of black: cloak, slouch hat, and gloves. The cloak went over his shoulders, the hat settled on his head. He was putting on the thin gloves, when the limousine turned a corner.

A rear door opened, toward the curb. With a deft twirl, The Shadow was gone from the moving limousine, closing the door as he completed his twist. Passing a parked taxicab, he spoke a whispered command to the drowsy driver, who immediately wakened from his fake sleep and remained alert.

It was The Shadow's own cab, its driver one of his secret agents.

Shiwan Khan's stress upon The Shadow's need for a long journey could well be camouflage to cover another point. Bound for the airport, The Shadow would be traveling away from the Oriental Museum, a place where things still could happen. With Shiwan Khan, things that *could* happen, generally *did* happen.

THEY happened quicker than ever on this occasion. The Shadow had scarcely reached the alleyway behind the museum, when he heard yells from the truckmen stationed there. They were husky, those fellows, but they looked puny as they scattered from the lighted doorway, for they were being shoved about by giants twice their size.

The Shadow knew the identity of those attackers. They were Mongols, huge fighters of the Ordos tribes, who served as guardians for the coffin of Temujin. They must have come to America on the freighter that carried the silver coffin.

The laugh that The Shadow delivered brought the Mongols full about. Perhaps they had been warned against the eerie mirth that they heard for the first time; for it wasn't in their nature to flee as quickly as they did. As The Shadow's guns, drawn from the coat beneath his cloak, began to serve out bullets, the Mongols used the shelter of the truck to reach the rear door of the museum.

By the time The Shadow reached that doorway, the Mongols were on the floor above. Following them, The Shadow saw six gigantic figures surge into the mummy room, where two detectives were retreating, firing wild shots. Cardona had gone out front, leaving his men to guard the silver coffin; but their flight was no discredit.

Mere bulk alone made the Mongols look like superhuman creatures out of a prehistoric past. Bullets didn't seem to bother them, as they flourished knives that were bigger than short swords. The detectives were diving to the corners of the gloomy room, hurling mummy cases into the path of the giant raiders.

Matthew came running in from the entrance hall swinging one of the huge Japanese swords. A towering Mongol plucked it from him, grunting as though pleased by a new toy. Then, contemptuously, the giant twisted the sword into a spiral shape and hurled it after the diving customs man.

Before The Shadow could open fire, a big Mongol flung a mummy case in his direction. The detectives had but tumbled those bulky cases, but the Mongol tossed it as if it were a piece of kindling wood. Dodging for a corner, The Shadow stabbed shots while twisting from the path of further missiles. His bullets were blocked by the nearest pair of Mongols.

Fierce howls told that gunfire could score results when a marksman took time to aim. But even blasts from .45 automatics could not stop the Mongols short. Bowled to a corner by the pair that he had wounded, The Shadow kept pumping bullets, while he wrenched away from mighty hands that could have snapped his back, had they gained a clutch.

The detectives threw themselves upon the bellowing pair and helped to flatten them. Matthew was joining the fray when Cardona arrived; the stocky police inspector drove for the same corner. Clear of the battle where he was no longer needed, The Shadow looked for the rest of the titanic band. He heard them, on the stairway.

Two of the Mongols were lugging the silver coffin that the six truckmen had found difficult to handle. The other pair slung knives, as they ducked below the stair top. The Shadow made a long, sideward dive at an angle that threw him into a sprawl. But the crazy leap was all that saved him.

One of the massive knives slashed the cloak that trailed from his left shoulder; the other actually grazed his right hip. One blade, at least, would have caught him, except for the angled dive.

Striking the floor, The Shadow rolled into the empty exhibit room; came up with his guns leveled toward the stairs. By then, the two Mongols were plunging down the steps to overtake the pair with the coffin.

Following the fleeing giants, The Shadow heard a clatter behind him. Trouble was ended in the mummy room. Cardona and the rest were taking up the chase. The Shadow was counting upon little help from the truckers in the alley; but he had expected, at least, that they had gotten away in their truck.

Instead, they had fled on foot. The Mongols were in the truck, the coffin with them. One of them knew how to drive, for the truck was whining backward from the alley when The Shadow arrived.

The Mongol driver must have nearly yanked the steering wheel from its moorings, as he neared the mouth of the alley, for the truck made a rapid spin and shot away with the speed of a motorcycle just as The Shadow opened fire. By the time the cloaked fighter reached the entrance of the alley, the big vehicle was swinging the next corner.

THE SHADOW'S cab whipped into sight. Too late to take up pursuit of the vanished truck, it was in time to serve the black-cloaked crimefighter. With a long stride, he reached the running board and was whipped forward at twice his own speed, just as a scrawny figure made a lunge from the roof of the museum.

A knife clanged the side of the cab, three feet behind The Shadow's clinging figure. Pointing an automatic upward, The Shadow fired before the assassin could dodge back to cover. There was an approaching wail as the scrawny creature plunged headlong to the alley.

The Shadow had settled one of Shiwan Khan's murderous spies—a lurking *naljorpa*, whose deadly aim had failed when The Shadow's speed had been doubled by the lift from the cab. Even Shiwan Khan would have commended the fate of that killer. The *naljorpa* had forgotten the Golden Master's promise of immunity until the plane took off.

Of course, the offer did not apply to the fighting Mongols. They were acting upon different orders; The Shadow had attacked them on his own. Their business had been to get away with the silver coffin, at any cost. They probably considered the job a complete success sweetened, in a way, by the loss of two comrades.

For the Mongols of the Ordos breed were sworn to protect the coffin of Temujin with their lives, and considered death a privilege when it occurred in the upholding of their cause.

As for The Shadow, he still had a privilege: to reach the airport within the limit allotted him by Shiwan Khan. He had taken up less than his extra fifteen minutes in rescuing helpless men from the attack of the mighty Mongols. Perhaps that was the reason why he flung back a trailing laugh for the rest of Shiwan Khan's hidden spies to hear.

Perhaps there was another reason. If so, it remained known to one person only: The Shadow.

CHAPTER V
THE MAN WHO RETURNED

BIG searchlights were playing high above the airport when The Shadow's cab arrived there. A ship was due in from the Pacific coast; it had flashed a radio report ahead, stating that one of the crew was in serious condition through sudden illness. An ambulance was waiting to receive the man in question.

Again in the guise of Cranston, The Shadow stepped from his cab, carrying cloak and hat across his arm as though they were ordinary garments. He stopped near the ambulance, where a physician was talking with airport officials.

Looking up, the doctor saw Cranston, caught the gaze of his steady eyes. An imperceptible nod passed between them. Strolling away, The Shadow approached the plane that awaited the takeoff signal for its flight to Miami.

Immediately after The Shadow's departure, the physician requested that a space be cleared near the ambulance. Very soon the vehicle was deserted, and standing in comparative darkness. Meanwhile, The Shadow had stopped at the door of the Miami-bound airliner.

Eyes were on Cranston, when he finally stepped aboard; then as the door was closing, the hawk-faced passenger did a sudden turnabout and stepped back to the ground. As the door slashed shut, he was almost beneath the wing of the great ship; it was quivering for the takeoff. He was whisking his cloak over his shoulders, pressing the slouch hat on his head.

Excited gestures came from a window as the airliner started forward. The Shadow had no chance to spot the passenger who served as spy for Shiwan Khan; nor did he bother about others among the onlooking crowd. He was gone, off into the darkness of the ground, choosing a quick course of his own.

When The Shadow's cab started away, very suddenly, another car followed it. There was a soft laugh from darkness, as The Shadow watched that blind chase. Certain spies, at least, had gone upon a useless trip; others, still on hand, would never know it until too late.

A pygmy thing was descending from the higher darkness into the spreading glare of huge searchlights. It was the plane in from the Pacific coast; it made a perfect landing. Men with a stretcher received a burden wrapped in blankets. They carried the hapless crew member to the ambulance; the physician followed the stretcher in through the rear door.

Curious things happened as soon as the ambulance left the airport.

First, the patient propped himself up from the blankets. His face was drawn and thin; his whole form was emaciated. Showing a scrawny hand to the physician, the human skeleton inquired:

"You're Dr. Rupert Sayre?"

The physician nodded.

"I'm Felix Bryson," declared the emaciated man. Then wolfishly: "Give me food!"

Sayre handed Bryson an apple; warned the patient not to devour it too rapidly. Between bites, Bryson talked.

"Guess you've heard about me," he declared. "I'm one of those saps that went away with Shiwan Khan. He took us to that wonderful place that he calls Xanadu. He gave everybody what they wanted: gold, jewels, jade, just like he promised.

"I wanted nothing"—Bryson cackled at the thought—"but he gave me jewels, too. Look at them." Bryson pulled a bag from beneath the blanket. "About half a million dollars' worth. I mean it. The place was lousy with them!

"So I took my share before I left. Why not? I'd donated a swell yacht to Shiwan Khan. It was my boat, the *Nautilus*, that took us on our voyage, after we listened to Shiwan Khan instead of The Shadow. Bah! What fools we were!"

BRYSON reached for another apple.

Sayre gave him one; the skeleton man finished half of it, then inquired anxiously.

"Do you think I'll ever get my weight back? You wouldn't think, to look at me, that I once weighted close to two hundred."

Sayre tested the scrawny arms, gave an approving nod. He remarked that they were solid enough, and had good muscle. Bryson gave a prolonged laugh.

"Muscle?" he queried. "You're telling me? You'd better hear the rest of my story first."

Bryson told the story—one of the most fantastic that Sayre had ever heard. Arrived at Xanadu, the happy followers of Shiwan Khan had been eager for their initiation into mystic ways. The Golden Master had given them that promise, and he fulfilled it.

First, he had trained them in the ways of the *naljorpas*, until they acquired a mystic force called *shugs*. To demonstrate that ability, Bryson placed his fingertips against Sayre's shoulders; the physician instantly felt a numbing electric shock. Throwing aside the blankets, Bryson chuckled while he gnawed the apple core.

"They wrapped me in these things," he said, referring to the blankets. "What do I need with them? I'm a *reskyangpa*, a guy with *tumo* powers. They call it *tumo* when you can sit in the middle of a snowbank and make it melt. It's a cinch when you learn it. You just chuck your clothes and concentrate.

"But it got too tough, when Shiwan Khan made us become *delogs*. A *delog* is a fellow who has visited the land beyond and seen all there is to know about it. The regular *delogs* just dream it, but Shiwan Khan put us through the mill.

"What he did was fake a *bardo*, or land beyond, and give us all the tortures that those wacky guys dream about. The 'short path' was what he called it. Short, maybe, but tough."

Sayre looked past Bryson, to the figure that had risen from the end of the man's cot. The silent passenger that Bryson did not see was cloaked in black. He let the cloak drop from his shoulders, drew away his slouch hat, to reveal the features of Lamont Cranston.

The Shadow had secretly entered the ambulance that was bringing in one of Shiwan Khan's former dupes without the knowledge of the Golden Master's spies!

Catching a cue from The Shadow, Sayre put a question to Bryson:

"How did you get away from Shiwan Khan?"

"We didn't, exactly," replied Bryson. "Shiwan Khan went away first. We were fed up by that time; that is, fed up with everything but food. So we walked out on his *naljorpas*, and they couldn't stop us. We knew the racket; they couldn't floor us with the *shugs*, because we knew all about it.

"We met a *lung-gom-pa* runner, somewhere in Tibet. Amazing fellows, those *lung-gom-pas*. They run along like antelopes, and keep it up for days without stopping. This fellow led us to a plain called the Chang Thang, where we met Lamont Cranston. He sent me home by plane; the rest are coming later."

As Bryson finished, he must have sensed that someone was in back of him, for he turned suddenly, to face The Shadow. Despite his occult training, Bryson showed amazement when he saw The Shadow's features.

"A *yidam*!" exclaimed Bryson. "A *yidam*!"

His eyes went glassy; he swayed, fell to the blankets. Looking toward The Shadow, Dr. Sayre showed alarm. He was met by a steady headshake.

"A *yidam* is an imaginary double," explained The Shadow. "Since he left Cranston in Tibet, Bryson naturally supposes that I am a creature of his imagination. He thinks that he has reached a higher sphere of understanding, and he has gone into a trance as the result."

A great fact dawned on Sayre. He had worked with The Shadow for a long while; always, he had supposed The Shadow to be Cranston, but he had never been sure. At last, Sayre understood.

There was a Lamont Cranston, an actual globe-trotter, who was at present in Tibet. While Cranston was absent from New York, as was usually the case, The Shadow adopted the globe-trotter's guise.

Evidently, there was an understanding between them. The Shadow must have requested Cranston to search for Bryson and other of Shiwan Khan's victims while in Tibet.

So Cranston wasn't The Shadow after all. The

fact didn't solve the riddle for Dr. Sayre. It merely put him up against a deeper question:

Who was The Shadow?

A WHISPERED laugh came as an answer to Sayre's perplexed frown. Then, resuming his cloak and hat, The Shadow spoke in a cryptic tone; his first words made Sayre forget the problem of the cloaked being's actual identity.

"Bryson said that Shiwan Khan has left Xanadu," declared The Shadow in a low, strange whisper. "He is right. Shiwan Khan is in New York."

Despite The Shadow's presence, Sayre could not repress a shudder.

"Take good care of Bryson," ordered The Shadow. "Get him out of town as soon as possible. Shiwan Khan must not know that he has returned."

Sayre nodded. He saw The Shadow point forward, and understood. The ambulance had reached Manhattan and was traveling through darkened side streets, its bell clanging loudly. Sayre told the driver to slacken speed and forget the bell. The patient was feeling better; there was no need to hurry.

"Bryson will be all right," declared The Shadow, glancing at the motionless man. "It is well that he returned. His story is valuable. He said one thing"—Sayre could see the glitter of The Shadow's reflective eyes—"that may prove of special worth."

Stooping, The Shadow reached the rear of the ambulance. He laid one hand on the door, thrust the other to Sayre. The significance of the handclasp struck the physician, as The Shadow spoke explanatory words.

"When Shiwan Khan meets opposition," declared The Shadow in a strange, sibilant tone, "he robs persons of their reason, and their identities. Bryson is fortunate. He lost both, but will recover them.

"I can afford neither loss, not even temporarily. But I shall avoid such experience. My intelligence can equal Shiwan Khan's. My identity"—The Shadow's tone carried a touch of whispered mirth—"is my own secret.

"I know the limitations of Shiwan Khan, as well as the extent of his powers. This is to be my own campaign, against a foe whose methods brook no quarter. It will be a battle to the death!"

There was farewell in The Shadow's grip, despite its firmness. As the ambulance swung a darkened corner, the door went wide; a cloaked form dropped off, into blackness.

Sayre saw the door sweep shut; heard himself repeating The Shadow's final words:

"To the death!"

CHAPTER VI
THE LONE THRUST

FROM a window of a musty, old-fashioned hotel room, a tall, gaunt man was staring out into the Manhattan dusk. His features, once bronzed, were the hue of pale copper; their lines showed the trace of worry. So did the gaunt man's stooped shoulders, although there was another reason for his posture; he was leaning heavily upon a cane.

The gaunt man was a forgotten hero. His name was Kent Allard; once a celebrated aviator, he had won high acclaim by his return from the jungles of Guatemala, where he had dwelt as a white god among a tribe of Xinca Indians, after a forced landing in his plane.

An observer, noting Allard at the window, might have supposed that the one-time hero was bemoaning the brevity of fame. The very streets that Allard viewed were those where he had ridden in triumph during a public welcome on the occasion of his return.

Today, few persons remembered Kent Allard; less recognized him when he walked along those streets. Rather than encounter proof of his vanished fame, Allard remained indoors most of the time. There was another reason for his lack of activity; his leg bothered him. He had injured it when he landed in Guatemala; since his return to New York, it had been getting worse.

Allard had some money; enough to live in simple style at this old hotel, and to keep a pair of trusted Xinca servants, who looked like squatty brown idols snatched from some Aztec temple. Thus, there was no mystery about Kent Allard; he was simply an ex-aviator, with no future.

Such, at least, was the impression that Allard successfully created; and there was a powerful motive behind his game.

Kent Allard was The Shadow!

There were times when The Shadow became himself, but only to keep up appearances. He was very careful about such appearances, in a peculiar way. As Allard, he made himself seem old, instead of youthful. His worried air was a pose; his constant limp a fake. Both were part of the all-important game.

Having proven that Kent Allard could *not* be The Shadow, because of his years of absence during the cloaked fighter's period of early fame, he did his best to continue the illusion, by making Allard seem decrepit, while The Shadow's activity increased!

There were long stretches when Kent Allard was never in his suite at this old hotel: but only two persons knew it. They were the faithful Xincas, silent sentinels who would never tell.

Allard's face was closer to the window. His eyes

showed a keen flash; the hawklike expression of his features was traceable, though it differed remarkably from Cranston's masklike visage. Night had come again, the third night since Cranston's disappearance. The Shadow's period of waiting was at an end.

Shiwan Khan was looking for The Shadow, but had failed to trace him. It was time for The Shadow to look for Shiwan Khan.

Otherwise, the Golden Master would strike, regardless. It was a sure thing that Shiwan Khan was preparing for supercrime; but, so far, he had not revealed his insidious hand. Whatever his schemes, Shiwan Khan would make provision for The Shadow's opposition; therefore, a longer wait would tend to help Shiwan Khan.

Three days had been necessary for The Shadow to sound out the situation. Through a contact man named Burbank, The Shadow had kept in cautious touch with certain secret agents who watched the underworld. From their reports, and his own secret forays into that terrain, The Shadow had proven the point that he suspected.

Shiwan Khan was lining up notorious men of crime, self-styled "big-shots" who had been idle during recent months. Willing lieutenants of the golden overlord, they were holding meetings among themselves. Through a lone thrust, The Shadow might hope to throw fear in their ranks, along with bullets, and thereby crimp the schemes of Shiwan Khan.

DUSK no longer reigned. Thick night was broken only by the glitter of Manhattan's lights, which would be few and far between in the district where The Shadow intended to go.

Limping from the window, Kent Allard paused wearily near the door. A stolid Xinca approached, held a cloak. Sliding his arms into the garment, Allard plucked a slouch hat from the servant's hand, clamped it on his own head as the Xinca caught the falling cane. The other Xinca opened the door, to let his black-cloaked master step out into the gloomy hall.

No longer Allard, The Shadow's wearied pose was ended. He became a swift, gliding shape of muffled blackness as he headed for a fire tower that offered a secret route to the outside darkness.

Through devious routes, The Shadow traveled a few blocks from the hotel before stepping into a cab, which was not his own. He was taking no foolish risks with his own cab, and its driver, Moe Shrevnitz. Both were valuable, and would remain so, provided they offered no link from The Shadow to the identity of Kent Allard.

Inside the random cab, The Shadow spoke in a tone that was neither Allard's nor Cranston's. Though surprised to find he had a passenger, the cabby offered no comment; he was only too glad to get a fare. Nor did he argue when he had completed a long trip to an East Side neighborhood.

The driver was too pleased over the five-dollar bill that fluttered into the seat beside him, accompanied by the order to "keep the change." Looking into the back seat, the cabby saw that his passenger was gone; on thinking it over, he realized that he hadn't gotten an actual look at the mysterious rider.

That didn't bother the cabby.

If modern ghosts had met with a mansion shortage in Manhattan and preferred to haunt taxicabs instead, they were quite welcome, so long as they passed out real five-dollar bills.

Moving through darkness, The Shadow neared the area he wanted. He passed an alley that ran through to the next street; noting the darkness of its walls, the odd shapes of the roofs above, he saw its double value as a lurking spot.

The narrow sidewalks were made to order for triggermen, the sort of lookouts that Shiwan Khan's lieutenants would bring with them. Slanted roofs were proper shelter for *naljorpas*, the type of watchers that the Golden Master would provide as added protection for the meeting.

Bullets fired at ground level could prove no deadlier than knives hurled from vantage points above. The alley could prove a place of close-range doom, no matter from which end The Shadow might approach. His goal, a three-story house in the exact center, seemed hopeless. Skirting the block, The Shadow entered a short passage that ended in a wall. The blind alley offered no direct route to his goal, but The Shadow was used to obstacles.

Scaling the wall, he worked his way into an empty building and up through to the roof. Crawling to a rear ledge, he reached a narrow gap between the empty building and the house he wanted.

The Shadow covered that space with a long diving leap from a crouched position. He was on the roof that he sought; near its rear, The Shadow found a trapdoor, tightly clamped from below. It wasn't the proper means of entry, for guards were probably stationed just beneath. Continuing forward, The Shadow veered to the side of the roof and paused.

He could see the depth of the alleyway ahead, and knew that the black three-story canyon was under expert surveillance. But the side wall of the house was likely to be clear of watchers, since they supposed that it could only be reached from the front.

Swinging over the side edge of the roof, The Shadow dangled in darkness, found a third-floor window with his feet. He was in luck—the window was unlocked, which saved him considerable time and trouble. Working the sash upward with his soft-shoed feet, The Shadow took an outward swing, then dropped as he swayed inward.

Slicing the darkness at a perfectly gauged angle, the cloaked invader landed inside the window, doubling his head and shoulders as soon as they were through the space. Then, with silent creep, he was moving toward a dimly lighted hallway, gun drawn in readiness for whatever might occur.

THE hall was empty; silent, except for murmurs that came from the front stairway. Listening, The Shadow gauged the position of those voices, and established who their owners were. The talking men were guards stationed on the second floor, very close to the foot of the stairway.

It meant that the meeting was taking place on this floor: the third.

Moving rearward along the hall, The Shadow came to a strong, tightly closed door. Probing its lock with a tweezer pick, he found the key and gripped it. Silently, with painful slowness, he turned the key. Slow motion was necessary, so that the twisting key would not be noticed from the other side.

The lock yielded. Pocketing the pick, The Shadow gripped the doorknob with one hand, advanced his gun with the other, to cover the narrow crack that he intended to open.

Inching inward under The Shadow's expert pressure, the door revealed a thin slit of light. The space was enough; two objects appeared at the crevice. One was The Shadow's eye; the other, the muzzle of his automatic.

The Shadow was looking right past the shoulder of a husky guard who had been stationed to watch the door. Interested in what was happening in the room, the guard had faced about, trusting his ears to warn him if anyone tinkered with the door.

Thus, like the guard, The Shadow was witness to events in the squarish room beyond; and one brief view was all he needed, as proof that he had chosen the right goal.

Shiwan Khan was not present in the meeting room, but The Shadow had not expected him to be there. The men on hand were the sort that The Shadow anticipated; if anything, they exceeded his forecast. Instead of just a few they numbered half a dozen.

Big-shots in their own right, notorious specialists in varied fields of crime, these were the public enemies who had rallied to the cause of Shiwan Khan. In becoming lieutenants of the powerful Golden Master, they had increased their evil status, instead of lessening it.

From their leering faces, the gleeful note in their raspy voices, The Shadow knew that he was to gain an insight into the plans of Shiwan Khan, from the lips of the very men who were to play a part in crimes to come.

Crooks had heard from Shiwan Khan; then were soon to hear from The Shadow!

CHAPTER VII
THE HIDDEN TRAP

SPOKESMAN for the six was Mike Borlo, a beetle-browed burly, noted as an all-around crook. Mike boasted that he had beaten eleven different raps, covering charges from arson to murder. Faked alibis, perjured witnesses, and legal technicalities always seemed to work in Mike Borlo's favor.

Next to Mike sat Snipe Shailey, a rat-raced character who considered himself handsome, which he was, in comparison to his present companions. Snipe had a long, sallow face, topped by sleek hair. His gimlet eyes were shrewd and glittery. Snipe's specialty was murder, but he confined his efforts to disposing of crooks who were muscling in on the rackets of others. It was difficult for the law to prove facts in such cases.

Straight opposite Snipe was Blitz Gandy, veteran of half a dozen sensational bank and payroll robberies. Coarse-featured and overbearing in his manner, Blitz didn't look as smart as the others, but he regarded himself their superior. At any rate, he had some claim to distinction; he had tried crime the tough way and was still at large.

The other three crooks likewise had reputations in the badlands. The Shadow noted Dobie Grelf, who specialized at cover-up work; Silk Laddiman, noted as a warehouse tapper; and Shag Flink, quite famed for his persuasive efforts in behalf of the numbers racket during its heyday.

"We've got together," announced Mike Borlo, "and that makes it all set. At our next meeting—"

"Why next?" demanded Blitz Gandy. "What's the matter with laying out the first job right now?"

"Shiwan Khan says to wait," put in Snipe Shailey, in a hard tone. "That's enough, ain't it?"

"I suppose you've been talking to this Shiwan Khan guy," retorted Blitz. "Like Mike here says he has."

"I've heard from him," said Snipe, coolly. "Maybe you will, too, Blitz."

Contemptuously, Blitz threw a look around the group. Tapping his forehead, he said scoffingly:

"You guys say it's all in the bean. Maybe it is, if the old bean's soft. This stuff of getting mental messages sounds wacky to me. I wouldn't have known about this meeting, if Mike hadn't told me."

The others offered only one argument; namely, that it was easier for one man to be soft in the brain, than five. It was Mike Borlo who finally voiced their sentiment, when he growled:

"All right, Blitz. Stay out, if you want. Only, I'm telling you I've talked with this guy Shiwan Khan, over a radio—"

"Over a radio?"

"Yeah, a radio with screwy lights, all different colors. Just when they get you feeling goofy, you hear Shiwan Khan. He told me there'd be two meetings—"

"Why two?"

"On account of Prex Norgan."

Blitz stared; then snorted.

"Prex Norgan?" he queried. "What're we going to do, heave posies over the cliff where he went off in his jalopy when the Feds were after him?"

"Prex Norgan isn't croaked, Blitz."

Blitz squinted, his big mouth opened wide. The others showed sudden eagerness to hear what else Mike had to say. This was the spokesman's first reference to Prex Norgan, formerly rated as the nation's Public Enemy No. 1, until his reputed death a year ago.

"I got it straight from Shiwan Khan," assured Mike, "the way he piped everything else. He says Prex Norgan is right here in New York, sticking in a hideaway. He's coming in with us, Prex is."

"A smart boy, Prex," commented Snipe. "An educated guy. Good stuff, Shiwan Khan bringing him back in circulation."

Rising from his chair, Blitz Gandy strode across the room, turning about to face the entire group.

"Another session is O.K. by me," declared Blitz, "if it means meeting up with Prex Norgan. If Prex is alive, and Shiwan Khan is wise to it, the guy must know everything. If this is the real McCoy, you can count me in. But I've got to lamp Prex, first."

BLITZ was turning toward the door. Mike told him to hold it. At Mike's suggestion, Snipe started to the door, pushed the guard aside, to take a look into the hall. When Snipe took a look for anything, he always had a gun ready. As he drew his revolver, the others did the same.

The door was shut, the key turned tight, when Snipe arrived. The Shadow saw no occasion to take on a roomful of Class A killers, under conditions which were to their advantage. With a lighted hall behind him and the crooks at the bottom of the stairway, he would be placed between two fires.

On that account, The Shadow returned rapidly to the side room by which he had entered.

From the edge of the doorway, he saw Snipe Shailey glance along the hall. The fellow's gimlet eyes noted everything, even streaky blackness on the floor. Watching for the patch to move, Snipe seemed disappointed. He returned to the meeting room, to join the others.

The Shadow waited for the whole group to appear. He was prepared to have a say regarding their next meeting; at least, to the extent of thinning out the participants. But the door did not open. Apparently, Mike Borlo had brought up some fresh subject for discussion, and all were staying to hear it.

Moving out through the hall, The Shadow reached the meeting room again, found the door unlocked. As he edged the door inward, no light appeared along the crack. The room was dark; empty, too, for The Shadow's ears could have caught even the slightest breathing. Carefully, The Shadow tested the darkness with a whispered laugh. Only echoes answered.

Remembering the trapdoor in the roof. The Shadow recognized that it was directly above the meeting room. For some reason, the crooks had taken that outlet. It might be that they had suspected the presence of The Shadow.

As he pondered upon such likelihood, The Shadow heard creaks from the stairs. Triggermen were on the move, upward. They must have received some tip-off from Mike and the departing big-shots. Turning a flashlight upwards The Shadow saw that the trapdoor in the meeting room was tightly shut. He didn't have time for further inspection of the place. Enemies were at the top of the stairs.

Wheeling, The Shadow greeted them with a strident laugh from the doorway of the meeting room. He was stabbing shots with one gun, while he put away his flashlight and drew another automatic, all in one move. Revolvers were answering, spouting wildly. With a surge, a wave of thugs flung themselves into sight, driving forward in a suicide charge.

Again The Shadow laughed, as he wheeled back into the meeting room. As he went, he was calculating the reason for that maddened charge; he was also hearing repeated echoes of his own mockery, which this time had reached a fierce crescendo.

Then, all of a sudden, The Shadow's twist became a long, wild spring. He had found the answer too late to prevent his whirl into the empty room. The place was a trap, a pitfall that the crooks had prepared before departure, in accordance with orders from Shiwan Khan.

The deserted room was floorless!

CHARGING crooks knew it; that was why they had begun their crazy surge. As The Shadow's gunfire broke off, his laugh cut short, too.

It was the crooks who were flinging gibes at their vanished foe. They hoped that The Shadow would have time to hear their taunts before he hit the cement basement, four floors below.

They also hoped that he would survive the plunge. They wanted to give him the finishing touches with their guns. Lunging to the brink, the thugs turned

Aiming thugs were greeted by a spurting .45 that staggered them.

their flashlights down into the cellar in search of their crumpled prey.

The glare revealed the near half of the floor, hanging from heavy hinges. There was another half across the room, dangling in the same fashion beyond the glow of the lights. But the crooks were concerned with the pit: they saw two guns against the grimy cement, but The Shadow wasn't there.

Then from across the meeting room came the quiver of a laugh. Aiming thugs were greeted by a spurting .45 that staggered them. One flashlight flinging upward from a hand that loosed it, gave a momentary view of The Shadow's new position.

Sensing the pitfall as he was wheeling into it, The Shadow had flung away his guns and made a tremendous leap across the room, hoping to reach a window ledge. Missing that mark, he had caught the upper edge of the half-floor on the far side of the room. Hanging on that slab, he had drawn one of the reserve guns that he carried when equipped for heavy battle.

Thugs were taking The Shadow's bullets. Two of those staggered foemen pitched forward, plunging into the pit intended for The Shadow. The rest made frantic retreat, some reeling as they took the brunt of The Shadow's barrage.

His gun emptied, The Shadow put it away and drew another. The last of his weapons was not needed for the present. He cloaked it, when he heard the last of the thugs stumbling madly down the stairway.

Working up to the window, The Shadow reached the ledge. Reaching for the trapdoor, he pushed his fingers in under the edge. Mike Borlo and the other aces hadn't tried to clamp the trapdoor from the upper side. They hadn't considered it necessary.

There were new sounds from the hallway. Defeated mobbies had summoned reserves from the front street. But The Shadow was through the trapdoor by the time the arriving triggermen began to test the floorless room with bullets.

Which way the big-shots had gone, did not matter. They were too far ahead to be overtaken. Returning along his own route, The Shadow went down through the empty house, out the window to the wall that marked the end of a blind alley. He did not forget that things might have happened elsewhere during the course of his trip.

From the wall top, The Shadow took a quick look upward, bringing his gun to firing position. He was just in time to sight a shape above—a wiry, scrawny *naljorpa*, like the one who had slung the knife from the museum roof.

This killer was on a rooftop, too. He had reached the roof that The Shadow had so recently left. Flinging half across the edge, the *naljorpa* loosed the knife so swiftly that the blade seemed to dart downward of its own accord.

The Shadow's gun spoke simultaneously. Blade and bullet must have passed in mid-flight. But only one missile was swift enough to find a target. It was the bullet.

Rolled from the wall edge by the recoil of his gun, The Shadow escaped the knife point that nicked the narrow stretch of brick. He flattened in the blind alley; as he struck, he heard a snarl coming from the darkness above.

It was the *naljorpa*, bound for a longer fall than The Shadow had taken. The snaky assassin landed with a bony clatter on the far side of the wall.

Shaken by his own short drop, The Shadow reeled off into the darkness, steadying as he neared the street. Aiming for the nearest corner, he nicked a triggerman who was coming into sight. The yell brought other thugs in that direction, while The Shadow was taking an opposite course.

Battle against a horde of lesser crooks was useless, particularly when *naljorpas* were in the offing. The Shadow had not made this trip to thin out ranks that Shiwan Khan could easily replenish, either from his own reserves or those of his lieutenants.

The Shadow's chief mission was accomplished. He had listened in on the assemblage of big-shots, learning who they were. Tracing them would not be difficult in the future. By damaging their efforts, The Shadow could eventually reach Shiwan Khan.

In the meantime, he would be ruining the Golden Master's own campaign, which seemed to be the launching of crime on an unheard-of scale. As for the traps of Shiwan Khan, they were not the sort that could ensnare The Shadow. Shiwan Khan had failed to use the proper bait.

Perhaps that very fact would strike Shiwan Khan, when he heard of The Shadow's latest exploit!

CHAPTER VIII
THE SECOND MEETING

NEWS always reached Shiwan Khan swiftly. Moreover, the Golden Master had rapid ways of transmitting it to others. When Mike Borlo reached the apartment where he lived, he turned on the radio that he had mentioned, just to see its lights flash.

Odd lights that blinked a medley of red, green and blue across the center dial. They always made Mike feel woozy, but he didn't always hear the voice. That depended upon Shiwan Khan. Mike didn't expect to hear from the Golden Master again tonight.

But the voice came.

It was like a bell, a thing that clanged inside Mike's head, leaving words there. When the voice ended, Mike turned off the radio; shaking himself from his daze, he reached for a telephone.

The telephone bell was already ringing. Snipe Shailey was on the wire. He, too, had received a message, after staring at a special electric light bulb that flashed dazzling colors.

Between them, Mike and Snipe agreed that the others must have heard from Shiwan Khan, with the possible exception of Blitz Gandy. Knowing where to reach Blitz, Mike said he would call him up. A few minutes later, he had Blitz on the wire.

"Get this," began Mike. "You know that rig we had to drop The Shadow, in case he showed up...? Yeah, the phony floor... I knew we set it, all right, but it didn't get The Shadow... Yeah, he showed up. He dropped in it and out of it, somehow...

"Anyway, the word was piped to Shiwan Khan... Yeah, some of those skinny guys must have passed it... We've heard from Shiwan Khan, all except you. He wants us to meet up with Prex Norgan, before The Shadow gets hep... I know where to go, so hop over here and I'll take you along..."

Blitz arrived within ten minutes. Mike took him on a subway trip, well downtown. They walked a few blocks eastward, came to an old building, where Mike rapped at a basement door. Blitz was looking across the street. He started to whisper:

"There's one of the skinny guys—"

The door swung open. Blitz thought he saw another slinky figure beyond it, but when they stepped into a gloomy hall, there was no one about. Mike led the way to a solid wall; glancing back, Blitz saw the door go shut.

But no human hand was visible. Except when they hurled their weight in knife flings, Shiwan Khan's *naljorpas* were capable at keeping from sight.

A panel slid up. Mike pointed Blitz through the wall. They came to another door, which opened at Mike's tap, while the panel behind them closed. Stepping into a subterranean room, they found the others waiting: Snipe, Dobie, and the rest.

The place was furnished lavishly; it made the most luxurious hideout that the visiting big-shots had ever seen. But Blitz wasn't interested in the furnishings. The coarse-featured crook stared at a motionless figure seated on a thick cushion.

Recognizing the wide-browed, square-jawed face, with its hardened stare and suavely smiling lips, Blitz exclaimed in his nearest tone to wonderment:

"Prex Norgan!"

The suave man rose from the cushion. His eyes showed a knowing glitter, as he shook hands with the new arrivals.

"I guess they told you that the Feds didn't get me," said Prex, in a smooth tone. "Kind of hard to believe, isn't it, Blitz?"

Acknowledging that it was, Blitz studied the public enemy. Once, Prex had been sleek; at present, he looked very thin. He had lost at least twenty pounds, by Blitz's estimate, during the past year.

Smiling, Prex pointed across the room; near a curtained doorway, Blitz saw another seated man. The fellow was rawboned; his ribs showed through his tawny flesh. Attired only in a loincloth, the man was evidently a native of the Orient.

"His name is Pashod," said Prex. "He is a *gomchen*; a hermit to you, Blitz, if you know what hermits are."

Blitz growled that he had heard of them. Addressing the others, Prex continued:

"Pashod is also a *guru*, or teacher. He has been training me in mystic ways, during the past few months. Watch!"

STEPPING to his cushion, Prex seated himself cross-legged in one easy motion. His eyes took on a fixed glitter. Like Pashod, Prex seemed completely entranced. Minutes ticked, while he remained immobile, his eyes upon a crystal ball across the room, the same object that held Pashod's gaze. Then, in a faraway tone, Prex spoke:

"I have heard. I shall obey!"

Snapping from his trance, he unlimbered as easily as he had seated himself. Pashod must have received the same mental command, for the gomchen also arose and retired to a corner, from which he surveyed the visitors without the slightest trace of curiosity.

"The credit goes to Shiwan Khan," declared Prex. "I'd have gone nuts in this dump, if he hadn't sent Pashod here. But after I took this yoga business, days went like that!"

Prex indicated the passage of a week by seven snaps of his fingers.

"Stick with this racket long enough," he told the others, "and you'll learn the whole works, too. You get so you don't even need to eat, and it puts you in trim. Look at Pashod; he's been living on a bowl of *tsampa* for ten days and hasn't finished it yet."

Blitz saw the bowl that Prex mentioned and didn't like the looks of its mealy content. He grunted that he didn't like Pashod's looks either; that he couldn't see any percentage in the starvation stuff. Prex merely smiled.

"If you don't think that Pashod is tough," he told Blitz, "Just make a pass at him."

Accepting the invitation, Blitz approached the *gomchen*, drew back his hand to deliver an open-palmed slap. It would not have mattered if Blitz had used his fist. He did not manage to even start the blow.

Hissing a snarl between bulging teeth, Pashod made a wide sweep of his thin hands. Blitz staggered back, as if jarred by an electric shock.

"Try it on me," laughed Prex, "if you want another dose. I can't dish it out as well as Pashod, but I'm plenty good!"

This time, Blitz declined. Finished with banter, Prex reached beneath a table, drew out a large coil of paper, and unrolled it. He motioned the others closer, to study the diagram that he showed them.

"Shiwan Khan doped this out," informed Prex, "and flashed it through to me. This is the lay for our first job, the Battery Trust. It's ready any time."

Detail by detail, Prex mapped out the plan for the most perfect bank robbery that any of the crooks could have imagined. It was to be staged at night, beginning with a false alarm that would actually bring the police to the premises, along with certain bank officials. Unwittingly, those arrivals would pave the way to the job.

Each big-shot was to play a part, and Blitz Gandy had the most important share, due to his experience in such jobs. Blitz swelled at the assignment, particularly because it gave him a higher rating than Mike Borlo, whose superior attitude had become annoying.

But Mike did not seem to care. He had been working for harmony among the lieutenants, and felt that this would satisfy Blitz. In fact, it seemed to suit everyone, until Snipe Shailey saw a loophole in the chart and questioned Prex about it.

"That's for The Shadow," explained Prex, coolly. "He'll be around, too."

Instantly, objections filled the air. Springing one trap for The Shadow had been good enough; but it wouldn't do to try the game again. Particularly when a few hundred thousand dollars were at stake, as with this job. Prex began arguments; his companions voicing him down with talk of dough.

Then, with a peculiar suddenness, the babble ceased. An icy stillness filled the hideout; of one accord, the mobsters began to turn toward the curtained doorway across the room.

What they saw, froze them rigid.

THE curtains had spread. Advancing from between the drapes came a figure clad in gold. Above the ornamented robe the big-shots saw a strange triangular face, lined with thin, curving brows and drooping mustaches. Those features seemed penciled upon the saffron complexion, except for the robed man's eyes, which shone with a greenish glitter.

To every brain, there sprang a name:

Shiwan Khan!

This was the famed Golden Master, who had influenced them from afar. His expression was unfathomable; his lips, when they opened, became parting slits of brown. His words had a bell-like tinkle.

"Of what use is money," spoke Shiwan Khan, "while our one real enemy remains alive?" He paused. The listeners realized that he had put a statement, not a question. Then: "To insure our plans for wealth, we must eliminate The Shadow."

Crooks found themselves ready to agree, though they did not say so. They were waiting to hear more from Shiwan Khan. His words had a note that made them expectant.

"Tonight was a mere test," continued Shiwan Khan. "It proved that no ordinary trap will do. We must have bait for our friend, The Shadow. I shall provide it."

He indicated a dotted line on the sheet, one that marked the path that the police and bank officials were due to follow. Again, Shiwan Khan was demonstrating his double methods.

Already, Prex had explained how people who arrived at the bank would pave the way to crime. Shiwan Khan was showing how those same persons could be used to bait The Shadow!

"Always, you have erred." There was a touch of reproval in Shiwan Khan's tinkly tone. "As men of crime, you have hoped that your deeds would escape The Shadow's notice. Such an assumption is ridiculous. The Shadow knows all—"

There was a long pause, broken only by Shiwan Khan's discordant laugh, which voiced a contempt far more subtle than any words.

"All except the ways of Shiwan Khan," completed the Golden Master. "Let him trace you. Let The Shadow gain an opportunity. Then, let him be confronted with a problem other than his own. Let him face a threat that will seal the fate of innocent victims, unless he attempts their rescue.

"That is when The Shadow will rely upon chance instead of wisdom. His mistaken policy of justice will prove his own undoing. Perhaps our victims will escape us, but their protector will not. The Shadow shall produce his own destruction!"

Those words left a tingle. Eyes on the diagram, the elated criminals realized the full extent of Shiwan Khan's remarkable scheme. Taking his cue from the Golden Master, Prex Norgan was pointing out how the mesh would close, in smooth, mechanical fashion. Finding their tongues, the whole group turned to babble their praise.

But Shiwan Khan had gone. All that they saw was a glitter of the golden robe, as the curtain closed behind the Unfathomable's departing form. All sensed a voice, however—even Blitz—a voice that could have been a product of their own thoughts.

Chiming, yet discordant, that tone was a token of farewell from Shiwan Khan. Not a farewell of the present to these lieutenants of the Golden Master, but a farewell of the future—to The Shadow!

CHAPTER IX
NIGHT OF DOOM

CROOKS were on the move again. Like slimy creatures crawling from beneath a lifted stone, they had come to The Shadow's attention. He was keeping close tabs on them personally, as well as through his agents.

Yet there was an oddity in their actions that might have perplexed The Shadow, had he not known the identity of the master plotter, who had coaxed big-shots from cover.

Last night, there had been a gun fray in an old house on the East Side. The law was still investigating, wondering what it was all about. The episode did not fit with the things that the law most feared, a thrust from Shiwan Khan.

But The Shadow knew that the hand of the Golden Master was behind the whole event.

As Allard, The Shadow was watching from his window while awaiting a call from Burbank. His own plans were fashioned. He had posted men to check on Mike Borlo, Blitz Gandy, Snipe Shailey—any of the others. A lead to one would be a lead to all.

Given an opportunity, The Shadow would move in turn; but, so far, those big-shots and their squads of mobbies were roving like flocks of honey bees, settling nowhere.

As yet, the crooks were thinking in terms of ordinary crime under the guidance of Shiwan Khan. More than a single crime, of course. They counted upon a run of evil opportunities that would mount into a crime wave. But how far that billow would carry was beyond their imagination. Only two persons could picture its ultimate possibility: Shiwan Khan and The Shadow.

Always, Shiwan Khan's power increased in proportion to success. He wasn't thinking of a crime wave that would subside, like others. He was looking forward to a tidal wave that would submerge everything. Each success would bring more crooks beneath his rule, until Shiwan Khan would be the mastermind of crime throughout the nation.

Thereafter, crime would pay. Old theories would be reversed. Crime with vast profit, swamping all opposition from the law, would become America's greatest industry. It would literally split the country into two groups, producing a national issue of a revolutionary size. When that happened, crime would win.

Long had The Shadow foreseen such dire consequences. There was nothing of the incredible about the proposition. The thing had occurred often in international affairs, when criminal nations imposed their iron will upon others that favored harmony and order.

All that crime had ever needed to dominate the nation was an absolute dictator. In Shiwan Khan, crime had found just such a master brain.

Yet the rise of Shiwan Khan, like that of other power-seeking schemers, could still be ruined if nipped in the early stages. The only solution was opposition from a fighter of equal mettle; and justice was fortunate to have such a champion in The Shadow.

It would mean a battle to the death, with the fate of a nation in the balance. With such an issue almost at hand, it was difficult to be patient, even for The Shadow.

Crossing the room in Allard's limping style, The Shadow took the telephone that a Xinca servant handed him. Calling Burbank, he found it difficult to retain his calm-toned style while asking for reports. No new ones had arrived. Crooks were still on the roam.

Across the wire, Burbank's voice carried a methodical note that was customary with the reliable contact man. Recognizing its value in this emergency, The Shadow gave a series of unusual orders.

"Await final reports," he told Burbank. "Then order all agents off duty. Immediately after delivering such instructions, prepare for an active assignment of your own."

It was an absolute reversal of The Shadow's usual process, but Burbank showed no traces of astonishment. He seemed to recognize that everything was working in reverse; perhaps even crime, since it was under the management of Shiwan Khan.

ELSEWHERE, in fact, things were quite in reverse.

Working late at his desk in headquarters, Inspector Joe Cardona was in a total quandary. So far, he hadn't managed to score a point in the law's campaign against Shiwan Khan. The mess at the Oriental Museum had led him nowhere.

The silver coffin, of course, was a matter of federal investigation, since it had caused a problem for the customs officials. Feds had come in from Washington to see what they could learn about it, but they were still stabbing in the dark.

There wasn't even proof that Shiwan Khan was really in New York. Cardona was forced to concede that someone other than the Golden Master could have entered as a passenger in the silver coffin. Tracing Shiwan Khan was worse than looking for a needle that wasn't in a haystack.

The only policy was to wait for Shiwan Khan to pop up somewhere. The thought gave Cardona an actual chill.

He was thinking that Shiwan Khan might pop in sight right in the middle of this office. It wasn't impossible. Shiwan Khan had done far more amazing things in the past.

His thoughts interrupted by the telephone bell, Cardona had a fleeting hunch that Shiwan Khan might be on the wire. Joe was laughing it off as he answered the call. In an instant, his manner changed.

Cardona knew the voice that spoke to him, recognized it as more important than Shiwan Khan's. It was the whispered tone of The Shadow, the one being who might solve the riddle of the Golden Master's return!

"Call the officials of the Battery Trust Co.," spoke the voice, in the sibilant tone that Cardona knew. "Tell them to meet you at the bank. Get there as soon as possible. Investigate the alarm that occurs, although it may prove a false one."

Heaving his shoulders in relief, Cardona set the telephone upon the desk. He was glad that he had heard from The Shadow instead of Shiwan Khan. It didn't occur to Cardona that there was one person who could fake The Shadow's tone.

Had he thought it over, Joe would have realized that such a trick could be staged by Shiwan Khan!

In twenty minutes, Cardona was outside the Battery Trust, talking with half a dozen anxious men. Finding everything quiet, as well as mysterious, Cardona rang the night bell. Two watchmen were on duty. One of them opened a massive door, while the other remained in the background.

The watchmen had seen nothing amiss. They were puzzled by the arrival of Cardona and the bank officials. But while the subject was still under discussion, a clangor occurred from deep within the bank. Cardona gave his companions a triumphant look.

"Don't worry," he told them. "It's likely to be a false alarm. That's what the tip-off said. We'll look into it."

Cardona had a small squad with him. His men were coming in from a patrol of the neighborhood, which they reported to be quiet. Leaving the outside patrol to Detective Sergeant Markham and two others, Cardona took another pair of men with him and entered the bank, followed by the worried officials.

One watchman went ahead to show them the way, the other remained on duty at the door.

It wasn't long before the trouble was located. It proved to be a short circuit in the alarm system, a broken wire running along a heavily barred window. But the thing had hardly been fixed before the clangor began again. This time, a short circuit was discovered on a balcony.

By then, the trouble seemed obvious. Someone had tampered with the alarm system, about as far as crooks could hope to get in a bank as stoutly protected as the Battery Trust. Nevertheless, Cardona decided upon a natural course to allay the worries of the anxious officials. He announced that he would make a full inspection of the entire premises.

Word was relayed back to the door. The inspection took on the aspect of a simple routine. The group made the rounds on the upper floors, then descended to the vault room, which was below the ground level.

Scarcely had the flashlights descended the steep stairs before events occurred outside the bank.

THE first thing happened at the door, where a lone watchman was on duty. A writhing shape detached itself from a cornice just above the doorway and plopped beside the watchman. As hands sped toward the watchman's throat, his whole body was numbed by a sharp shock. Then, choked into submission, he fell silently upon the tiled floor. A wily *naljorpa* had handled the first task swiftly.

The officers who patrolled the block were similarly attacked, with equal skill and speed. The only remaining man was Sergeant Markham. As he approached the doorway, he saw the watchman's huddled form and stooped beside it. The first *naljorpa* bounded from the inner darkness and numbed Markham before he could give a shout.

Of burly build, Markham managed to put up a struggle, despite his numbness. The *naljorpa* whipped out a knife, was about to loose the deadly *phurba* for Markham's heart, when a gold-sleeved arm moved in between, supplying a long-nailed hand that stopped the thrust.

In curious jargon, the gold-robed arrival dismissed the *naljorpa* as other men appeared upon the scene. They dropped from passing cars, to settle Markham in rough and ready fashion, binding him along with the watchman.

They were mobbies, these arrivals, headed by Shiwan Khan's new lieutenants. Roving crooks had converged at the given time to take up their appointed stations. One band followed Shiwan Khan into the bank; the group was headed by Blitz Gandy.

A human beacon in the gloom, the gold-robed Shiwan Khan led the way to the vault room. Descending with silent stride, he signaled for the others to be cautious on the stairs. Shiwan Khan reached the lower level to find Cardona and the officials standing in front of the massive vault door, which they had opened.

A long-nailed hand made gestures to the men above, slitted lips delivered a tinkly challenge. Cardona swung about; his hand stopped before it reached his gun.

There was hypnotic power in the greenish gaze of Shiwan Khan. His very presence carried a numbing force. Beneath the glow of the vault room lights, he seemed a fiend materialized from some lost limbo. But behind the mental sway of the Golden Master was a visible, physical threat.

Blitz Gandy and his crew had arrived with bristling guns. While a pair of crooks kept the victims covered, Blitz and the rest rifled the vault in rapid, effective style.

The officers who patrolled the block were attacked with skill and speed.

Sending men upstairs with stacks of currency that filled their arms, Blitz advanced with his two triggermen. Imitating Shiwan Khan's cold glare with an ugly leer, Blitz backed Cardona and the bank officials into the vault.

Then the crooks were moving away at a chimed command. Alone, Shiwan Khan was standing at the entrance of the vault. The glitter of his eyes was more ominous than guns; he held Cardona and the other prisoners paralyzed.

Slitted lips gave an off-key chortle. With an imperious sweep of his golden arm, Shiwan Khan swung the great door shut. The *clang* of the huge barrier was echoed by fragmentary tinkles, like the shattering of glass. Shiwan Khan had throated that threat of doom.

Alone, outside the vault door, Shiwan Khan turned off the lights. In darkness, he stepped toward the stairs, where Blitz and the last two mobbies had already gone.

The first scene was ended, with Shiwan Khan predominant. The next act in the tragedy would bring The Shadow. Not as a rescuer, but as another victim in the scheme of doom.

Such was the strategy of Shiwan Khan!

CHAPTER X
THE SHADOW'S TURN

CRIME had moved ahead of The Shadow, but not by many minutes. He had received reports from several quarters as soon as bands of roving crooks began to converge. All indications pointed to the Battery Trust as the common target.

Leaving his hotel, The Shadow made a quick trip to that vicinity, picking up Burbank on the way.

All was quiet around the bank. The door had been closed, apparently for greater safety. From their cab, The Shadow and Burbank saw a patrol car passing, keeping on its way. The officers had evidently been informed that the place was under the law's own control.

To The Shadow's eyes the scene was too quiet. As the cab swung a corner, he noticed cars pulling away from the next block. In doorways, he spied glittered reflections that had the glint of gun muzzles.

The ease of the departure, the presence of the cover-up men, indicated that crime could already be completed. Still, nothing had been heard from within the stony walls of the bank building. The silence intrigued The Shadow.

He whispered a command to Burbank. The contact man told the cabby to stop in the middle of the next block. Alighting in a rear street, The Shadow waited until Burbank had dismissed the cab; then beckoned his companion with green glimmers from a tiny flashlight.

Carrying a bulging satchel, Burbank followed the blinking beacon into total darkness. The Shadow was threading a course through spaces that few others could have found.

Blocked by a low wall in a narrow, blind alley, he scaled it. Muffling green flashes within his cloak folds, he reached down for Burbank's bag, then gave the contact man a helping hand to the wall top.

Though a comparatively low building, the Battery Trust towered above the squatty houses of this neighborhood. Its gray granite walls were topped by a flat roof, with a severe cornice that offered little chance of concealment.

Quite sure that no *naljorpas* could be close, The Shadow looked for a means of entry into the formidable structure, and saw one. Where a jutting corner of the bank building met the extension of a low garage, a square, barred window was in easy reach.

The light was blinking green again. The Shadow had dropped in darkness beyond the low wall, and Burbank followed. They were near the corner of bank and garage, when the light flashed red. Stopping, Burbank heard The Shadow's approach, only because the cloaked investigator uttered a whispered command.

Receiving a coiled wire from the bag, The Shadow ascended the wall, using a wedging process between the granite blocks of the bank and the brick surface of the garage.

From the top, his light blinked green; Burbank caught the end of the wire that sizzed downward. The light blinked red. While watching for the next signal, Burbank put on a pair of insulated gloves from his kit.

A green flash called for the bag. Burbank sent it up by the wire. When the wire came down again, it was Burbank's turn. His heavy gloves proved valuable protection, when he lashed the wire tightly about his wrists. At a green flash from above, Burbank began his own attempt to scale the wall.

Ordinarily, his clutches would have been inadequate, and his toe holds were uncertain. But the wire was drawing upward under The Shadow's haul. It gave the needed support whenever Burbank floundered. The Shadow could actually sense his agent's progress by the varying strain upon the wire. At last, Burbank flopped over the roof edge like a landed fish.

They were atop the low garage, The Shadow and his agent. A big blot approached the barred widow of the bank; it was The Shadow, cloak outspread to hide the figure within it. Under that shelter, The Shadow began to probe the bars with the tiny beam of his flashlight, which had turned to white.

Then he was whispering for tools that Burbank, crouched close by, provided from the bag.

A low laugh stirred the darkness as the barred

frame came free. Taking it as a summons, Burbank crawled closer. The Shadow showed him two ends of a cut wire, part of the bank's alarm system. Though no one had previously entered by this route, the way had at least been cleared from within the bank itself.

ENTERING, The Shadow and Burbank were within a little office that concealed old furniture, quite out of keeping with the modern style of the bank. A slight glow from the window showed a word on the glass panel of the office door. The reversed letters read: SUPERINTENDENT.

In a corner, a watchman's dinner pail was resting on a table, a half-finished cup of coffee beside it. Instructing Burbank to find out what he could about the damaged alarm system, The Shadow moved ahead alone.

The superintendent's office was in an isolated corner of the mezzanine. It enabled The Shadow to hear whispery sounds that carried from the high-roofed banking room. Following along the balcony rail, he saw occasional flashlight glimmers. At times, the whispers rose to the tone of voices.

Crooks were stationed everywhere. Little by little, The Shadow could picture the whole arrangement. One mob, probably headed by Blitz Gandy, had staged a robbery. Others were covering, here inside the bank, while more were outside. Each group was probably under the control of a separate big-shot, such as Mike Borlo or Snipe Shailey. Perhaps Prex Norgan was also present.

Just who the leaders were, and what their duties, did not matter at the moment. At least the crooks had left the superintendent's office unguarded. Maybe they intended to use it for a getaway, which would be very nice from The Shadow's standpoint.

With that office as a pillbox, The Shadow could stand off the combined crews until the law arrived. But as for attacking crooks in their present entrenched positions, behind tellers windows and solid-walled entries, the attempt would be suicidal. Even The Shadow recognized limitations when it came to pitched battle against assembled hordes.

Returning to the superintendent's office, The Shadow found Burbank examining a switch box. A special lock controlled the alarm system. Someone had broken the lock and gotten at the wires.

The Shadow could picture one of Shiwan Khan's sneaky *naljorpas*, secreted in the bank, ready for such duty. But he could also visualize the deed producing an alarm throughout the bank, unless some short circuits had troubled the system earlier, in which case there would have been localized alarms.

The Shadow was gaining definite clues to what actually had happened.

Burbank was examining big switches hooked to the high-tension circuit that provided the bank with light and power. That system had not been touched. Burbank was announcing the fact, when a sharp buzz interrupted.

It came from the other side of the office accompanied by a blinking light. Stepping across, The Shadow found a special telephone in the wall. The instrument was labeled with a single word: VAULT.

Lifting the receiver, The Shadow spoke in one of his between tones, which could not be identified with anyone. He recognized the voice that responded; it belonged to Joe Cardona.

It was fortunate that The Shadow had not used his sibilant whisper. If he had, Cardona would have supposed him to be Shiwan Khan, for the inspector had by this time guessed the Golden Master's trick. Hearing a voice that might be anybody's, Cardona talked, figuring that he had nothing to lose.

"We're in the vault," informed Joe, "talking over an emergency phone. The watchman is locked in here with us, but we thought there might be a chance of somebody showing up in the super's office.

"We've got air enough to last us a while, but not too long. There's a guy with us that knows the combination. If you come down to the vault room, whoever you are, you can let us out. I'm Inspector Cardona. Listen while we give you the combination—"

THE voice cut off with a groan. Cardona had just heard an interrupting whisper. It was The Shadow's tone, but Joe didn't believe it. Thinking that he was talking to Shiwan Khan, Cardona was starting to hang up when The Shadow pressed a button that produced a buzzing clatter over the wire.

Jarred to attention by the sound, Cardona heard The Shadow's tone again and decided that it might be real, since its owner was so insistent upon continuing the conversation. Again convinced that he had nothing to lose, Cardona repeated the combination as he received it from one of the bank officials.

Mechanically, The Shadow wrote down the numbers as Cardona droned them; but all the while his keen brain was ferreting other facts. The course that lay ahead was entirely too logical. It made The Shadow cold to his usual urge of supplying rapid rescue.

Chance could have brought about an unguarded window in the very room where the call for rescue would come. But The Shadow was dealing with Shiwan Khan, the crime master, who invariably turned chance to his own evil advantage!

Hearing a reflective laugh across the wire, Cardona's hopes went flickering again. But The Shadow's next words produced a change in the suspicious police inspector. The Shadow was talking in terms of rescue, but with a new slant.

He asked Cardona to describe the interior of the vault door. Cardona said that it consisted of a big sheet of plate glass, set in a heavy metal frame. He could see the vault's mechanism through the glass.

The Shadow wanted a description of the mechanism. Cardona gave it. The Shadow must have recognized the type, for he was soon talking, while Cardona listened. The Shadow asked if members of the party were equipped with penknives. Cardona answered yes.

"We've got guns, too," he began. "If you can get us out of here—"

"The penknives come first," interrupted The Shadow. "Unscrew the metal frame and remove the glass. Use the knives to throw the tumblers in the combination mechanism. The blades will do it, easily. Here are the exact instructions—"

As The Shadow whispered details, Cardona repeated them to the others in the vault. Slight *clangs* across the wire told that men were setting to work with the great steel box, while The Shadow still continued with instructions.

Then Cardona was listening to orders that were understandable, yet baffling in their purpose.

"When you open the door," said The Shadow, "push it two-thirds wide. Move everyone to the front corners of the vault room, as silently as possible. Cut the telephone wires and connect them to the hinges of the vault door."

"The telephone wires?" echoed Cardona. "But they'll be no good—"

"They will not be needed for the telephone," inserted The Shadow, "after the vault is open. Listen carefully while I explain their purpose."

Cardona was not the only man who heard The Shadow's next statements. Burbank had drawn close; he was checking the details, too, for they concerned him. When The Shadow had finished, Burbank got to work without awaiting an order.

From the open satchel, Burbank brought tools and lengths of wire. Tilting a flashlight toward the superintendent's switch box, Burbank began methodical operations.

The Shadow was asking Cardona how many guns he and his companions had. Joe counted four—his own, two belonged to captive detectives, and one in the possession of the watchman with them. The Shadow told him to station two guns on each side of the stairway that led up from the vault room.

Then came Cardona's tense announcement that the door had yielded. The Shadow told him to move the prisoners out. Listening intently, The Shadow could hear slight sounds from the receiver; when they ended abruptly he knew that Cardona had cut the telephone wires.

Turning to Burbank, The Shadow approved the competent technician's rapid work and gave him further orders. Moving out from the little office, The Shadow glided silently along the balcony, to pick a route below.

Whispers had ended below. Barricaded crooks were awaiting their zero hour. They knew that the time was near for the stroke that Shiwan Khan had arranged, the sure-fire thrust that would mark the finish of The Shadow.

Shiwan Khan had made the plans—it was The Shadow's turn to execute them, to the black-cloaked fighter's own undoing.

Unless The Shadow, too, had ways of turning chance to suit his own design!

CHAPTER XI
THE PERFECT SNARE

ALL during his descent to the subterranean vault room, The Shadow was aware that crooks were following his progress. The vantage points where enemies were posted were like lairs in a web provided by Shiwan Khan's *naljorpas*.

Brushing threads in the darkness, The Shadow could feel them tighten and break. He knew that mobsters, crouched in safe spots, had felt those snaps, also. There were times when the floor gave slight crackles, despite the caution of The Shadow's tread.

Shiwan Khan's mystics had strewn those places with fine-grained sand that matched the color of the tiled door. The crunches were audible to listening crooks whose ears were laid to the floor.

Those tokens were supposed to be unnoticed by The Shadow; at least, he was not expected to divine their full significance. Shiwan Khan recognized that The Shadow would suspect the presence of crooks, but had calculated that it would not change the cloaked rescuer's quest. So far, The Shadow was performing according to the schedule. He was going to the vault room.

His methods seemed entirely true to form.

Once below, he would release the prisoners, confident that crooks had not spotted him; after that, he would return to offer battle. A simple process, typical of The Shadow. But on this occasion it was slated to end in disaster.

The faintest of crunches told that the black-cloaked master over crime was descending the lowermost steps. Not an eye had seen him; ears had merely detected The Shadow's direction, not his actual location. But the fact that he was going down the steps was quite enough. A squarish chunk of wall moved forward from beneath a metal counter in the main banking room.

The thing was a movable shield, mounted on rubber-tired wheels. Behind it was Dobie Grelf, the cover-up specialist, flanked by two triggermen, who were to aid him in a task of swift murder. The snout of a machine gun poked through the metal shield and pointed toward the lower stairs.

When the shield reached the steps, its wheels found tracks. The stairway had an ornamental baseboard, running from top to bottom. The projecting tires fitted neatly upon those ornamental strips. Of its own weight, the heavy gun shield drew the assassins downward.

Behind Dobie and the two men with him, came other members of the murder mob. Dobie's pale face carried a pleased grin upon bloated lips. The Shadow wasn't going to stand a chance tonight.

All the way down, the gun and its shield moved noiselessly. The whole contrivance was rubber mounted and geared so that its descent would be even. Not only was it a silent juggernaut, equipped to deliver a rapid, deadly hail; its bulk served to muffle all sounds behind it.

Even The Shadow's keen ears could not have heard the mob descending by the stairs. As for sneaking crooks above, they were far out of earshot. Other lieutenants were moving their mobs to new positions. One group was working toward the balcony, the other in the direction of the watchman's door, where they had laid the bound forms of Markham and other prisoners.

Blitz had already gone with the swag. After Dobie ripped loose with the machine gun, it would be his turn for a getaway. The remaining mobs would cover his flight, then depart on their own. In turn, they would be covered by outside crews.

It was like a game of giant leapfrog, this system instituted by Shiwan Khan. Best of all, the last leap would be covered by the craftiest of rear guards, Shiwan Khan's corps of *naljorpas*, who were waiting a few blocks distant. No one would ever trace those slinkers of the night.

For the only person capable of trailing a *naljorpa* would be dead: The Shadow!

The smoothly descending bulwark had halted at the bottom of the stairs. Peering over the top of the shield, Dobie watched for a glimmer of light. He and his men had followed while The Shadow was still somewhere on the stairs; had the cloaked fighter turned to challenge them, they would have drilled him in greeting.

But it was preferable that The Shadow should be below in the squarish vault room, where he couldn't find a place to dodge. The Shadow couldn't possibly have opened the vault by this time, even if he had the combination. That was why Dobie was watching for signs of a flashlight. He expected The Shadow to use one when turning the dials.

No sparkle came. It didn't seem possible that The Shadow could manipulate the combination in total darkness; nevertheless, Dobie wasn't going to let him get way with it, should he be capable of such a feat. The light switch was on the stairway wall near Dobie's elbow. Nudging the gunners to be ready, Dobie pressed it.

The sharp *click* produced no light. Someone had cut off the current. Instantly, a whispered laugh came from the vault room, a chilling tone that gathered menace from the many echoes that rose with it. It seemed like mockery from nowhere, a rising taunt that could bring shivers even to murderers like Dobie Grelf.

The laugh of The Shadow!

AT Dobie's snarled order, the machine gunners cut loose, spraying the vault with a terrific avalanche of bullets. The chatter drowned The Shadow's mockery. The crooks thought that they had ended the tone forever.

Reaching to the top of the shield, Dobie turned on a spotlight. It was hooked to dry cell batteries. The thing gleamed like the triumphant eye of a mighty Cyclops, above the smoking muzzle of the machine gun.

But the wide circle of light showed no trace of a black-cloaked figure on the floor in front of the vault. Nor did it reveal the shiny surface of a steel door, that Dobie expected to see tight shut.

The vault was open, its door swung at a two-thirds angle. The vault's inner walls were scarred by machine gun bullets, but the yawning steel-lined cube showed vacancy. The Shadow had disappeared before the crooks opened fire!

Then came new mockery—a taunt that Dobie located, not by the shivery sound itself, but through a streak of blackness that traced itself upon the wall, then vanished.

Dobie recognized the hawkish profile. Momentarily, The Shadow had thrust himself into the glare, then twisted back to cover.

He was behind the slanted door of the vault, protected by its bulk. He seemed to be inviting crooks to come and take him, bringing their machine gun with them.

The idea suited Dobie. He saw a way to make The Shadow's laugh a short one. The open vault was exactly what he wanted.

While he and his pair of henchmen were pushing across the room, the rest of the mob could take the vault as shelter. If The Shadow tried to hurdle the big shield, he would become a target for the men in the vault. With its steel walls, the vault made a perfect pillbox.

Turning about, Dobie snapped the order. He and the machine gunners heaved, pushed the big shield clear of the jamming stairway, started it rolling toward the open door of the vault.

As the big contrivance cleared from the path, five triggermen leaped from the stairs and made for the vault. Two were veering to throw their weight against the door, hoping to jam The Shadow in back of it, while the other three were ready to cover.

Meanwhile, the side of the rolling shield had almost reached the door edge when The Shadow wheeled from cover, diving past and below the muzzle of the machine gun. Dobie's men swung the shield on its pivot.

Even before the big shield struck the door edge, the air was riddled with sparks. The crackling spurts came as Dobie's triggermen reached the vault. They were jolted, twisted, by some devastating force; their clattering guns sparkled like short-circuited wires.

Then, as Dobie sprang about to view those lashing forms, the steel shield took the juice. Blazing with spurts of artificial lightning, it relayed the current into the men who handled the machine gun. The rubber insulations did not help. They had been packed in place to produce silence, not to stop a current of some thousand volts.

Where metal touched metal, sparks flew. Only Dobie was clear; the rest of his men, machine gunners included, were tossing about like balls of fat in a hot skillet. Yells were ending, as Dobie dived for the stairs; in his mad flight, he fancied that he could hear his mobbies sizzle.

It was all a result of The Shadow's foresight, plus the cooperation of Burbank. Some credit was also due Joe Cardona.

Up in the superintendent's room, Burbank had carefully hooked the high-tension circuit to the telephone wires that Cardona had attached to the hinges of the vault door. The simple pull of a switch had transformed the steel walls and the door into a high-powered frying pan that did not show its nature until tested.

The right men had tried it. Dobie's crew of murderers had reached the equivalent of the electric chair in a rather novel form. They had found a hot box, instead of a "hot seat."

HIGH-POWERED current burned out the spotlight. The sudden darkness enabled Dobie to reach the stairs. Finding remnants of his mob who had remained to cover the stairs, he yelled for them to be ready for The Shadow.

The triggermen weren't fast enough. Big guns spouted before their revolvers could talk. Sprawling crooks heard the laugh of The Shadow, as he drove up among them in pursuit of Dobie. At the top of the stairs, Dobie yelled for other big-shots to aid him; as he howled, he ran for the far door.

Guessing that he couldn't make it, Dobie spun about and jabbed shots for the stair top. His aim was just a trifle high. Flattening below the uppermost step, The Shadow picked his target and jabbed a reply.

Dobie was shooting at a blackened square that represented the stairway. The Shadow chose a much better mark; Dobie's spurting gun. The Shadow's shot drove home. Jolted, Dobie lost his revolver, and sprawled upon the weapon as it clattered to the floor.

From his present position, The Shadow could cover every avenue of approach. Secure in that stronghold, he was backed by four other gunners. Cardona and the rest had come from the front corners of the strong room, where they had been safely placed while The Shadow was drawing Dobie's mob in his own direction.

Two groups were putting up a fire: Mike Borlo was giving orders from the outer door, Snipe Shailey from along the balcony. The Shadow not only answered those shots, he delivered a welcoming laugh that invited his enemies to attack. Hearing The Shadow's mirth, Burbank cut off the circuit to the bank vault.

When lights glimmered from the vault room, The Shadow knew that the machine gun was no longer electrified. He sent Cardona and others down to get it. Meanwhile, Burbank finished repairing the alarm switch. Brazen throated bells began a clangor from all over the bank.

Mike's crew fled out by the doorway fearing that arriving police would cut them off. Springing from his safety spot, The Shadow followed, peppering them with bullets to prevent them from killing the prisoners who lay in the doorway.

The crooks managed to take a few cripples along, including Dobie, but they abandoned Markham and the other captives. Reaching the prisoners, The Shadow released them. He told them to arm themselves with guns that thugs had dropped.

The Shadow's sprint across the banking floor was so unexpected that he was halfway to his goal before Snipe and the balcony mob began to open fire. They missed him with their wild shots, and their chance at better aim was spoiled by Cardona's action with the captured machine gun.

Tilting the shield straight upward with the aid of the men about him, Cardona kept drilling bullets along the balcony rail, even after The Shadow had completed his dash.

Snipe and his gang made for their only outlet, the window of the superintendent's office. They were well back from the rail, to avoid Cardona's rattling fire; but The Shadow picked off a few of them by long-range shots from the door.

With pals dropping like the moving targets in a

shooting gallery, Snipe and the rest did not stop. They dashed through the superintendent's office and sprang from the window to the garage roof, without encountering Burbank at all. The contact man had discreetly stepped into a closet, knowing that he could not combat so large a mob alone.

Burbank was using a gun, however, when The Shadow arrived. Firing slowly, but carefully, the methodical contact man nicked a pair of Snipe's tribe, while the rest were dropping through an opening into the garage. All had gained cover when The Shadow reached Burbank's window.

The garage route offered a good exit. The Shadow took it, accompanied by Burbank. Cars roared away into the night, before The Shadow could overtake them. Snipe's mob was off to join the others, as Shiwan Khan had ordered. The beaten crooks had managed to get clear before the law closed in.

Moe's cab had come warily into the neighborhood. With Shiwan Khan's followers vanished, mystics as well as thugs, The Shadow decided that it would be safe to use the cab without danger of leaving a trail. He and Burbank entered it.

AS the cab rolled away, a strange thing happened. A long, limber creature twisted from a doorway and broke into a trot. In his stride, the elongated runner seemed to bounce like a rubber ball. His lopes were amazingly long, and so swift that his feet touched the ground in fleeting fashion.

The man was a *lung-gom-pa* runner, a mystic of the strange type that Bryson had mentioned during his ambulance ride. Eyes fixed dead ahead, the *lung-gom-pa* kept them on The Shadow's cab, and held to the course through the darkened, narrow streets that Moe preferred.

There were moments when the runner loped into the light, revealing himself as a brown-faced man, clad in a short, ragged tunic. Under his arm the *lung-gom-pa* clutched a phurba, and his long fingers were the sort that could loose the enchanted dagger with all its reputed accuracy.

Never did the runner remain long in the light. His swift pace always carried him into darkness before eyes could notice him.

To the *lung-gom-pa*, the side streets of Manhattan were a better racetrack than the grassy plains of Tibet. When the cab went beneath an elevated structure, the runner followed, keeping away from the traffic lane except when he swerved to pass the steel elevated pillars.

He was on the trail of The Shadow, whose keen eyes did not spy the lung-gom-pa during occasional glances back from the cab. Victor over massed men of crime, The Shadow had postponed his search for Shiwan Khan only to be trailed in turn!

CHAPTER XII
MIND VERSUS MIND

THE gaunt features of Kent Allard showed their usual worry, but this time there was a cause for their expression. Not that The Shadow was actually worried; he had long ago forgotten how that emotion felt. But he had, at least, lost some of his usual confidence.

Two nights ago, he had fought a terrific battle and had won it, saving the lives of others through tactics that had outmastered the strategy of Shiwan Khan. The Shadow had expected further results from that victory, but they had not come.

Crooks who had been easy to trace were gone entirely from the scene. Shiwan Khan had spirited them away, as effectively as if they had been creatures of a dream. Neither The Shadow nor the police had obtained a clue to the whereabouts of the missing big-shots.

Certainly, Shiwan Khan had not disposed of them. Even their failure to eliminate The Shadow could not have enraged the emotionless Golden Master, particularly when the blame rested upon only one man: Dobie Grelf.

They had been real enough, those fighters, as The Shadow could testify. They had not been *yidams*, or other phantom creatures, that Shiwan Khan claimed he could produce by mental means. They had left too many of their number on the field.

Nor could Shiwan Khan have transported them into a *bardo*, or land beyond. Such a world was imaginary in itself. If Shiwan Khan wanted a *bardo*, he had to fake one. It followed, therefore, that the missing crooks were still somewhere in Manhattan; but that did not prove that they could be found.

One public enemy, Prex Norgan, had been in town almost a year without being discovered.

There was something else that impressed The Shadow, none too favorably. Despite his precautions to protect his identity of Allard, he could sense that he was being watched. Such a sensation was a tricky thing to analyze, but The Shadow had been able to check its actuality.

The Xinca servants were his index. Those stolid servitors were restless. Their tribal instincts, that made them keep together when jungle beasts approached, were at work here in New York. Perhaps the Xincas did not realize that their watchfulness had increased, but The Shadow could observe it.

This night was drizzly. Darkness was very thick outside the window. Extinguishing the light, The Shadow dropped his limping pose; he raised the sash and swung across the sill. Clinging to the ledge, he stretched out and peered toward the corner wall. He saw a scrawny form sidle from sight like a spider seeking a crack.

Dropping back into the room, The Shadow closed the window. He turned on a lamp as he passed it, and approached the door, leaning on his cane.

The Xincas were slow, reluctant, as they brought him his black garments. Speaking reassuring words in their native tongue, The Shadow garbed himself in cloak and hat, dropped the cane and made a quick wheel out into the hall.

He had a gun in readiness, but it was not needed. No living creature was in sight.

Descending by the fire tower, The Shadow adopted a most unusual policy, which he continued after he reached the street. At intervals, he openly showed himself, only to fade from sight with quick, evasive twists. If *naljorpas* were in the offing, the only course was to draw them out and meet them in combat before they could return to Shiwan Khan.

Ending a long whirl in a doorway, The Shadow gave a quick look along the street. His eye detected motion near an opposite doorstep. Following its direction, The Shadow's keen eyes spotted a loping figure that appeared fleetingly, some yards away. The thing was gone by the time he realized what it was.

A *lung-gom-pa*!

FIXING his eyes on the corner, The Shadow saw the runner turn. Taking a route through an alley, The Shadow reached the next street and stepped into a cab. He passed the driver a ten-dollar bill; his hat removed, The Shadow let the driver glimpse the face of Allard.

"Go exactly where I tell you," said The Shadow in a crisp tone. "I'm looking for something; when I see it, I'll let you know."

What Allard was looking for, the cabby never guessed. He was too busy following the orders that his eccentric passenger gave him. At times Allard called for speed, then sudden halts. He pointed to corners, then changed his mind about turning them.

He seemed to prefer the worst streets, and the darkest ones, and his whole course was a zigzag. The meter had ticked off two of the ten dollars when they reached an area filled with old-fashioned houses. There Allard kept the driver going around the block, until they had made three circuits.

The tour satisfied him. He dismissed the cab, without asking for any change. As he stepped to the curb he became The Shadow. Sidling from one basement entry to another, he reached an old house that looked no different from any others in the block.

But The Shadow was positive that he had seen the *lung-gom-pa* take a final lope up the brownstone steps of that particular residence. In his turn, The Shadow chose the basement door; he picked its lock, and entered with drawn gun.

The whole basement was dark. Using the tiny spot of his little flashlight, The Shadow found a stairway and went up to the first door. There was a dim light in the hallway; avoiding it, The Shadow looked for the *lung-gom-pa*, but saw no sign of the missing runner.

Moving up to the second floor, The Shadow noted dust streaks on the banister. The whole house seemed empty and deserted, but the light in the lower hall meant that there must be occupants. A few moments later, The Shadow had actual proof.

The second floor was dimly lighted. Crouching on the stairs, The Shadow saw two figures approaching with slow, deliberate stride. The stairway ended at the center of the hall; the patrollers were coming from the ends.

They were brownish men, with fixed looks on their thin faces. They wore baggy trousers, drab robes that came to knee-length, and their heads had short-clipped hair. Though they resembled Shiwan Khan's *naljorpas*, The Shadow identified them as a different breed.

These men were *dubchens*, skilled wizards, of a higher class than the *naljorpas*. They carried daggers of the *phurba* type, but seldom used the weapons. Where a mere *naljorpa* fought at close range by temporarily paralyzing an unwary opponent, a *dubchen* had the reputed power to strike at a distance.

Hailstorms, floods, even avalanches, were believed to be the product of *dubchens*, when they chose to stir up such elements. Such was the belief in Tibet. While such exaggerations could scarcely be credited, it was a certainty that any *dubchen* was stronger than a *naljorpa* in all forms of combat.

As they met, the *dubchens* stared mutually for several seconds; then, as if in response to a mental signal, they turned away from the stairs and faced a door directly opposite. They bowed solemnly, then paced away, each in an opposite direction.

Both sentinels had turned their backs, but they seemed quite unconcerned. Silent in their tread, their thoughts focused on their duty, they had an air of confidence, as though able to detect anything that happened behind them.

Whatever their ability, it did not apply in The Shadow's case. His glide was silent as he crossed the hall. He had time to test the door before the dubchens swung about. The test was all he needed. The door gave when The Shadow turned the knob.

Inside were curtains at the end of a little entry. Silently, The Shadow closed the door. Drawing an automatic, he stepped to the curtains, whisked them boldly aside and swept into the room beyond.

In the dim glow, he saw a stooped form seated on a low throne across a small room. With a challenging laugh, The Shadow aimed his .45 straight for the enthroned figure.

Surprise tactics were the only way to deal with Shiwan Khan. For once, The Shadow was tempted to be over-quick with his trigger, but he managed to restrain his finger until the enthroned man lifted his head.

As the face came up, the room lights rose. The Shadow's hand relaxed, his gun sank toward his cloak.

THE man on the throne was not Shiwan Khan, nor was he attired in a golden robe. Instead of the satanic features of the Golden Master, The Shadow saw a benign countenance that might have been a hundred years old, judging from the parchment texture of its flesh. Steel-gray eyes gazed toward The Shadow; their flash seemed to carry welcome.

Thin, dry lips wrinkled in a smile. As they did, they spoke in a tone that was truly musical:

"I am Marpa Tulku. You are welcome here, Ying Ko. I was confident that you would follow my messenger."

The name of Marpa Tulku was sufficient. The term *tulku* signified a living deity, and this man, Marpa, was regarded as such in Tibet. His robe, striped with deep-shaded colors, was one token of his rank. More important was his odd-shaped hat, which bore a huge, glittering diamond in its center.

The hat itself was yellow, which meant that Marpa Tulku was a *Gelugspa*, or member of the Yellow Hats, the predominant group among Tibetan mystics. Never before had a true *tulku* been known to travel far from the Land of Snows. That fact told The Shadow why Marpa Tulku was in America.

Though not a word had left The Shadow's lips, Marpa Tulku smiled again. Once again, he addressed his visitor as Ying Ko, the Chinese name for The Shadow.

"You are correct, Ying Ko," declared the *tulku*. "I have made this journey because of Shiwan Khan. His schemes of conquest do not concern me, because it is a worldly affair. But there is another matter that demands a settlement.

"Shiwan Khan has made false claims." Smiling lips had straightened, their tone had lost its music. "He has proclaimed himself a *tulku*, like myself. He has lured treacherous *naljorpas* into his service. He has even induced a *gomchen* to aid him in schemes of evil.

"These things are wrong"—the tone was slower, solemn—"and I have come to rectify them! I have learned, Ying Ko, that your cause is the same as mine: to destroy the power of Shiwan Khan. Let us, therefore, seek the way together."

Descending from his throne, Marpa Tulku drew a handful of roundish pebbles from the folds of his robe. Solemnly, he laid them in a circle. The Shadow knew his purpose. Marpa Tulku was forming a *kyilkhor*, or magic diagram. He intended to perform a *dubthab* ritual.

The proceeding was not claptrap. It was Marpa's way of reaching a state of intense concentration, that would enable him to exercise clairvoyant powers. Ability to see distant scenes was so common in Tibet that it was accepted as an ordinary phenomenon, not as some supernatural accomplishment.

But there were few who could exercise that faculty to its full degree. Of those few, Marpa Tulku was one.

SEATED in the center of the *kyilkhor*, Marpa Tulku drew his body erect. His eyes closed; color welled into his ancient face. He pressed his long hands tightly against his chest. His breath fully drawn, Marpa Tulku held it for minutes.

As he exhaled, he spoke. His words seemed far away.

"I see Shiwan Khan." He paused, drew in a spasm of breath. "It's Shiwan Khan in his robe of gold... I see the glitter of his eyes... They are watching—"

A convulsion shook the *tulku*. His breath left him with a sigh. He drew another long supply of air, then continued:

"He is watching men... They are men that you have met, Ying Ko... They are in a room, a low room... It is somewhere underground. I can hear their words—"

With a violent gesture, Marpa Tulku threw his hands in front of his closed eyes. The color left his face as he recoiled. His dropping hand brushed aside the stones from the surrounding diagram. Roused from his trance, the *tulku* faced The Shadow with a solemn gaze. Marpa Tulku recognized what had happened.

"As I listened," he said, "my thoughts became identical with those of Shiwan Khan. He has telepathic powers. Not only can he send messages on the wind, he can receive them. He sensed the interference and injected disturbing thoughts.

"Further effort would be useless at this time. Later, I shall perform another *dubthab*, perhaps with results. What I have told you so far, Ying Ko, is accurate. I am sure, moreover, that Shiwan Khan is planning another crime, like the one that you defeated."

Rising, Marpa Tulku stepped through the curtains. Opening the door, he signaled the patrolling *dubchens*. They halted while their master again addressed The Shadow.

"My cause is yours, Ying Ko," repeated Marpa Tulku. "You may call upon me for any aid that you require. My servants are yours, whenever needed."

Returning the bow, The Shadow stepped from the room. A *dubchen* followed him down the stairs and ushered him out into the night. It was not until he had merged with distant darkness, that the black-cloaked venturer delivered a whispered laugh.

The Shadow had solved the riddle of the spies who had kept so close to him. They belonged to Marpa Tulku, not to Shiwan Khan. The Shadow's true identity, that of Kent Allard, was safe with Marpa Tulku. But that was not the reason for The Shadow's mirth.

He was thinking of his interview with Marpa Tulku. He had come to a complete understanding with the Tibetan master; they had formed a lasting alliance toward the destruction of Shiwan Khan.

Yet, in that entire interview, The Shadow had not spoken a single word!

CHAPTER XIII
THE CORPSE THAT LIVED

THEY were in their low-built room, the lieutenants of Shiwan Khan, exactly as Marpa Tulku had described them to The Shadow. The place was lavishly furnished; thick rugs strewed the floor. But the walls were of roughly finished stone; his impression of that surface had given the *tulku* the fact that the place was underground.

Prex Norgan sat at the head of the conference table, acting as spokesman for Shiwan Khan. Neither he nor any of his companions knew that Shiwan Khan was watching them through a curtained doorway at the end of the room, behind Prex.

The distant vision of Marpa Tulku had disclosed a fact that had escaped observers close at hand!

Prex Norgan was flanked by Mike Borlo and Snipe Shailey. Farther down the table were Silk Laddiman and Shag Flink; they were keeping silence, glad that they rated among the big-shots. But Blitz Gandy, at the far end of the table, was having plenty to say.

Blitz regarded his end as the head, and with good reason. He had pulled the real job, two nights ago. He had gotten away with the gravy, while others were bungling things. Blitz didn't hold that against them; he simply felt that it went to his credit.

In the midst of a loud statement, Blitz was interrupted by Prex's cold tone:

"You talk too much, Blitz."

"Dough talks, don't it" countered Blitz. "Who got the dough from the Battery Trust—you or me?"

"You did," conceded Prex. "But a lot of good it was. It's all listed currency. That makes it hot."

"Shiwan Khan wanted it," argued Blitz, "so I got it. That puts it up to him to freeze it."

"He'll handle that all right. He handles everything."

As Blitz began an objection, Prex came to his feet. Despite his months of mystic training, Prex was losing his temper.

"Lay off the big talk, Blitz!" he stormed. "Shiwan Khan figured out the job. He fixed up this slick hideaway for us. We're all set here, with our mobs. We're ready for another job, and nobody can stop us, not even The Shadow!"

"Yeah?" Blitz growled. "He did some stopping the other night. What about those guys that fried? He wiped out Dobie's mob, The Shadow did. What's more"—Blitz glanced from Mike to Snipe—"some of the rest of us lost good triggermen."

"We've got more than we need," retorted Prex. "They come a dime a dozen."

"You mean guys like Dobie?"

There were murmurs, ugly ones from the group. Blitz's argument carried weight. Dobie Grelf had died in transit from the bank to this hideaway. His death was something that the others did not like; not just on Dobie's account.

They had been told that in the service of Shiwan Khan, they would be immune from personal danger. Such immunity had been specifically implied in case of battle with The Shadow. Mike and the other listeners agreed with Prex that mobbies and gorillas did not count. But they sided with Blitz, in the matter of Dobie Grelf.

Before Prex Norgan could think of anything to say, the curtains parted behind him. Mutiny smoldered, though it still existed, when the lieutenants saw Shiwan Khan step into the room. Imperiously, the Golden Master approached the table. At his gesture, Prex yielded the seat at the head.

Greenish eyes studied the group. The others let their own heads turn, even Blitz. They didn't like to meet those eyes, at all. No one guessed that mere words from Shiwan Khan would have forced them to face his gaze. The Golden Master could have turned them into mere machines, had he so chosen.

Had Shiwan Khan wanted automatons, he could have created them from ordinary mobbies. He valued his present lieutenants because they had individual abilities. He preferred to hold them without recourse to dominating powers of a hypnotic sort.

But Shiwan Khan was quite willing to provide a phenomenal demonstration that would convince them that he was more than human. With such a scheme in mind, he spoke mildly; his tone even had an abject touch.

"These men are right," Shiwan Khan told Prex, who was standing close by. "I promised them life. Dobie Grelf received that promise. Of course, in a sense, Dobie was merely wounded—"

"He was as good as croaked!" interjected Blitz, angrily. "Ask Mike. He's the guy that lugged Dobie out of the bank."

"He was still alive," put in Mike, who felt uneasy sitting so close to Shiwan Khan. "If we'd had a medico on the job, right then, why maybe—"

"Maybe nothing!" stormed Blitz. "Dobie was through, and you know it! Anyway, we didn't have a saw-bones with us. So what?"

Shiwan Khan raised a gold-sleeved arm. His tone carried a melodious tinkle. Only Prex caught the ugliness behind that tone. It occurred to him that he might soon be Shiwan Khan's only lieutenant.

But Prex was wrong.

"I have only one course," announced Shiwan Khan. "I must keep my promise. Let me assure you, however, that it is exactly what I intended. It is the reason why I came here."

Lifting his hands, he clapped them three times, very slowly. In from another room came two Mongols, so gigantic that they had to double their bodies to get through the low door. Blitz did not like the size of those Ordos tribesmen. He shifted uneasily, was reaching for his gun, when he saw the burden that the Mongols carried.

It was a stretcher, bearing the body of Dobie Grelf. Rising, Shiwan Khan approached the stiffened corpse.

FROM that moment onward, the Golden Master was watched by riveted eyes. If ever a man was really dead, Dobie Grelf could be so classed. But Shiwan Khan, master of the incredible, was ready to challenge any physical fact.

Clawlike hands stretched above the dead man's sightless eyes, Shiwan Khan distorted his own features until they were hideous and livid. From deep in his throat came the high-pitched utterance: "*Haik*!"

The odd shriek rang through the low room. Shiwan Khan repeated it, then gave other syllabic utterances. He was bounding like a dervish; all the while, his greenish gaze was fixed on the dead man's glassy eyes.

Suddenly, Shiwan Khan flung himself beside the corpse, gripped its hands with his and stretched them wide. His livid lips were breathing upon those of Dobie, as if to stir their bloated death-grin.

At times, Shiwan Khan wrenched the body upward; at first, Dobie's neck went back, as if hinged. But on the final attempt, Shiwan Khan's jerk of the extended arms affected the head as well.

It stayed upright; so did the half-lifted body, as Shiwan Khan relaxed his grip. Then, tightening his hold upon the hands, the Golden Master pulled the dead form to its feet.

Other lieutenants shrank away as Shiwan Khan swung the corpse in their direction. Then, to their utter amazement, the figure of Dobie Grelf began a slow pace forward, under the guidance of the Golden Master. Glazed eyes still bulged, but they looked alive. The bloated lips were moving, almost uttering words!

Taking Dobie's shoulders, Shiwan Khan started him toward the curtained door. Pointing with one hand, he pressed the walking corpse forward with the other. Then, releasing Dobie entirely, Shiwan Khan stepped aside and lifted the curtain so that the slow-pacing figure could go through!

Gradually, the Golden Master let the curtain drop. He gestured to the Mongols; they took away the stretcher. Through the curtain, Shiwan Khan spoke words; after tilting his head to catch a reply, he nodded and spoke again. Turning about, he resumed his seat at the head of the conference table.

"I promised life," announced Shiwan Khan, "and I have given it! Of course, we must expect a slow recovery. It will be weeks, perhaps longer, before we can depend upon Dobie for further duty."

The lieutenants were shrunk in their chairs, mopping at their foreheads. They were used to seeing living men turned into dead ones; in fact, they all had dabbled in such business. But to see a dead man brought back to life rather horrified the group of murderers.

They were wondering how they would stand, if certain dead persons came back among the living and told all they knew. They were thinking in terms of the electric chair, when it struck them, one by one, that they could even beat as tough a rap as that, if they remained loyal to Shiwan Khan.

What he had done for Dobie, he could do for them! From his place at the head of the table, Shiwan Khan watched the looks of gleeful confidence that swept the faces of his lieutenants.

Turning to Prex Norgan, Shiwan Khan suggested: "Proceed with your unfinished business."

"Our next job is Traymer's jewelry store," Prex told the lieutenants. "We can go over the lay tomorrow. The main point is this: we're giving the job to Silk Laddiman—"

"Why to Silk?" interjected Blitz with a growl. "He handles warehouses. A jewelry store comes in the bank class."

Blitz's argument didn't make a hit with the others, particularly Silk Laddiman. Their faces tightened, as Blitz began again to brag about how he had handled matters at the Battery Trust. All eyes turned toward Shiwan Khan.

"The point has merit," declared the Golden Master, calmly. "We shall let Blitz repeat his competent work."

Grumbles ended. No one cared to dispute a decision made by Shiwan Khan. But Blitz was chuckling triumphantly, bragging more than ever, as he and others went from the room to their quarters in the huge underground hideaway.

Only Prex remained. Shiwan Khan had gestured for him to stay. The Golden Master conducted Prex through the curtained doorway. On the floor, just beyond, lay the crumpled form of Dobie.

"A *rolang*," confided Shiwan Khan—"a corpse that dances. It was better to keep the performance impressive."

"I know," nodded Prex, "Pashod told me about them. It takes more than *shugs*, though, doesn't it?"

"The warmth of *tumo* is necessary," declared Shiwan Khan. "It requires long practice, to transfer vital energy from a living body into a dead one. Ordinarily, the demonstration is useless"—Shiwan Khan seemed weary, as he spoke—"for it can be no more than temporary.

"But on this occasion, it proved its worth. I can depend upon my chosen lieutenants. They will no longer fear death. Later, when I have shown them the short path to understanding, they will know that death is a mere illusion."

Prex agreed. He had completed the "short path," under the tutelage of Pashod, and believed in the things that he had learned. But Prex was still interested in worldly matters.

"About Blitz," he began. "Giving him the jewelry job will make the others pretty sore."

"They will be recompensed," stated Shiwan Khan, with an off-key chuckle. "They will relish whatever may happen to Blitz Gandy. No one will insist that I again demonstrate my ability to bring the dead to life."

"You're getting rid of Blitz?"

"He is useless alive. In death, he may serve us. Where he goes, The Shadow will follow, believing that the way is safe. Death to Blitz can mean—"

Shiwan Khan had stepped to the curtained doorway. He paused, as he lifted he drape; he completed his statement as the curtain fell. His words, though the finish of a sentence, were a harsh-chimed promise in themselves:

"Death to The Shadow!"

CHAPTER XIV
CROOKS LEAD THE WAY

AT noon the next day, Prex Norgan called the lieutenants together and showed the plans for the next job. Again, they were intrigued by the way in which Shiwan Khan had prepared for everything. Their only objection was that the job looked too easy.

Blitz Gandy took the statement as an insult. He argued that every job was tough for the guy that did the real work. Warming up to an angry heat, Blitz put himself in perfect fettle for the next step ordered by Shiwan Khan.

As soon as he was alone with Blitz, Prex used some subtlety that the Golden Master had suggested earlier in the day. He began by agreeing that the job was tough.

"How about getting some new gorillas?" queried Prex. "If you've got a bigger mob, the thing will be lot easier."

"I like things tough," returned Blitz. "Besides, why should I borrow any monkeys from lugs like Mike or Snipe?"

"Who said to borrow any?"

"You mean you want me to sign up some new gorillas, on my own?"

"That's the idea, Blitz. A big guy needs a big mob."

Prex put the final comment suavely. It flattered Blitz. He *was* a big guy, right enough, and he could picture himself becoming bigger than any of the other lieutenants. Bigger, even, than Prex Norgan, who at present enjoyed Shiwan Khan's chief favor. But Blitz, despite his love for brag, was shrewd enough to keep the final sentiment to himself.

As for suitable mobbies, Blitz could name a half a dozen to amplify his fair-sized band. The question was how to contact them without leaving this hideaway where Shiwan Khan was keeping his lieutenants and their followers thoroughly secluded. In fact, Blitz didn't know the location of the underground stronghold; he had come here in a covered truck.

Of all the lieutenants, the only one in the full know was Prex Norgan.

"Don't bring the new gorillas here to begin with," declared Prex. "There's a phone at the base where you're going to start from. Call them up when you get there; not all six of them, but just one or two. Have those guys get hold of the rest."

The suggestion suited Blitz. It naturally meant that he and his mob would have to start early. Prex advised him not to tell the new recruits where to come, until they had all assembled at some suitable place, where they could stand by for another call.

Later that afternoon, Blitz and his original crew left the sizeable hideaway by a passage that had once been a water main. It brought them to a small garage, managed by a couple of Prex's men.

Blitz and the thugs entered a furniture van. Driven by a muffled Mongol, the vehicle set out; tightly sealed in the interior, Blitz and his bunch began a pinochle game by the glow of an electric lantern.

They didn't care where they had started from. Their destination was more important. They reached it in about half an hour. Backed into a blind alley, the van unloaded its thuggish freight; under its shelter, the crooks slid down through an opened cellar grating to reach their new base.

Blitz used the telephone soon afterward; calling

two recruits, he told them to contact the others. They were to hear from Blitz again, by nightfall.

They were to hear from The Shadow, too, though Blitz did not know it. Such was the design of Shiwan Khan.

The Golden Master knew that his cloaked foe would still be keeping tabs on the underworld, seeking any clue that would lead him to vanished big-shots like Blitz Gandy. Any gathering of new candidates for Blitz's mob would prove conspicuous in the badlands, so far as The Shadow's surveillance was concerned.

For at present, The Shadow's only method was to keep close check on scattered small-fry, who were hoping that former acquaintance with the missing biggies would make them eligible for future service in crime's greatest, and most mysterious push.

AT dusk, six boastful thugs were gathered in the rear room of an underworld dive. Blitz Gandy was consistent; he preferred other braggarts as members of his mob. These thugs had covered their tracks in clumsy, elephantine style.

When Blitz's call came through, they moved out from the meeting place, exchanging comments as they went. Two of them actually named their destination, while they were crowding into a sedan that was parked in the rear street.

Even before the sedan had started, a black-cloaked figure was sliding off through darkness. A block away, The Shadow blinked a green signal that brought Moe Shrevnitz's cab. In a few minutes, the swift driver was taking The Shadow straight to his goal, which he could easily reach ahead of the recruits, who were at least smart enough to take a roundabout route.

As the cab rolled into a side street that led toward Times Square, The Shadow noted three buildings.

The first was a corner jewelry store, the large house of J. C. Traymer & Co. It bore no signs; everyone was supposed to know where Traymer's was; people who didn't, could not be regarded as proper customers for so select a concern.

There was a main entrance on the avenue, a small one on the side street. Past Traymer's was a narrow parking place, paved with cement. The next building was an old theater, which had lately been remodeled.

The theater was named the Pandora, and it was open for business, presenting Shakespearean drama. Already, patrons were arriving for the evening performance, which was to be "The Merchant of Venice."

Beyond the theater was a squatty building, one of the nineteenth century type. It was closed; a big sign on the front stated that a certain wrecking company would soon demolish the old structure. The Shadow studied the squatty building quite carefully, as he passed it in the cab. It was to be his first stopping place.

The cab swung corners and reached the next street, in back of the condemned building. Dropping off in darkness, The Shadow let Moe continue through. On foot, the cloaked investigator approached a blind alley, stopping in a doorway short of it.

Queer-shaped roofs dominated both sides of the street; good lurking places for *naljorpas*. The Shadow could almost sense the electric presence of the murderous mystics who served Shiwan Khan. The scene was quite as he expected it. Mobsters would be passed through, but the *naljorpas* were on close lookout for any intruders.

One invader could pass that cordon: The Shadow. He had worked through such meshes before. But even he found it necessary to pick a favorable opportunity. One knife, skimmed from darkness before The Shadow could spot its launcher, would be enough to end the cloaked fighter's career.

Calmly, The Shadow awaited his opportunity. It came, in the form of Blitz's new recruits. Alighting from their sedan, they began a cumbersome sneak into the alley, moving in by pairs. No lurking *naljorpas* could have failed to identify them, for each pair had a flashlight.

When the final brace of crooks entered the alley, The Shadow followed. One thug had a gun; he was gesturing it about, while the other sprayed a flashlight along the cobbles, from one side of the alley to the other.

But the shape that trailed them closely was never in the glow. As darkness kept closing behind the shoulders of the advancing pair, The Shadow's solid form came with it, part of the very gloom.

Reaching the opening in the base of the building wall, the crooks slid through. Being the last of the scheduled arrivals, they clanked the grating tight in place above them. Hardly had their flashlight moved off through the cellar, before gloved hands were at work.

Deftly, silently, The Shadow raised the hinged grating and squeezed through the narrowest of places. It was swift, that entry, and The Shadow let the grating settle down in place almost in the same move. Watching *naljorpas* could not possibly have seen the blackish motion, nor heard the slightest of sounds.

ONCE inside the building, The Shadow's only problem was the matter of Blitz's mob. Once he had handled that crew, he could choose any exit, even the alley. Getting in had been the difficulty. In getting out, The Shadow could use the shelter of the cellar window, while baiting *naljorpas* with his laugh and battering them with his bullets.

But it would take more than pitched battle to

settle Blitz's oversized mob. The Shadow's only course was to let the crooks move along their road to crime; to thin their ranks by nibbling tactics, then find an advantageous spot from which to ambush them.

Such was The Shadow's way of nullifying heavy odds. Certain masterminds were familiar with The Shadow's strategy. Among such masters was a great brain named Shiwan Khan.

Elsewhere, Shiwan Khan was putting plans of his own into action. One of his locations was the Pandora Theater, that lay midway between the old office building and the jewelry store. A limousine had pulled into the parking space that flanked the theater. The big car had blackened windows; it's chauffeur was a Mongol.

Prex Norgan stepped from the car as soon as its rear door opened. He was followed by two other big-shots, Mike Borlo and Snipe Shailey. Three more men joined them, smooth-looking trigger experts. One belonged to Prex; another to Mike; the third to Snipe.

Instead of going around by the box office, Prex rapped at a side exit of the theater. An usher opened the door. Prex showed him six tickets. A five-dollar bill greased the usher's objections to the irregular procedure. Taking the tickets he conducted the six patrons to a curtained theater box near the exit.

In the gloom of the box, the big-shots and their right-hand men were indistinguishable only by the starched fronts of their tuxedo shirts. They could easily be taken for a respectable theater party.

The curtain was rising as the six took their chairs. The crooks heard the opening line, from the lips of Antonio:

"In soothe, I know not why I am so sad—"

"Hear that," undertoned Prex, with a chuckle. "There's a guy that's sad right at the start of the show. But I know a bozo that will be a whole lot sadder before it's over."

Though Prex Norgan did not specify the person, he meant The Shadow. The one lieutenant in Shiwan Khan's full confidence, Prex knew all the details of the Golden Master's latest scheme to rid crime's pathway of the black-cloaked fighter who alone had managed to dispute the rule of the mighty Shiwan Khan!

CHAPTER XV
THE TRAIL BELOW

PACKED in a room that was cramped with cigarette smoke, Blitz Gandy and his thugs were ready for their coming venture. They had guns and flashlights drawn; they were merely awaiting a buzz from the telephone to signal the moment for advance.

Blitz still hadn't mastered the ability to catch mental messages from Shiwan Khan. Perhaps that was another reason why the Golden Master had decided to discard the argumentative lieutenant.

At the door, Blitz had posted two lookouts. It would have been suicidal for The Shadow to attack the massed mob while watchers were alert. In a darkened passage outside, The Shadow was continuing his waiting policy.

There was a buzz from the muffled telephone bell. Blitz answered; he leered his recognition of the crystalline voice that spoke across the wire. Shiwan Khan had given the word. Dropping the telephone, Blitz turned to a corner of the cellar room.

There, he bashed the cement with gun butt. Astonished mobbies saw the stone fall apart. It wasn't cement, but merely a layer of plaster over a strip of wallboard. Having gashed a jagged hole in the wall, he stepped through and ordered the others to follow.

The mobbies filed after Blitz, leaving only the two lookouts. One of those thugs turned to admire the trick opening in the opposite wall. While he was studying the gap, he heard a thud behind him; something like an echo of Blitz's gun strokes.

It wasn't an echo, though. The thump had been delivered by another gun butt, straight to the skull of the watcher at the door. The turning lookout saw his companion crumple; then, across the sagging figure, came a shape cloaked in black.

The Shadow reached the second crook before the fellow could fire. Again, a long hand, shoving forward, planted a hard stroke with a reversed automatic. The heavy handle of the .45 carried the effect of a sledge-hammer. The second thug collapsed.

Picking up the telephone, The Shadow made a call to Burbank, told the contact man to phone police headquarters and give Inspector Cardona an accurate tip-off, by way of variety. Then, after swiftly binding and gagging the unconscious lookouts, The Shadow took up the trail below.

Soon clear of the office building, he entered the cellar of the theater. Across a wide room stacked with scenery and props, The Shadow came to a short passage that led to another section of the theater cellar.

The passage ended with a steel door, its lower half solid, the upper half criss-crossed bars. The door served as a barrier to a subcellar, which contained most of the theater's machinery. The door was unlocked, for Blitz considered the place safe from invasion.

Descending half a dozen stone steps, The Shadow reached the subcellar. It was lighted; the glow showed dynamos and other machinery, a long row of fire extinguishers along one wall.

On the far side of the subcellar was a metal partition; from it The Shadow heard a muffled *thrumming* sound. It was the fan room, important to the theater's air-conditioning system.

In a corner to the right of the partition, The Shadow saw a black, irregular gap in the wall. Blitz had hacked through another well-faked section of stone. Through an underground passage beyond it, the big-shot and his crew were taking a direct route to the jewelry store!

REACHING the gap, The Shadow listened. He heard muffled scrapings ahead; peering through the break, he saw flashlights pointing upward. The crooks were evidently working their way up into the store, this time prying solid stone from their path.

Sappers had probably dug the entire tunnel while the theater had been under repair; but they had necessarily stopped short before it was completed. Blitz was superintending the remaining task—that of actually puncturing a path into Traymer's.

Again, The Shadow waited. He wanted to give the police time to arrive and throw a cordon around the entire block. He calculated that Cardona had heard from Burbank by this time. Earlier, The Shadow had made sure that Joe was in his headquarters office.

Could The Shadow have viewed the interior of the jewelry store and watched events there, he would not have been so certain of the future.

The store had a watchman, who was patrolling the main floor, along broad aisles that ran among cloth-draped counters. Hearing taps from somewhere on the floor, the watchman stopped to listen. The wide gleam of his flashlight included a stairway that came down from a balcony, but the watchman did not see what happened there.

The light gave off a dazzling reflection, as a golden shape weaved close to it. A robed figure grew from the steps; green eyes, monstrous in their gaze, studied the watchman. Like a jungle creature on the prowl, Shiwan Khan had found his prey.

He spoke; his tone was metallic. The startled watchman sprang about, saw clawish hands advance beneath the green eyes. Those flowing orbs petrified him; so did the clang of the repeated voice. Approaching hands stopped short of the watchman's throat. Choking methods were unnecessary. Shiwan Khan's work was done.

Numbed by some shocking force that seemed to spark from the claw-tipped fingers, the watchman swayed. His body stiffening, he fell prone upon the floor, shattering the flashlight as he flattened.

Shiwan Khan turned, ascended the stairs to the balcony. Stepping into a little office where he had remained, unnoticed, since the store's closing hour, he picked up the telephone. His ways unfathomable as ever, Shiwan Khan made a call direct to police headquarters!

He heard an angry voice over the wire: Cardona's. For a half hour, the inspector had been trying to check upon a long-distance call that had come to the office. The operator claimed it was from Washington; Joe supposed it must be from the F.B.I., never guessing that the whole thing was a fake.

Shiwan Khan had seen to it that Cardona's phone was constantly busy, in order to prevent the inspector from receiving any word from The Shadow.

Cardona's anger turned to astonishment, when he heard the voice of Shiwan Khan. Tonight, there was no fakery in the tone. Shiwan Khan was speaking as himself!

His words were brittle. They left a ringing tone, like the stroke of a table knife against a half-filled goblet. Shiwan Khan offered no apologies for his past misdeeds; nevertheless, he had an explanation for them.

"My purpose is to control crime," he told Cardona, icily. "Such can only be accomplished when all criminals avow a master whose power they fear. I am to be that master!"

Cardona was interested. He grunted: "Go on."

"Those who do not obey my mandate," continued Shiwan Khan, "must take the consequences. Tonight, such men are engaged in a most daring robbery. They have entered Traymer's jewelry store through the side door, and are at present rifling the premises.

"They are gluttons, those criminals. Eager for spoils, confident that they are undetected, they will remain long in the place. Long enough, Inspector, for you to find them still at work."

ABRUPTLY, Shiwan Khan ended the call. He descended from the balcony; heard louder tapping beneath the main floor. Picking up the paralyzed watchman, he carried him to the side door and propped him just within it. Coolly, the Golden Master unbolted the door and left it ajar.

Returning to the balcony, Shiwan Khan took an observation post behind a table that was topped by a large, well-ornamented porcelain vase. The tapping was almost below the spot where he stood. So motionless that he seemed a part of the gilt-decorated wall behind him, Shiwan Khan awaited results.

The floor gave with a clatter. Blitz and his clumsy crew bowled up from below like hobos rushing a breadline. They were greedy—as Shiwan Khan had described them—but not for food. Springing for the draped counters, they ripped away the cloth covers and began to smash glass panels with their gun butts.

Blitz was even greedier than the rest. He did not fear interruption; he had been assured that any watchmen would be handled before he and his mob arrived. But Blitz, fascinated by the glitter of many gems, was anxious to make a complete haul.

He intended to take all the swag to Shiwan Khan. Not that Blitz was honest; he was merely shrewd enough to calculate that the Golden Master might have appraised the stock beforehand. Since he wasn't going to pocket any gems for himself, he was anxious that his mobbies would play fair, too.

Wherever flashlights turned, they produced beckoning sparkles from massed arrays of jewels. Blitz's eyes followed every gleam. He kept ordering his vandals to pile the gems in the cloth coverings that they had taken from the counters.

They obeyed, and aided Blitz by checking on one another. Moving all about the floor, Blitz picked up the separate cloths and brought them to a corner, dumping the contents into one group.

Soon, Blitz had an actual sack-load of bracelets, necklaces, pendants, and assorted rings; a great, brilliant pile, of staggering weight as well as value. Knotting the corners of the cloth, Blitz formed one bundle, then began another, which grew as rapidly as the first.

He had tied the second sack, when growling gorillas complained that they were running out of good pickings. Blitz looked toward the balcony, saw some showcases near the stairs and sent men up to rifle them. He told the rest to scour around and gather what they had missed. He wasn't going to quit until he had a third bundle the size of the other two.

From the far side of the balcony, Shiwan Khan had ceased to watch the outspread crooks. He was staring straight downward, his glistening gaze fixed on the hole in the floor. He could see the top of a ladder, but the rest was blackness. Motionless black, that showed no trace of an occupant.

Shiwan Khan was looking for The Shadow. As yet, he had no proof that the cloaked fighter was on hand.

Then come sounds that made the Golden Master shift his gaze. He heard footsteps, creeping in from the obscure side door, and knew that the arrivals were Cardona and his squad. Reaching behind him, Shiwan Khan pressed a switch on the wall.

The clamor of a big alarm reverberated throughout the store. Hearing the bell, Blitz Gandy sprang from the big bundles that lay half obscured behind a corner counter.

At Blitz's yell, the thugs leaped to join him near the center of the floor. Ever quick to spot danger, Blitz pointed his gun toward the side doorway, just as Cardona and a headquarters squad surged into sight.

Blitz's followers were as swift as their leader. With all their clumsiness, the mobbies acted like a well-drilled team. Stirred to rapid action, they actually gained the bulge on the police and would have scored first blood, in plenty, except for the sudden intervention that came to the law's aid.

Fierce, challenging in its mockery, a laugh rose through the gloom, riveting the aiming crooks. They knew that taunt, and feared it. It seemed to come from everywhere, uttered by a being who had materialized from empty space.

It was a laugh that carried triumph, even before battle had begun.

The Shadow's!

CHAPTER XVI
THE FINAL STROKE

BEFORE the chilled crooks could fire, The Shadow was among them. He had come from the gap in the floor, stretching a long, upward leap into a tremendous lunge. Only by striking into the very center of Blitz's congregated crew could he offset the opening advantage that the crooks held.

From the balcony, Shiwan Khan saw that sweep; his green eyes supplied a vicious glare. The Golden Master had relaxed his watch for The Shadow at just the wrong moment. He had expected The Shadow to start shooting from the pit, where he could be easily reached, not by crooks but by Shiwan Khan himself.

Instead, The Shadow had preferred close-range tactics. He was among Blitz's mob before Shiwan Khan could snap a dagger from the sleeve of his golden robe and fling it for the cloaked fighter's back.

The crooks had become a mass of whirling bodies; the core of that spinning medley was a fighter in black. Arms lashing right and left, The Shadow was slugging down the opposition with the big guns that projected from his gloved fists. Some of the mobsters were slashing back at him; others were shooting at the police, but firing wildly.

The Shadow had turned the mob into a pinwheel of spurting guns, that was traveling fast but getting nowhere.

Then Cardona and his squad had reached the melee, holding their own fire because The Shadow was in the mess. The Shadow's slugging tactics ended; his guns began to pump. So did those of the police; like The Shadow, they fired when their muzzles were pressed squarely against human targets.

Smart enough to dive away, Blitz yelled for the rest to do the same. Mobbies heard his shout amid the gun blasts and scattered for the counters. Of their number, nearly half remained upon the floor. The ranks of the police were scarcely crippled. The headquarters men went after the diving crooks.

A long piercing call came from the balcony. The Shadow recognized the cry. He had heard it long ago, when traveling the deserts of Mongolia.

The call told The Shadow that Shiwan Khan was present. Furthermore, it signified that he was summoning a new, and stronger, breed of fighters: his Ordos tribesmen.

They could only be coming from outside. With a wide veer through the darkness, The Shadow reached the side doorway. He met the surge as it arrived; instantly, he was swept backward by a wave of giants. He managed to twist clear, long enough to carry the drive toward a corner. Otherwise, he might have been downed by bullets, instead of the swordlike knives that the Mongols handled.

For Cardona and his men did not see the cloaked figure that the yellowish wave engulfed. They were turning to open fire on the giant tribesmen, when The Shadow changed direction.

Blitz Gandy saw a chance for escape; he did exactly what Shiwan Khan expected. Clearing a counter, Blitz bounded for the hole to the cellar and went down it like a hasty rat. His scattered followers saw him beckon as he dropped; they made for the hole, too—the few who were still able.

Thinking that The Shadow had diverted the Mongol attack, and then eluded it, Cardona shouted for a pursuit of Blitz's mob. Like Blitz, Cardona was acting as Shiwan Khan had planned.

Whatever Cardona started, he liked to finish. Settling the mobbies was his immediate goal. Joe wanted to overtake them before they reached a stronghold; moreover, he foresaw that he and his own men would be better placed, below, if they had to stave off a Mongol attack.

Judging by the smallness of the hole, Cardona doubted that any of the Ordos giants would be able to squeeze through it, which made the route all the better. Besides, Cardona judged that Blitz and his companions had filled their pockets with jewels. Reclaiming the swag was part of Joe's job.

Firing back at the Mongols in haphazard fashion, the whole headquarters squad went through the hole, taking a few slightly wounded members with them. The last man was hardly on the ladder, when counters clattered in the far corner of the store.

The Shadow had twisted from the clutches of the Mongols; but two of the giants were looming over him as he turned to find some vantage spot.

CONTINUALLY slashing with his guns, The Shadow had done no more than ward off knife thrusts. He had planted a few bullets, but the Mongols had taken them like buckshot. Even a blast from a .45 could not stop one of those fighters, unless it reached the giant's heart.

There was only one refuge for The Shadow: the same hole through which Cardona's squad had followed the remnants of Blitz's mob. The Shadow knew the exact length of the passage to the subcellar of the theater. He could hold it, even if the Mongols did manage to squeeze through.

The Shadow's race across the floor was an odd one. He could have outdistanced the Mongols, might even have turned and put in some accurate gun stabs of the sort that he had been unable to give before. But The Shadow needed those Mongols as temporary cover against Shiwan Khan.

One sweeping blade sliced The Shadow's cloak from shoulder to hip. The other cut the brim of his hat, just as he made a quick twist of his head, fortunately in the right direction. Then, almost beneath the balcony, The Shadow put everything into a sprint.

He shot from under cover of the Mongols like a human cannon ball leaving the muzzle of a spring gun. Twisting as he reached the hole, The Shadow grabbed the rungs of the ladder at the moment of his downward plunge.

At that instant, Shiwan Khan gave a short, low-wailed command. The two Mongols stopped in their tracks, then dived away.

Over in the far corner, the remaining giants were halted beside the loaded bundles of jewels, actually wondering where The Shadow had gone. They thought that their two companions had followed the imaginary fugitive, until they heard Shiwan Khan's new call.

Shiwan Khan wanted his huge fighters to accompany him in his own departure, taking the loaded jewels out through the side door, which had become an open pathway. But first, the Golden Master intended to apply a cure for a certain troublemaker called The Shadow.

So far Shiwan Khan had not managed to deliver a personal stroke against The Shadow. There were moments when he could have flung a knife, but never with certainty. He had given Blitz's crew their opportunity; allowed the Mongols one, as well. Both hordes had failed him; but it did not matter.

The time had come for the final stroke, and Shiwan Khan was pleased, for it was to be his own. Moreover, according to his own estimate, Shiwan Khan never failed.

Though The Shadow had dropped into the pit below and was swallowed in total blackness, he was not beyond the reach of Shiwan Khan. With a mere touch of his fingertips, the Golden Master tilted the big porcelain vase that stood upon the table by the balcony rail.

The vase went over the edge. It was placed exactly above the pit; therefore, it did not stop when it reached the level of the main floor. Instead, it plummeted down into the pitch-black hole, while the halted Mongols listened for its crash.

They did not hear the vase shatter. Instead, a huge blast came from the pit; the force of the explosion made the whole floor shudder. Great chunks of tile heaved upward; broken loose, the smashed slabs roared into the widened pit, to meet the cloud of smoke that was pouring upward.

As the echoes died, a chiming voice spoke from the balcony. The tone was Shiwan Khan's farewell to The Shadow. Whether or not the cloaked fighter had escaped the blast or not was something quite immaterial to Shiwan Khan.

The explosion had accomplished its purpose. It had closed the only path of retreat. Down below, The Shadow would be unable to return; he would have to go ahead, through the cellar beneath the theater.

Should The Shadow still be able to take that route, it would lead him to certain doom, according to the calculations of Shiwan Khan. The end of The Shadow would be a matter of mere routine.

That was why the Golden Master congratulated himself upon having delivered the final stroke in crime's death struggle with The Shadow!

CHAPTER XVII
WHERE GUNS FAILED

PREX NORGAN and his companions were enjoying the show in the Pandora Theater, but in a manner different from the rest of the Shakespearean audience. While Prex was watching the stage with a deadpan expression, Mike Borlo and Snipe Shailey were exchanging wisecracks.

"We ought to have Blitz with us," chuckled Mike. "Say—he's so dumb, he'd think this guy Sherlock was a dick."

Prex leaned forward to halt the guffaws.

"The name is Shylock," he told Mike, "and that makes your joke a flop. Lay off the ha-ha stuff. I'm listening for something more important—"

The thing that interrupted Prex was a muffled reverberation that sounded like a distant explosion. Prex knew that it was closer than it sounded. It was the signal that he awaited.

"Sit tight, guys. Have your gats ready."

With that warning, Prex pressed a concealed switch beneath the box rail. Smoothly, noiselessly, the interior of the theater box slid downward. The others staring in surprise, lost sight of their companions as the floor descended into blackness. But Prex was talking, soothingly.

"I told you there'd be another act," he said. "We're the guys that are going to stage it. Get ready, like I said."

By then, the other five realized that the floor of the box was an elevator, and a cleverly contrived one. Not only did the floor go down; a ceiling followed it, from beneath the balcony box above. All sounds and other occurrences below would be cut off from the theater audience.

Dull lights appeared. The crooks saw a criss-crossed grating pass them. Then they were behind a half barrier of solid steel, peering through the grillwork. It was the door to the subcellar of the theater. The elevator had filled the passage above the stone steps. A *click* told that its descent had snapped the lock of the barring door.

Stooping forward from his chair, Prex poked a gun muzzle through the close-knit grating, and told his companions to do the same. As they watched, they saw men sprawl from a jagged hole in a far corner of the subcellar. One bulky figure raised itself, crawled forward and rolled face up.

It was Mike who mouthed recognition:

"Say—that's Blitz Gandy!"

"Too bad, isn't it?" spoke Prex, smoothly. "Well, we can ask Shiwan Khan to put some life into him, like he did with Dobie Grelf. How about a vote on it?"

Growls showed that the vote was in the negative. Having turned down the proposition of Blitz's revival, the others began to question Prex further.

"Who nicked Blitz?" queried Snipe. "Got any idea about it, Prex?"

"Keep watching the corner," advised Prex. "You'll see."

Other men came into sight. Despite the dullness of the light, the crooks promptly recognized them as Joe Cardona and a group of headquarters men.

The whole squad looked rather shaky. They had finished Blitz and his fugitive mobbies with bullets, only to find themselves flattened halfway along the passage by an explosion that had occurred in back of them.

"They're groggy," declared Mike. "Let's be nice and rub them out while they won't feel it much."

"Hold it," ordered Prex. "When I give the word, start shooting. But don't hit anybody. Aim for those fire extinguishers over along the side wall."

CARDONA was close to the center of the sub-cellar, his companions right behind him, when Prex gave the word. Six guns tongued from the grilled door. Immediately, Cardona and the detectives began to fling themselves to cover. They found shelter behind dynamos and other machinery.

Human targets had been spared, but the line of fire extinguishers was wrecked. Gas was sizzling from the big containers, through the holes that the crooks had drilled. The stuff was visible; it formed a greenish vapor, that crept like a rising fog along the floor below the steps.

Prex was still watching the exit from the passage. He saw a vague stir in the darkness.

"The Shadow," said Prex, coolly. "Get him!"

Those mobbies came nearer to getting The Shadow than any other gunners ever had. Their failure was to be blamed on Prex. He wanted to be the first to fire, that he might take credit for the fatal shot.

But Prex's gun wasn't enough. It needed a barrage to drop the black-cloaked figure that wheeled suddenly from the gaping corner and launched across to closer shelter. Prex fired a trifle wide; by the time that other guns were barking along with his, The Shadow had reached a squatty dynamo and was close behind it.

His laugh was more than a challenge. It was a threat of future retaliation that made the crooks huddle lower. The sinister mockery drowned the hiss of the escaping gas. Quivering echoes were ominous, as they tongued from the stone walls all about. The passage in the far corner seemed to catch the mirth and throw it back.

"Don't let that fool you," argued Prex in an undertone. "The Shadow has handed us that ha-ha twice too often. Give him a little while to dope out what's really up. He won't laugh a lot longer. If he does, it won't mean anything."

Tense seconds went by. The whole scene had the appearance of a stalemate, with the crooks firmly barricaded and The Shadow entrenched along with the police. But the absence of The Shadow's laugh told that he had scented something.

Looking toward the leaking extinguishers, The Shadow saw the escaping gas. He distinguished it not only by its color, but by the odor that he could trace in the air. It was a chlorine gas, non-inflammable and heavier than air.

Its purpose was apparent. The leaks were too many to be stopped. Once it had filled the subcellar, the gas would bring death to all the occupants. There was no chance of retreat to the jewelry store; the passage was on the same level as the subcellar. The explosion that The Shadow had barely outdistanced, had completely filled the vertical outlet.

While death crept closely about The Shadow and his hapless companions, Prex and the other crooks would be quite safe. The passage to the upper cellar was just high enough to keep them comfortably above the level of the rising gas.

It was a far better trap than the one at the Battery Trust. Here, The Shadow again had helpless men to save; but to accomplish it, he would have to lead an attack upon the grilled door. There was a chance, a very long one, that such thrust could save the others, but only at sure sacrifice of The Shadow's own life.

Only The Shadow had the swiftness and the stamina to keep on driving forward, though riddled by a hail of bullets. Perhaps, by a dying effort, he could thrust his hand through the barred section of the door and get a death grip that would release the catch. That done, the police could push on through to do battle with the crooks.

The chance was so slight that Prex and his trigger specialists were eager to accept it. With The Shadow dead, they were willing to meet Cardona's squad on even terms; but they doubted that they would be forced to such a sequel.

WARILY, The Shadow tested the steel lattice with shots. The crooks kept below the solid portion of the door. Their guns were poked through openings; they answered with random fire. The Shadow could take chances; not they. When he drove for the steps, any kind of shooting would find him as a target.

Meanwhile, the gas was working for the crooks. Writhing clouds of ugly vapor were enveloping the crouched headquarters men, bringing hackish coughs from their tortured throats. His cloak sleeve across his face, The Shadow tightened for the desperate charge, that would be worthless if delayed a half minute longer.

Perhaps worthless even at this moment. It wasn't the thought of his own sure death that made The Shadow pause. It was the fact that even a heroic sacrifice might fail to rescue the other men from doom.

In planing this trap, Shiwan Khan had made just one mistake. The Golden Master had given The Shadow too little chance. The Shadow could consider sacrifice, but not sheer suicide. His hesitation enabled him to note another sound, scarcely audible amid the sizzling of the gas.

It was the *whir* that he had heard before, from the metal partition at the far side of the subcellar. The tinny wall was just behind The Shadow's back. Still crouched, the cloaked fighter wheeled about and blasted shots at the partition.

Thin metal caved. Leaping for the ruined sheeting, The Shadow was away from gunfire, thanks to the lowness of the subcellar ceiling. Hammering, with the butts of his empty guns, he completed the wreckage that his bullets had begun. With gloved hands, he seized a half-dangling chunk of the partition and ripped it wide away.

The roar of the fans drowned the gas. A great gust of wind howled from the gap, with the force of a typhoon. The air from the huge fans caught up the weaving gas, swirled it away from the choking police, and drove the greenish cloud straight for the grilled barrier where the entrenched crooks crouched with their guns.

Along with that cyclonic whirl came a strident, triumphant laugh that seemed to burst from the center of the greenish twister. It was The Shadow's mockery, telling men of crime that they—not their victims—were caught in the toils of their evil master, Shiwan Khan!

CHAPTER XVIII
THE CURTAIN FALLS

AS the cloud of poison gas engulfed them, the crooks flung aside their chairs and fled from their useless stronghold. They were taking the quickest way to escape the deadly chlorine—out through the passage behind them, to the main cellar of the theater.

The gas was coming in billows. It piled up at the steps, rose in cloudy mass and sent a wave through the grating; then, subsiding like some greenish monster, it became a crouching thing that gathered strength and leaped again.

Working at speed far greater than the leaking cylinders, the big fans cleared the subcellar in less than half a minute. Driving for the barred door, The Shadow threw his cloak across his eyes, merged with the last gathering cloud of green, and shot his hand through the grillwork to reach the catch.

The door went wide. With its opening, the vapor leaped away from The Shadow like a thing released from bondage. It carried up the steps and through the passage, in a last deadly wave that followed the fleeing crooks.

Seeing The Shadow start up the steps, Cardona coughed for his squad to come along. Willingly, the rescued men took up the trail, prepared to aid The Shadow in a death combat with the murderous crooks ahead.

Prex and his pals had reached the next cellar and were trying to get outdoors. Choking sounds told that the gas had bothered them badly, although they were surviving its fumes.

Spreading when it reached the main cellar of the theater, the vapor had thinned considerably. But in slashing a path to the outdoor air, the mobsters had created a draft that carried the gas along with them.

At the grating in the alleyway, the crooks popped out like demons from an inferno, for the green clouds that came with them seemed the products of hell itself. Stumbling blindly for the street, they were shouting for assistance, hoping that some outside mob would be on hand to give it.

The Shadow emerged from the opened grating, enveloped in the last wave of the gas. His black shape was not discernible in the green-tinted gloom. Sidestepping, he dropped to a corner of the blind alley and delivered a long, throbbing laugh, a mockery that reverberated from surrounding walls.

The taunt brought whizzing knives directed for the outlet that the cloaked figure had just left. As the blades clattered, The Shadow opened fire for spots along the roofs. He couldn't see the lurking *naljorpas*; they remembered the fate of others and were keeping well to cover. But The Shadow's shots completed the task that his challenge had begun.

His laugh had drawn the stingers from some of those human hornets. Having flung their blades, they could make no further thrust. The Shadow's shots were a barrage that drove back remaining lurkers, sending them along with the others.

The assassins were on hand to spot persons entering the alley; not to cover a getaway. Shiwan Khan had wanted The Shadow to get through, and had arranged to close the path behind him.

No getaway was on the schedule. Blitz and his clumsy crew had been marked for annihilation. Prex, Mike, Snipe, and their triggermen were supposed to return up into the theater on the elevator.

As for The Shadow, the *naljorpas* had been told not to expect him at all. His laugh, issuing from darkness, had utterly amazed them. They actually believed that they were hearing a laugh from the *bardo*, the invisible world that only *delogs* visited. They had flung their knives hurriedly, almost as a mere gesture. Even *naljorpas* could not battle a creature that did not exist!

THE SHADOW'S barrage cleared the way for other comers. Cardona and his squad poured out into thc allcy and dashed for the street. They saw the big-shots and their subordinates streaking past the theater, toward the parking lot.

Gunfire drove the police to cover. Outside mobs were on hand, managed by Silk Laddiman and Shag Flink. But they were far along the street, near the parking lot, and their opening fire was wide. Moreover, it got them into trouble.

Patrol cars had arrived at the jewelry store, attracted by the blast. Though too late to head off Shiwan Khan and the Ordos tribesmen who carried away the swag, these police were quick to battle the cover-up crews.

Neither Silk nor Shag was as handy at this work as Dobie Grelf had been. Instead of making a stubborn retreat, they jumped into cars, their mobbies with them, and took the police off on a running chase. They knew where they would find a closed van that would take them back to their hideaway, wherever it might be. They wanted to get there in a hurry.

Prex and his pals dodged into the parking lot, waved their guns at scared attendants and sent the fellows scurrying to shelter. Reaching the big limousine, they piled into it and waited, expecting the car to start. When it didn't, Prex guessed the reason.

"There's coppers around," he declared, savagely. "Cardona and those headquarters dicks must have seen us duck in here."

"Why don't we get started anyway?" demanded Mike. "This mongrel that's driving for us is supposed to be tough, ain't he?"

"He's tough, all right," put in Snipe, "but he's got some sense, too, or he wouldn't be working for Shiwan Khan. Sitting tight is the right idea. How about it, Prex?"

"It would be," gritted Prex, "if we had only the bulls to think about. But we've got to figure on The Shadow, too."

Opening the door a trifle, Prex saw that the police had passed the limousine. The dull black of the windows made them seem deep; gave the big car an empty appearance. The front windows were black, too, and the windshield was of special glass, which gave only one-way vision, from the inside. The Mongol at the wheel was quite as invisible as the crooks in the back seat.

Parked near the limousine was a small, open-topped roadster, a very innocent looking car. Since the weather was chilly, a lap robe lay on the seat beside the wheel. Prex noted a bulge beneath it. He gave a satisfied chuckle, as he turned to his companions.

"There's an old jalopy here," he told the others, "that belongs to us. Shiwan Khan didn't have anybody bother to take it away. I'll hop in that buggy and get started. I'll get the bulls away, so you fellows can clear."

"Yeah?" queried Mike. "How are you going to get back to the hideaway?"

"I'm one guy that knows where it is," returned Prex. "I'll meet you there later."

"Which way will you head?" asked Snipe. "Out toward the corner?"

"No." Prex shook his head. "That's where the coppers are. I'll have to go the other direction, to get a good start on them."

Promptly, something occurred to both Mike and Snipe.

"Say!" began Mike. "If you go past the theater—"

"You'll run into The Shadow," interrupted Snipe. "When the bulls all go one way, he usually covers from the other."

Prex nodded.

"That's right," he agreed. "I *want* to run into The Shadow. If you guys keep your eyes and ears open, you'll find out why."

EASING out to the parking lot, Prex raised himself in front of the limousine's windshield and made gestures that the Mongol driver could see and comprehend. Drooping low, he reached the roadster, slid behind its wheel and started the motor. The small car shot toward the street.

Cardona was yelling for detectives to prevent the getaway, but they leaped for the running board too late. Sprawling on the paving, they came to hands and knees and fired after the rocketing roadster; but it was away. By then, Cardona was in another car; as he started after Prex, detectives joined him.

As announced, Prex swung past the theater. He hadn't much of a start, but the roadster was speedy and could increase his lead. As the police car reached the street, the limousine nosed forward, ready to take the opposite direction as soon as the chase had turned the corner. Their faces to the crack of the partly opened door, Mike Borlo and Snipe Shailey watched events.

Unconcerned by the blasts of police guns behind him, Prex Norgan was driving with his left hand. His right had tossed aside the lap robe, to pick up a roundish object on the seat. The thing was a bomb, of the type that Shiwan Khan had used in the porcelain vase.

Some yards beyond the theater was the alley that led into the cellar of the squatty office building. The mouth of the alley was Prex's objective. As he veered toward that darkness, he raised his hand to chuck the pineapple. Prex was confident that The Shadow was still lurking in the darkness, waiting to head off just such an escape as this.

It wouldn't take careful aim to finish The Shadow. A quick chuck of the bomb would do the trick. Rising from behind the wheel, Prex let his hand dart forward. It hadn't moved an inch before a gun spurted from the gloom.

Prex's arm jolted. His clawing fingers juggled the bomb. The Shadow's bullet had cracked his wrist, but Prex was still trying to complete the throw. His left hand veered the car outward to the center of the street, but he was twisting, hoping to make a clumsy thrust across his shoulder.

What happened was his own fault, not The Shadow's. Prex could have let the bomb drop to the street and twisted the car clear before it struck. Wounded, he would have had to surrender to the law; that was one reason why Prex didn't stop. Another, he couldn't give up his thought of vengeance against The Shadow.

The bomb skidded from Prex's fingers, as his arm made the cumbersome fling. The bulbous object glanced from the crook's right shoulder. Frantically, he tried to elbow it away from him but failed.

His jab was a mistake; it diverted the falling bomb from the car's cushioned seat to the wooden floor.

It wasn't just the bomb that blasted. The whole car split to atoms. With a thunderous gush of flame, the roadster was gone and Prex Norgan with it. Chunks of twisted metal cluttered the sidewalks; oil spattered the cracked paving of the street.

Prex Norgan, chief of Shiwan Khan's lieutenants, had met the death that he intended for The Shadow.

As the police car shrieked to a stop, Joe Cardona sprang out. He didn't look back toward the parking lot; hence he failed to see the limousine that started in the opposite direction. Cardona was worrying about The Shadow; he wondered how close the cloaked fighter had been to that blast of sudden death.

Joe didn't find The Shadow in the alleyway, nor in the cellar route below. Gas had cleared, so Cardona made a search, but discovered nothing. One thing, however, surprised him. As Joe remembered it, there had been some theater chairs in the passage that the crooks had used as a pillbox. Those chairs were gone.

The audience in the Pandora Theater was wondering about disturbing sounds from outdoors; people noticed, too, that the place was getting stuffy, as if the ventilating mechanism had gone awry. One person could have told them the reason for those annoyances.

He was Kent Allard, seated alone in a theater box. Cloak and hat discarded, The Shadow had come up by way of the camouflaged elevator, to watch the finish of the play. When the curtain fell on the final scene, Allard limped out from the theater, wincing as though sorry that he had not brought his cane.

Across his arm, the cloak looked like an ordinary topcoat; the slouch hat was concealed beneath it. But there was nothing ordinary in The Shadow's gaze, as he studied the outside scene. His eyes were keenly looking for stray hoodlums or secret spies of Shiwan Khan. The Shadow saw none of either breed.

Night's curtain had also fallen, upon a drama more startling than the Shakespearean brand; a play of life and death, wherein The Shadow had carried the leading role!

CHAPTER XIX
FROM THE DEAD

THERE was gloom in the many-roomed hideaway where Shiwan Khan had secreted his lieutenants and their mobs.

Gloom that Mike Borlo shared, though he now rated as the Golden Master's chief lieutenant. The promotion did not offset the loss of Prex Norgan. The crooks had begun to lose their confidence, believing that there were certain dead who could never return.

The Shadow had found a way to wipe them from the earth, and had demonstrated it in Prex's case. The revival of Dobie Grelf, in which the mobsters thoroughly believed, was no longer a comfort. They were afraid that they would meet Prex's fate, not Dobie's, if Shiwan Khan kept up his campaign against The Shadow.

Despite his own doubts, however, Mike was trying to stifle the mutiny that the other lieutenants displayed. As they gathered in their meeting room, he handed each a chamois bag.

Opening them, they found large, unset jewels: rubies, emeralds, sapphires. Even to their unpracticed eyes the stones were matchless; too good to have come from any jewelry store.

"Shiwan Khan is getting rid of the hot stuff," explained Mike. "These rocks are ones he brought from China. We won't have any trouble peddling them."

"We've got to get out of here first," growled Snipe Shailey. "This joint is safe enough while we're in it; but the bulls are getting pretty close. They trailed the van a long way, the other night."

Snipe shot an angry look across the table at Silk Laddiman, who shrugged as though the blame belonged to Shag Flink. Observing a rift among the other lieutenants, Mike Borlo took advantage of it. He pointed to a radio cabinet in the corner of the room.

"Scram, you guys," he ordered. "I'm going to make my mind concentrate, and see if I can pick up a flash from Shiwan Khan."

Alone at the radio, Mike pressed the switch. Colored lights flashed in varied fashion. Entranced by the ever-changing glare, Mike could hear a faraway voice: the chiming tone of Shiwan Khan.

"All is well," spoke the Golden Master. "Soon you will be joined by your friend, Prex Norgan."

Mike gave a hollow gasp.

"Concentrate hourly," said Shiwan Khan, "for periods of ten minutes. The others must be with you. When your minds are as one, Prex will return among you."

The stroke of a distant gong sounded in Mike's brain. Coming from his trance, the lieutenant went out to give the good news to the others.

ELSEWHERE, two persons sat in silent meditation. Kent Allard, otherwise The Shadow, was with Marpa Tulku in the little room that the *tulku* called his *ritod*, or hermitage. Gazing toward the far wall, Marpa Tulku spoke:

"It is clear, Ying Ko."

The Shadow saw the thing that Marpa Tulku meant. It was a moving image against the wall; a shape that seemed struggling to wrest itself from the flattened surface and take on a solid form. Already, it had gained a resemblance to a human figure.

"It is a *tulpa*," defined Marpa Tulku. "An illusion which Shiwan Khan is seeking to produce by the power of his great mind. We are more sensitive to such impressions than the persons he hopes to influence. Should he succeed, however, as he doubtless will, they will see the *tulpa* suddenly in its full form."

The Shadow was quite familiar with the process. He had delved deeply into the history of ghosts and phantoms and knew their scientific cause. Such illusions were produced by telepathy, or thought transference; picked up by sensitive brains, they were easily converted into hallucinations.

Sometimes, such hallucinations required added suggestion. Thus, a person receiving a telepathic call from a dying friend might not gain the hallucination for days or weeks. When it came, under circumstances conducive to hallucinations, the image would naturally impress the viewer as a ghost.

In Western nations, such facts were doubted, regarded often as pure superstition. But throughout the Orient, particularly in Tibet, telepathy and its byproducts were studied and cultivated like any other branch of psychology.

In fact, telepathy was better understood than some simpler mental reactions. Such emotions as fear and sorrow, for example, were considered nonexistent by many Tibetans.

Crass brains like those of Mike Borlo and the remaining lieutenants were not the sort that could pick up distant impressions easily; but Shiwan Khan had obtained some results with them. In a way, the situation helped him; for, as Marpa Tulku declared, if they should see the *tulpa*, it would strike them as an actual being.

In fact, the phantom was already taking on a complete solidity in the eyes of Marpa Tulku and The Shadow. It was The Shadow who saw and recognized the wide-browed, square-jawed image, with its hard eyes and suavely smiling lips. He spoke the name:

"Prex Norgan."

"It is a *yidam*," declared Marpa Tulku, solemnly. "The double of a man who no longer lives. They will believe the *yidam* to be real, those others, when it appears to them."

The Shadow inquired how soon results might come. Marpa Tulku estimated that it would require three or four periods of concentration, at least. While they spoke, the *yidam* faded, obliterating itself against the wall.

"A hard strain upon Shiwan Khan," asserted Marpa Tulku. "He is putting every ounce of mental energy into his task. He will be pleased when it is over."

There was a soft laugh from The Shadow. He took on some of the quality of a *tulpa*, as he left the ritod. Marpa Tulku watched the cloaked form fade from the doorway of the little room, out past the patrolling *dubchens* who were on duty in the hall.

It was night. For the next few hours, The Shadow's course was untraceable, though there were intervals when he momentarily appeared in a neighborhood where police had been making a search all that day.

It was the area where they had last seen the van that carried away Silk Laddiman and Shag Flink, with their combined mobs.

The Shadow finally struck results, some three blocks outside the suspected area. He did not find the garage; its front was cleverly camouflaged to resemble an old, empty house. What The Shadow did discover was a basement entry to a residence that had been converted into a small apartment house.

The entry was floored with wood, as a protection to cracked cement beneath. With an ordinary house, it would not have mattered; but this building had been partly reconstructed, and new cement should normally have been installed. When The Shadow tested the boards, a portion hinged upward. He found a passage beneath.

HAVING found one of the secret inlets to the hideaway, The Shadow soon reached the rooms themselves. He recognized that they were the deep foundations of some incompleted structure.

Recalling a warehouse in the neighborhood, he decided that it had been built upon a site originally intended for a skyscraper. Such changes in building plans were not unknown in Manhattan.

Shiwan Khan had evidently tapped into the foundations through water mains, abandoned subway exits, and other suitable passages. As it stood, the vast hideaway was a veritable stronghold, with so many outlets that it would be almost impossible to trap the occupants.

Guards were on duty, members of the various mobs. But they had become accustomed to security, and were lax. Alert enough to detect massed invasion by the law, they were satisfied with their own vigil. They hadn't calculated upon The Shadow making a secret trip into the midst of their domain.

Reaching a small room, The Shadow saw a curtain just beyond. He heard pacings outside the door that he had entered, knew that guards had come on duty. There were voices beyond the curtain; tones belonging to Shiwan Khan's lieutenants.

The Shadow, it seemed, had come into another trap; one more dangerous than those which had actually been prepared for him. In this stronghold, with crooks everywhere, escape would be hopeless once the cloaked fighter was discovered. But The Shadow was not troubled by the situation.

Whipping off his cloak and hat, he tucked them underneath a small table, where they lay in darkness. Stretching his hands ahead of him. The Shadow parted the curtains and deliberately stepped into the light, letting the drapes close behind him!

Mike Borlo was sitting at the head of a table, his back toward The Shadow. The chief lieutenant was talking to the others.

"Didn't Shiwan Khan send the sparklers?" demanded Mike. "Pashod brought them, and he'll bring more every time we pull a job for Shiwan Khan. He's come through every time, Shiwan Khan has. It may sound screwy, him saying that Prex will show up, if we think about it long enough. But I'm telling you—"

Mike didn't tell the rest. He was looking at Snipe Shailey, who was at the far end of the table. Snipe, in his turn, was staring at The Shadow!

Such a sight was remarkable in itself. Even more surprising was the fact that Snipe did not see The Shadow. He saw Prex Norgan!

After leaving the abode of Marpa Tulku, The Shadow had disguised himself as Prex. He remembered the dead big-shot's features well enough to imitate them for his present purpose. The Shadow had correctly analyzed the opinions of crooks like Snipe and knew that they would not expect to see Prex exactly as he had been.

The Shadow's disguised features were chalkish. The brow and chin were constructed. The eyes, lacking something of The Shadow's burn, were good enough. As for the lips, they were perfect. The Shadow had no difficulty imitating the suave smile of Prex Norgan, for it had been a forced expression, even with the crook himself.

Snipe Shailey uttered one word:

"Prex!"

The others turned, saw the living ghost that faced them. Far better than the *yidam* that Shiwan Khan was trying to create, The Shadow held his viewers in awe. Where a *yidam* could not have spoken, except in the minds of those who saw the phantasm, The Shadow voiced real words.

"I have come," he declared in Prex's smooth tone, "to prove the power of Shiwan Khan. Later, when my new life is complete, I shall be with you as I was before. For the present, I return to our master, Shiwan Khan."

LOOKING at Mike Borlo, The Shadow saw the fixed effect of the chief lieutenant's gaze. With a gesture suited to Prex Norgan, The Shadow waved the others from the room. Lifting his hand, he pointed to the radio. Mike understood.

Turning on the varicolored lights, Mike contacted Shiwan Khan. The moment that he heard the bell-like tones of the Golden Master, Mike voiced his story.

"We've seen him," he exclaimed. "Prex! He's here!"

The Shadow could almost sense the jangling laugh that Mike received from Shiwan Khan. Then Mike was hearing other things. The Shadow waited until the chief lieutenant turned.

"It's all set, Prex," declared Mike. "There won't be any hitch, now that the rest have seen you. Do you know what Shiwan Khan just told me?"

The Shadow smiled as if he, the false Prex, knew all. But his suave grin also invited Mike to tell the rest.

"Tomorrow night," asserted Mike, "Shiwan Khan is going to bring Joe Cardona and those headquarters boobs to his own joint, wherever that is. He's going to finish them himself. Those guys, and somebody else—"

"The Shadow?"

"Yeah, The Shadow," nodded Mike, pleased by Prex's interruption. "Where they go, The Shadow will show up too, like he did before. Only, this time, he'll meet up with Shiwan Khan!

"All I got to do"—Mike nudged a big thumb toward the radio—"is wait for a flash. That'll mean for me, and the rest of us, to come along and help the mop-up."

Remembering that Snipe and the other lieutenants were supposed to hear the news, Mike turned toward the far door. He was halfway there, when he thought of something.

"How about you, Prex?" he questioned. "Are you sticking here, along with us?"

"I return to Shiwan Khan," replied The Shadow in a suave, but cryptic, tone. "We shall meet again tomorrow night."

As soon as Mike was gone, The Shadow sprang to the radio. Rapidly, he found the gadget that controlled the flashing lights and noted its contacts. Removing bulbs of different colors, he changed them to other sockets. He transposed red with blue, green with yellow.

Going beyond the curtains, The Shadow picked up his cloak and hat. Back through the meeting room, he took the exit that Mike Borlo had used and found a clear passage beyond it. Again garbed in cloak and hat, The Shadow threaded his way from the underground stronghold.

When he reached the open air, The Shadow laughed. He had done a favor for Shiwan Khan, by visiting the crooks ahead of the *yidam* that the Golden Master was trying to produce. More important, The Shadow had turned that favor to his own account.

Not far from the underground hideaway, The Shadow encountered the *lung-gom-pa* who belonged to Marpa Tulku. He was not surprised because the runner had trailed him to this neighborhood; in fact, he was quite pleased because Marpa Tulku was concerned about his safety.

The Shadow was depending upon Marpa Tulku.

He gave a message to the *lung-gom-pa* and told him to carry it to his master. Then, with a whispered laugh, The Shadow was gone into the night.

CHAPTER XX
THE WRONG CALL

THE all-important evening had arrived. The one man who did not know it was Inspector Joe Cardona, who was pacing his office at headquarters. Cardona had never been confronted by such a dilemma before. Usually, he knew whether he was right or wrong; tonight, he didn't.

Anything might be right—or wrong. Joe had followed tip-offs—one that he thought came from The Shadow; another that he knew had been from Shiwan Khan. He had followed both of them and put himself in wrong, only to have things turn out right.

Cardona was used to being criticized for mistakes that he hadn't made. At present, he was being commended because of his mistakes. All that he could do was hope that his luck would hold; probably it would, if The Shadow stayed around.

But Cardona wasn't even sure that The Shadow was around; not after the explosion near the Pandora Theater. As for Shiwan Khan, he was certainly around, but the question was to find out where. Even with the right answer, that question was likely to bring a one-way ticket to the morgue.

Of one thing, Cardona was sure. At present, he was receiving praise for having mopped up two notorious big-shots and their mobs: Dobie Grelf at the Battery Trust; Blitz Gandy at Traymer's. But the newspapers were beginning to talk about the funds that had gone from the bank and the gems stolen from the jewelry store. Soon they would be asking why Cardona had not reclaimed the swag.

The total of the two hauls exceeded half a million dollars, and it bothered Joe worse than the national debt annoyed Congress. Cardona was ready to accept a gold medal with one hand, and pass in his resignation with the other. It was about time that the Feds took over; for once, Cardona wished that they would.

He was muttering those sentiments, when he thought that he heard the telephone bell ring. That was just it; he *thought* he heard it, but he wasn't sure. Picking up the telephone, he gruffed a hello and waited.

After long, interminable moments, he heard a voice that spoke the single word:

"Come!"

It was the crystalline tone of Shiwan Khan, but it hadn't told Cardona all he wanted to know. Finding that he still had a voice, Cardona queried:

"Come where?"

The voice gave instructions; Cardona repeated them aloud. The summons was from Shiwan Khan, but it was worthwhile to listen. He finished with the query:

"When do I start?"

"At once," replied Shiwan Khan. Then: "You may bring men with you, but all must come together. When you have started, you will remember my instructions."

The call ended; Cardona rubbed his forehead. He understood what Shiwan Khan had meant by the word "remember"; for all the instructions had been wiped from Joe's mind. It dawned on him that if he picked a squad and left headquarters, he would recall the route as he went along. Such was the significance of Shiwan Khan's final statement.

But it struck Joe, also, that if he tried to outwit the Golden Master by ringing in lot of reserves, Shiwan Khan might find it out. It was better to play along on Shiwan Khan's own terms. Why not take a squad and go to it?

"Why not?"

Putting the question aloud, Cardona found that he was talking to Fritz, the janitor, who was standing in the doorway. Fritz was a stoop-shouldered, dull-faced fellow who was dumb enough to work overtime without getting paid for it. He had cleaned Cardona's office earlier, so apparently his day's task was finished.

"Get out, dope," growled Cardona. "Don't you have enough sense to go home?"

Fritz turned and shambled away. As he went downstairs, his lips repeated the instructions that Cardona had heard and temporarily forgotten. Those recollections pleased Fritz so much that he laughed when he reached his locker. His mirth was the whispered tone of The Shadow!

LAYING aside a mop and bucket, The Shadow gathered a cloak and hat from the locker. Stepping out by a basement door, he met a lurky figure in the darkness. It was the *lung-gom-pa* runner.

The Shadow repeated words in a strange tongue; the racing mystic loped way. His run was not a long one; he was picked up by Moe's cab, which was to carry him to Marpa Tulku, and return.

Up in his office, Cardona was debating whether to take along a squad of bluecoats or plainclothesmen. Uniformed officers could recognize each other more easily than the others; still, plainclothesmen could move into places with more efficiency. Cardona had just made his decision and was shouting it over a telephone, when he heard a whispered laugh behind him.

Dropping the telephone, Cardona turned to face The Shadow. The cloaked intruder spoke firmly, steadily.

"Summon your squad," The Shadow told Cardona. "Follow the instructions of Shiwan Khan. But do not start until you receive my command."

The tone ended in a whisper that carried singular mirth. It told Cardona that The Shadow, too, had plans for this night's adventure. While whispery echoes quivered from the walls, The Shadow was gone.

SEATED in the central room of their expansive hideaway, Mike Borlo and his fellow lieutenants were awaiting the promised summons from Shiwan Khan. Colored lights were spinning, blinking with erratic sparkles. Rubbing his hand over his forehead, Mike turned to Snipe Shailey.

"I'm groggy, Snipe," said Mike. "The lights have kind of got me tonight. They seem different. I'm hazy in the bean."

"Show more concentration," argued Snipe. "That's what you need, Mike. Don't let us bother you."

Mike concentrated on the lights. Gradually, his lips began to move. Then, aloud:

"I'm getting it," he said, slowly. "Yeah, I'm getting it. Stick close, all of you, and listen—"

Ten minutes later the big-shots and a picked crew of followers were sneaking through darkness outside an exit from the hideaway. They were picking their own path tonight.

Forming little groups, they took cabs when they found them, and rode southward. They met again on a gloomy side street, and approached a darkened house.

The door above the brownstone steps was open. They moved into a dimly lighted hall, up a flight of stairs, to a door just opposite. At each end of the hall they saw brown-skinned men in tunics; rigid sentinels, who made no move. Inside the doorway, Mike beckoned the others toward a curtain.

"This is the real McCoy," he said. "Shiwan Khan's own joint. Let him do the talking. You guys listen."

The room was dark. The crowding thugs had filled about half its space, when lights glimmered, rising to show the scene. The crooks saw an enthroned figure; not until the lights had considerably increased did they guess that it was not Shiwan Khan.

On the throne sat Marpa Tulku!

The aged Tibetan master fixed his gaze upon the visitors. His expression tonight was anything but benign. His eyes had a stern glitter that each viewer felt was directed straight at himself. They were eyes that bored with phenomenal power.

Not a single crook stirred. Hands that had moved toward guns were motionless. For a minute, perhaps longer, Marpa Tulku held the whole group spellbound. It was Mike Borlo who managed first to wrench himself from that amazing mental sway.

"Snap out of it," rasped Mike, to the others. "Maybe this guy can put the hyp on one of us, but not on a whole bunch together. It can't be done!"

Mike's fingers found a gun and drew it; when Snipe Shailey copied the action, other mobbies began to stir. Hands were slow in their motion, for Marpa Tulku, his fixed gaze unchanged, did have some semblance of control. But the spell was breaking; Mike recognized it, as he snarled:

"It's curtains for you, old crab-face!"

Only Marpa Tulku, staring straight ahead, saw the shape that entered behind the crooks. But the big-shots and their mobbies heard the laugh that put an end to gunplay before it even began. Turning numbly, they let their guns drop as they faced The Shadow.

He held two automatics, moving them slowly from side to side, to keep the whole tribe covered. Flanking The Shadow were the mystics from the hallway, Marpa Tulku's *dubchens*, drawn daggers ready in their hands. Behind The Shadow were other men, who pushed gun muzzles into sight. They were The Shadow's agents, recalled to duty for this task.

Disarming the crooks, the agents and the *dubchens* lined them up and forced them, one by one, to Marpa Tulku's throne. The Shadow's guns had taken over where the power of the *tulku* left off, but again, the ancient Tibetan held sway. He was taking evildoers individually, placing each man beneath a powerful hypnotic spell.

In a corner stood The Shadow. Beside him was a device with flickering lights, tuned to the rotation of Mike Borlo's radio dial, but with the colored bulbs in the new arrangement that The Shadow had provided. Shiwan Khan had flashed a summons to Mike this evening, but the chief lieutenant had not received it.

Instead he had tuned in on Marpa Tulku, who was as great an adept as Shiwan Khan. On his first attempt, Marpa Tulku had put through a message that Mike had accepted as one from Shiwan Khan.

Leaving the rest to Marpa Tulku, The Shadow moved past the curtains, to a telephone downstairs. He called headquarters and spoke to Joe Cardona in a tone that the ace inspector did not doubt. This was the message that The Shadow had promised.

Tonight, Joe Cardona had received another wrong call; but its evil was nullified. The inspector had listened to The Shadow's call, instead. Whereas, the lieutenants of Shiwan Khan had been tricked in Cardona's stead. They had missed the right call from the Golden Master, and taken a wrong one from Marpa Tulku.

Only once had a message from Shiwan Khan been supplanted by another. But that one wrong call was vital to The Shadow's purpose: the destruction of the Golden Master!

CHAPTER XXI
HOUSE OF GOLD

FORGOTTEN in the mid-section of Manhattan stood a great, dark mansion once the property of a millionaire, who had died at the turn of the century. Built to endure, tangled in legal controversies between disputing heirs, the mansion had remained as a landmark of the Gay '90s.

Its appearance had changed little during forty years. It still stood like a fortress, somber behind the great brown walls that fenced its grounds from the corner of a secluded avenue and a quiet side street.

The mansion had been sold to another millionaire, who seldom came to New York at all. Why he had bought it was a mystery that could have been explained by Shiwan Khan. The real purchaser of the mansion was the Golden Master.

Long had Shiwan Khan reserved the structure for some future use. It had the proportions of a palace, suitable for an owner who had kingly ambitions. For the present, however, the Golden Master regarded it partly as a fortress wherein he could stave off any attack.

Always ready to strengthen his strategy by a total reversal of his plans, Shiwan Khan had the qualifications of a real dictator. Tonight, instead of wanting visitors to stay away, he was inviting them to his great mansion. First, he had summoned men of the law; later, men of crime.

Between those two sets, Shiwan Khan expected another visitor, a lone one. He was depending upon The Shadow to be present at this housewarming. Since leads to crooks had been well covered, Shiwan Khan was quite sure that The Shadow would be checking the moves of the police, in hope of finding some trail to crime.

Only Shiwan Khan would have risked an open invitation to Joe Cardona. The Golden Master was quite sure that the police inspector would follow its exact terms. His trick of giving instructions, then having the listener forget them temporarily, was a stunt familiar to all hypnotists.

It was called post-hypnosis, and Shiwan Khan had perfected it. He had given Cardona a series of suggestions, so that with each step along the way, Joe would remember the next.

Under such conditions, Cardona would naturally obey the admonition of bringing a squad, without reserve. He would have to make sure that the thing wasn't a hoax, before making a big issue out of something that he couldn't fully explain.

There were eyes in the mansion, peering from curtained windows. They saw figures moving in through the unlocked gate: a chunky leader in plain clothes, followed by a squad in uniforms. The cautious invaders reached the mansion's grime-encrusted walls, began testing doors and windows.

Then the watchers observed another figure that sidled past the lamplight beyond the gate. It was the cloaked shape of The Shadow, casting a momentary streak of blackness upon the sidewalk. Moving into darkness, The Shadow trailed the squad ahead.

The mansion's big door was unlocked. Clustered invaders crept into a great hallway, where a soft, dim light outlined them. It was impossible to discern their faces in the half-gloom, but their slowing strides betokened astonishment.

Everywhere, the scene was golden. Walls of gold, stairs of gold, furniture crusted with the same precious metal!

This was the abode of Shiwan Khan, the Golden Master.

PRESSING past curtains woven from gold cloth, the entering men saw other rooms, more lavish even than the hallway. Those rooms were decorated with jewels that sparkled from every quarter.

Green emeralds, glittering like the eyes of Shiwan Khan; ruddy rubies, like those of his *naljorpas*. Perhaps the Golden Master and his fiendish servants were on watch, though the silence gave no token of it. Shiwan Khan had turned his premises over to the law, to let the police decide the next step.

In the rear wall of a great side room was a door, its outline marked with jewels. The door was of gold, but that did not make it conspicuous in this mansion. The door seemed important because it was closed. It invited the invaders to pass beyond it. They accepted the invitation.

Hardly had the door closed behind the uniformed squad, before a blot of blackness moved in through the front hall. Usually, dim light muffled the cloaked figure of The Shadow; but against the golden background, the black form showed more plainly than those that had gone ahead.

Shiwan Khan had expected The Shadow to observe the disadvantage and act accordingly. True to form, the cloaked arrival moved swiftly along the path that the others had taken. Reaching the golden door, he opened it quickly and stepped beyond.

Figures showed in a mellow light that spread through a huge room of glass. The room had once been a conservatory; Shiwan Khan had turned it into a hothouse, easily identified as such by its humid atmosphere. Great tropical plants were visible, rising toward the high ceiling. The floor was thick with foliage, like a jungle.

On the far side of the mammoth hothouse was a solid wall. There, above a low platform, was a doorway hung with golden curtains. Lights were stronger in that quarter; the gold drapes formed a subtle lure.

From somewhere—beyond the curtains, perhaps—came low strains of barbaric music known only in

Tibet, for the instruments were peculiar to that Land of Snows. Wailing notes were provided by a type of oboe called a *gyaling*; the low accompaniment, with a trumpet's tone, was provided by a *rag-dong*. Strange drums, identified by other bizarre names, kept up a thrumming cadence.

Strange that this music of the lofty Himalaya Mountains should be heard in a tropical atmosphere!

That paradox did not restrain the men who were crunching through the foliage. They were seeking the platform, the curtains beyond it. At moments, they stumbled; their shoulders were lost among the plants. At other intervals, they halted.

Occasionally, there were sounds like grumbles, that became suddenly stifled. The piping music was rising to a higher pitch; the instruments were still Tibetan, but the tune carried thoughts of India. From the near side of the tropical room a solitary black-clad figure waited, watching for those ahead to reach the platform.

Blue uniforms did not appear. A low laugh sounded; sibilant, but with a touch of harshness. Gloved hands drew big automatics; the lone venturer started through the foliage. Drums welcomed that advance with a new beat, like the pound of tom-toms.

Then from the brush along the floor came a coiling thing with little, glittery eyes, that spied the cloaked form in the darkness. Leaves rustled as a great serpentine shape wrapped itself around the man in black. Like those in uniform ahead, he was dragged downward, helpless, his guns useless!

Golden curtains were flung apart. Onto the platform stepped Shiwan Khan, his catlike eyes ablaze. His laugh, harsh, discordant, was a call for lights. The tropical scene was flooded with a glare. While music throbbed, Shiwan Khan enjoyed a hideous sight.

Looking for Inspector Joe Cardona, Shiwan Khan saw a stocky form entangled in the coils of a great python. All about were men in uniform, fighting against the grip of other massive snakes.

Beyond, at the very start of the jungle route, was the greatest python of all. Close to forty feet in length, it held The Shadow, wound from head to foot, in spiral twists!

SHIWAN KHAN was speaking, his tone chiming with the music, as he picked a trail through the plants. He was followed, at respectful distance, by Pashod, the *gomchen* who had given full allegiance to the Golden Master.

"You have disturbed my snake temple," Shiwan Khan told the victims, with a chiding laugh. "These serpents are my friends; I brought them from Penang. As my friends"—his tone was harsh—"they show no mercy to my enemies! When the music stops—"

Shiwan Khan had reached The Shadow. Pashod was stopped beside Cardona. As Shiwan Khan whipped away The Shadow's slouch hat, Pashod yanked a felt one from the head of Joe Cardona.

A vicious snarl came from Shiwan Khan. As Pashod echoed it, the python hissed, filling the room with a sibilance that seemed a pronouncement of doom for the coil-entangled victims.

Doom it could be, but not for the victims that Shiwan Khan wanted. He was staring at a face that he recognized and knew as a real one. Not a face belonging to The Shadow, but the sallow, rattish visage of Snipe Shailey!

Pashod wasn't looking at Joe Cardona. The man whose hat the *gomchen* had ripped away was Mike Borlo. Nor were the other helpless men police. Uptilted faces were those of Silk Laddiman, Shag Flink, and members of their mobs.

Into the heavy beat of drums came a crash like that of a dozen cymbals, as a side door of the conservatory shattered, flinging living darkness inward.

From the hidden lips of a real black-cloaked invader came the sardonic laugh of The Shadow, challenging Shiwan Khan to a duel of death!

CHAPTER XXII
TO THE DEATH

WITH a snakish twist as swift as the lashes of his trained pythons, Shiwan Khan sprang for the nearest refuge, the golden door leading into the front of the mansion. Despite his speed, he could not have beaten The Shadow's shots, had not the music stopped.

As the instruments halted, knives flashed from the curtains past the platform, followed by scrawny forms that loosed them. The musicians were *naljorpas*, rallying to Shiwan Khan's defense. Quick though their attack was, they had no opportunity to reach The Shadow with their blades.

The stopping of the music had warned the cloaked fighter of the thrust. The Shadow had wheeled to outer darkness, as the knives skimmed in his direction. His one loss was a chance for an immediate settlement with Shiwan Khan.

As the golden door clanged behind Shiwan Khan, The Shadow spun into sight again, his guns blasting toward the platform. The *naljorpas* scattered, thinking it was safer. They were wrong.

In behind The Shadow surged a squad of plainclothesmen headed by Joe Cardona. For once, they were finding *naljorpas* out of cover. They made the most of it.

Scrawny men somersaulted before they could reach the tropical foliage. Some who actually gained the brush were riddled by bullets that mowed through the fringing plants. All the while, Pashod was screaming imprecations, that ended when Cardona sprawled the *gomchen* with a well-placed shot.

Pashod had been yelling at the *naljorpas*, shrieking for them to play music. It was the only way to make the pythons uncoil, thereby releasing the four lieutenants and the mobsmen. But the music never came. Its cessation doomed the crooks.

Lulled to varying degrees by the changes in the tunes, the pythons had so far been lenient with their human prey. Without any form of music, the great snakes were totally unrestrained. Twining tightly, they crushed their victims utterly.

No bullets could have saved Mike Borlo, Snipe Shailey, and the rest. Nothing short of an explosive shell could have shredded a python's tightened coils.

Shiwan Khan's allies, the pythons, had disposed of another set of warriors that served the Golden Master—the crooks who were the charter members in his long-planned empire of crime!

The Shadow had reached the golden door and was in full pursuit of Shiwan Khan. Cardona and his squad followed, circling the tropical garden to avoid becoming python fodder. The snakes were still too busy to be looking for fresh victims.

Shiwan Khan was halfway up the great stairway, when he heard The Shadow's laugh behind him. Wheeling on the landing, the Golden Master thrust forth a long hand. A knife, sliding from within his golden sleeve, was plucked by fingers that aided it on its way.

Expecting the blade, The Shadow had dropped back. The dirk went wide by more than a foot. The Shadow's gunshot, fired while he twisted, was also wide but only by an inch. Lucky to escape that bullet, Shiwan Khan kept on his way.

Though he knew nothing of Marpa Tulku's alliance with The Shadow, Shiwan Khan could guess the events that had ruined his best-laid schemes. Lured from their hideaway, the gang lieutenants and their crew had been placed under a powerful hypnotic influence.

Guided by the commands of another mind, Mike Borlo and the mobbies had impersonated Joe Cardona and a squad of bluecoats, while Snipe Shailey, given cloak, hat and gloves, had fancied himself to be The Shadow. As such, they had come, instead of the expected invaders.

The Shadow, meanwhile, had restrained Cardona and a squad of plainclothesmen from approaching the mansion until the others were inside. All of which informed Shiwan Khan that The Shadow must have overheard the phone call that the Golden Master made to Joe Cardona.

But Shiwan Khan was concerned with other matters. His one thought was escape. With it, he hoped still to control the tide of battle by the one form of counterattack that was still within his power.

DASHING across a second-floor hall, Shiwan Khan yanked open a door to a centrally located room.

The walls of the room were draped with gold. From the doorway, Shiwan Khan gave a shrill call that brought new fighters to his aid. Great Ordos tribesmen sprang from doorways; with them were a few snakelike *naljorpas*.

Dropped at the stair top, The Shadow greeted them as they came. The scorching fire of his guns produced results. The *naljorpas* launched their knives, at an angle far too high, then dived rapidly for cover, getting their scraggly forms out of harm's way.

The Ordos bodyguards of Shiwan Khan, coming onward despite The Shadow's rapid fire, were finally sprawled by a supporting bombardment supplied by Cardona and several detectives, who had reached the stair top during the fray.

Lunging between a pair of drooping giants, The Shadow cleared another of the Mongols as the giant fell. Reaching Shiwan Khan's doorway, he saw that the Golden Master had whipped away a curtain, to get at the wall beyond it. Standing beside Shiwan Khan was the silver coffin of Temujin; it was upright, its lid half-opened, like a door.

Shiwan Khan was yanking a chain set in the wall. It snapped; with a backward twist, the Golden Master recoiled into the silver coffin just as The Shadow opened fire. One of the bullets must have scored a hit, for the gold-clad shoulder drooped as it disappeared.

Then the coffin lid clanged shut, catching a portion of the golden robe, which remained outside, in sight. If Shiwan Khan expected concealment in the coffin, he had found it, but in an ostrichlike style.

Clangs were still coming from the silver coffin lid, produced by The Shadow's bullets. The cloaked fighter had only to spring across the golden room, yank open the coffin front, and get at Shiwan Khan. Instead, The Shadow wheeled full about and hurled himself upon Cardona and arriving detectives, flinging them back into the hallway.

It was a timely move, speeded to the limit, because The Shadow knew the ways of Shiwan Khan. Double purposes, always. The Golden Master had not chosen his present shelter merely as a protection against bullets. The Shadow remembered the chain that Shiwan Khan had torn from the wall.

A vast rumble came from deep below. The foundations of the massive mansion trembled, as a mighty explosion ripped upward in volcanic style. Its target was the floor of the golden room, where Shiwan Khan had hoped The Shadow would be.

The blast split the floor, lifted its spreading timbers through the roof. Curtained walls heaved outward; the force of the concussion hurled The Shadow and the detectives almost to the stairs.

With the cataclysmic roar came flames like great tongues from a blast furnace.

From cellar to roof, the center of the mansion had become a tremendous chimney; black smoke, gushing with the flames, proved that the blast had set off an oil tank. Sucking air from every floor, the fire was beyond restraint.

Crackles from the floor below meant that the golden walls were mostly painted gilt, another sham of Shiwan Khan's. The mansion was ablaze; it behooved all occupants to make a quick departure before the billowing fire became a holocaust.

The Shadow pointed Cardona and the others down the stairs; as they started for safety, the cloaked fighter turned about. He didn't have to look for the doorway of the golden room; most of the walls were gone.

Through flame and smoke, The Shadow saw the silver coffin. It had been hurled outward by the blast, off through the opposite wall. It was flat on the floor, the strip of Shiwan Khan's robe still showing from the lid. The Golden Master still expected rescue; The Shadow could see an open path to a balcony beyond.

In from shattered passages came staggering Mongols; the wounded fighters had crawled through other rooms, to reach the space beyond. They were stooping, tugging at the coffin. Dropping back to the stairway, The Shadow made a dash, took a long leap straight through the smoke and flame.

THE room was more than a dozen feet across, not too long a jump, provided that the far floor was solid. Timbers cracked as The Shadow struck; he went knee-deep in the debris. Catching the end of the silver coffin with one hand, he stabbed shots at the Mongols with the gun that he carried in the other.

Great knives hacked wildly, as the Ordos bearers tried to beat off The Shadow and still retain the coffin. His gun was bashing away their slashes, his bullets sagging them. They lunged, unwillingly, coffin and all; then tried, too late, to crush The Shadow with their mighty burden.

The coffin was swinging at an angle. Rolling in the other direction, The Shadow escaped it and jerked his feet clear of the broken floor. He was past the Mongols, almost to the balcony, when he turned.

Rallying, the mortally wounded giants made a last effort to drive the coffin toward the balcony doorway, which was open. The Shadow aimed.

Out of swirling, pitch-black smoke came a grimy *naljorpa*; though weaponless, he attacked, driving his bony hands for The Shadow's throat.

Stooping, The Shadow caught the attacker in a quick grip, propelled him over head and shoulders, turning the fellow's lunge in a long dive that sent him through the balcony rail.

The Shadow's gun was spurting when the rail crashed. Dying Mongols caved under battering bullets. The coffin struck the sagging floor; its weight splintered the beams that the flames had weakened.

With a topple, the silver casket went across the brink. Its lid flopped upward as it twisted. The Shadow glimpsed the writhing figure of the gold-robed occupant. A solemn laugh was The Shadow's farewell to Shiwan Khan, as the coffin plunged, end first, to the depths of the mighty furnace that the Golden Master had himself created.

The heat of that inferno would melt the coffin of Temujin. Like its human contents, the casket had gone to absolute destruction. Before choosing that refuge, Shiwan Khan should have remembered The Shadow's terms of battle:

"To the death!"

Flames roared upward, as though inspired by the fuel they had just received. Wheeling from their gush, The Shadow reached the balcony. From below, Joe Cardona saw the cloaked victor swing through the splintered rail and drop to the darkened ground below.

A laugh trailed amid the roar of the mounting flames. Shivery echoes blended with the fire's crackle. Mirthless, the laugh told of triumph over Shiwan Khan, the fiend who had defied The Shadow's vengeance!

THE END

INTERLUDE by Will Murray

Supervillains are the focus of this Shadow volume. It's a theme we've explored often. But in this case this may be the last time we revisit it for a pairing of tales.

From The Voodoo Master to The Wasp, we've reprinted all the classic multi-story face-offs between the Master of Darkness and a recurring opponent. Here, we conclude with a final deadly showdown between The Shadow and The Golden Master, Shiwan Khan. To round out the package, we offer a sly sequel to the Voodoo Master trilogy. More on that later.

Written in October of 1939, our initial offering, *Masters of Death,* saw print in the May 15, 1940 issue of *The Shadow*. Here, the Dark Avenger and The Golden Master bring their long-running duel to the death to a ferocious finish. The descendant of Genghis Khan is bent on global conquest. Three times before, The Shadow managed to checkmate him.

The origins of Shiwan Khan are not difficult to determine. Sax Rohmer's Dr. Fu Manchu was the first Asian supercriminal to capture the global imagination. Rohmer had revived him in the 1930s, and there followed films, radio programs and imitation pulp magazines such as *The Mysterious Wu Fang* and *Dr. Yen Sin.*

In 1939, Rohmer released the first Fu Manchu novel since 1936's *President Fu Manchu. The Drums of Fu Manchu* was followed by a Republic Studios movie serial, *Drums of Fu Manchu*, which focused on the search for the tomb of Genghis Khan and was released in 1940. Since both his editors and Gibson himself had up until this point in the series scrupulously avoided the cliched Fu Manchu-style supervillain, this revival must have influenced their thinking.

Walter once addressed this issue with typical Gibsonian humor:

> Shiwan Khan was a supervillain. He came from Tibet. There were four stories, and all the way through The Shadow matches wits with Shiwan Khan, with all this invisibility stuff. Incidentally, I'll give you a really humorous touch on that. People always try to find origins of The Shadow stories, and when I came out with the Shiwan Khan stories—Shiwan Khan was supposedly the lineal descendent of Genghis Khan, this superfoe from the East, some people thought that it was probably inspired by Sax Rohmer's Fu Manchu. In fact, somebody referred to Shiwan Khan as "the poor man's Fu Manchu."
>
> I was asked point-blank the other day, "Well, after all, did you ever read Sax Rohmer?" and I said, Yes. "Well, didn't you get any ideas from Sax Rohmer?" I said, "You know, I just don't recall that I did. But you know Shiwan Khan may have read about Fu Manchu—and that's why he had the ideas he had!"

Robert Kelland (left) and Henry Brandon in *Drums of Fu Manchu*

Gibson's comment is a bit on the disingenuous side. He once told a reporter that before he was approached to write The Shadow, he had created a strange protagonist who was as sinister as Rohmer's famous creation.

"I had some plots and a mysterioso character stranger than Fu Manchu," Walter recalled. "They said, 'Submit it, and if we like it, we'll buy three more.'" Beyond Dr. Fu Manchu, Gibson was also inspired by Kublai Khan, grandson of Genghis Khan, whose capital was Xanadu, the modern-day Shangdu. Kublai was the subject of a famous opium-inspired vision experienced by Samuel Taylor Coleridge, who produced a poem based on this vision, which unfortunately was never completed due to the poet being interrupted during its composition.

There's no question that The Golden Master was created in the vein of Dr. Rodil Mocquino, The Voodoo Master, who gave the Dark Avenger a serious challenge over two superb novels published in 1936, and was brought back by popular demand in 1938. This unprecedented third story probably sparked the editorial thinking that produced a new foe so formidable that The Shadow needed four novels to finally conquer him.

The two superfoes were unalike as characters, but their ability to control others ran in parallel. One had his zombies, while the other specialized in psychically manipulated dupes. In that sense, Shiwan Khan can been seen as a variation on The Voodoo Master. But in his final encounter with The Shadow, The Golden Master outperforms Dr. Mocquino when he telepathically reanimates the dead! Never before has Maxwell Grant strayed so far into the occult. Needless to say, he never went there again.

The Shadow's true identity of aviator Kent Allard returns after a long absence, portrayed in rather forlorn terms, since Gibson had all but decided that Lamont Cranston would continue as the Man of Mystery's main cover identity. Although he had been present in Theodore Tinsley's *Prince of Evil* novel published only the month before, the last time Gibson wrote Allard into a story was *Silver Skull,* penned back in 1938. So this is Allard's true return—although he will not be around for very long.

Speaking of Allard, very few knew of his connection to The Shadow, only criminologist Slade Farrow and Allard's Xinca Indian servants. This strange story introduced a third, but Tibetan mystic Marpa Tulku was never heard from again.

Shadow editor John L. Nanovic, in talking about the story in the issue before *Masters of Death*, segued into this one:

> When you have finished the novel, you don't have to wonder whether the next one will be as good. It will be better! For here, finally, The Shadow comes face to face with Shiwan Khan, that master of Oriental wizardry who has thrice matched wits with The Shadow, and thrice escaped personal obliteration, although his schemes were always thoroughly smashed.
>
> Two individuals cannot keep up in such a battle

forever. One of them has to take desperate measures to bring things to a conclusion. And it is The Shadow who is forced to do this in the meeting of "Masters of Death," the complete novel in the next issue.

Shiwan Khan, calling forth all of this treachery, his scheming, and his Oriental magic, gives The Shadow the toughest, most exciting campaign of his entire existence. You have all met Shiwan Khan before, and know what an antagonist he can be. In "Masters of Death" he reaches his heights. Don't miss the next issue, unless you want to miss a masterpiece of mystery fiction.

Nanovic whipped up reader expectations even further when the story rolled around in *The Shadow*:

> Our old friend, Shiwan Khan, is back again! He's met The Shadow before; he's matched wits with the Master of Darkness on previous occasions. But he's always managed to escape, even if he saved nothing else but himself in the flight.
>
> Can he do so again? Will the battle between The Shadow and this Oriental wizard go on forever? The two antagonists realize that it cannot be so; that one or the other must meet his finish, at least insofar as their separate purposes are concerned. Will Shiwan Khan succeed in evading The Shadow and accomplishing his preordained task, or will The Shadow completely smash his plans?

If you read the fiery climax of *Masters of Death* carefully, you'll see that Maxwell Grant left himself an out to bring Shiwan Khan back for a fifth battle. He never did during the run of *The Shadow* magazine's original run, but in later years, Walter Gibson began a new Shadow saga in which The Golden Master did indeed return. Alas, he did not live long enough to finish that tantalizing tale...

For these stories, Gibson revisited an idea that went back to *Circle of Death* and *The Python*—that of a mysterious neon sign used for evil purposes. He revived it for Shiwan Khan's debut, *The Golden Master*, and explores it further in this tense tale.

This was part of his traditionally realistic approach to the series. As he once told a reviewer:

> I can tell you what it was like forty years ago, or a little less. I tried to make all the Shadow stories informative, and I was surprised how well I did. For example, I used to see Harry Blackstone frequently with his magic show, and he had a new assistant, a young fellow in his twenties, and the fellow grabbed me immediately and wanted to know if they had fifty-story buildings in New York, or whether that was just something fanciful that I put into The Shadow. I said, "Oh no, they're all there." And I said if there were any facts or statistics, well, they were all based on fact. Well, he liked that, and he couldn't wait to get to New York to see them. I used to try to play that up in my plots. The fifty story building is very apropos. I'd start a scene in a big room up on the fiftieth floor, and there were these men around a big table, and they were pausing to look out the window because some ships were going down through The Narrows. And it happened that that was a steamship line that they owned, and they were talking about the ships like little toys, and at that moment somebody was getting ready to sink one of their ships.
>
> In other words, I tried to keep the things in tempo with the times, and really make them informative, and I think that gripped the readers and carried them along with it. I know that the comics are a great field for that because there you can actually...the thing is realized in a visual way. I did quite a few comics; I adapted the regular stories into the *Shadow Comics*.
>
> There was one scene in The Shadow on the elevated. I used to ride the elevateds a lot, the old Third Avenue El, and they had expresses on that that went up a middle track, and whenever they would get to an express station—those were far apart—why that center track would climb so it went to a higher platform. There was no problem with it being a single track because the expresses

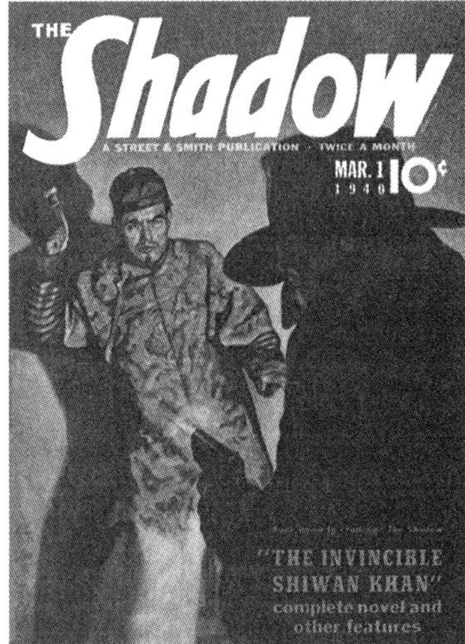

Babette Rosmond

Walter B. Gibson

came in in the morning and they went out in the evening. Well, in one story I had The Shadow corralled by some crooks on an elevated platform, and it happened to be an express stop, and he raced up the steps to the express level above. Well, the single track had platforms on each side. Now you can visualize the width of a single track of a subway or elevated, probably about twelve feet wide, I'd say, at least. As they were after The Shadow, an express was coming in, and he just took a flying leap right in front of the train and grazed it, and as he went by the front and landed on the other platform, the express came right through and blocked the pursuit. Well, I would use scenes like that.

This brings us to our companion novel, *Voodoo Death*. Written in January 1944, and published in the June, 1944 issue of *The Shadow*, it sounds like a sequel to the classic Voodoo Master stories. It's not. But in another way it is!

Professor MacAbre, the voodoo priest villain of this story, does not rise to the heights of Dr. Mocquino, but he is clearly in that sinister vein. His goals are not to conquer the world, but he is a menace on a smaller scale—as The Shadow and Margo Lane discover. For we are in the digest era of *The Shadow*, where it reflected the radio series, then starring Bret Morrison. The voodoo theme is also a comfortable mirroring of typical Shadow radio episodes. Even the editorial blurb screams radio:

> Strange drums throbbed through Margo Lane's head as she rode to a rendezvous with destiny—destiny aided by Professor MacAbre and the monsters who served his malignant will. But would the spell of voodoo tom-toms cloud the plans of The Shadow, master of darkness who ruthlessly righted wrongs?

In later years, Walter had said that he considers this story to be the unofficial fourth appearance of The Voodoo Master. It's hard to comprehend how Dr. Mocquino could have survived his fiery finish at the climax to *Voodoo Trail* back in 1938, but Walter knew what he was talking about. We're just going to have to take him at his word.

When *Voodoo Death* saw print, Shadow readers were puzzled by its unfamiliar byline—Walter Gibson! A similar mistake was made with the March 1944 issue of *Doc Savage*, which carried the byline of "Lester Dent."

This unexpected development seems to have been triggered by a letter request Dent made in October, 1943, inquiring of interim editor Charles Moran if the "Kenneth Robeson" house name could be dropped in favor of Lester's honest name.

By the time both stories reached print, Moran had moved on. Walter later recalled that a female editor was the responsible party. That was probably Babette Rosmond, who worked under new editor William J. DeGrouchy.

Both Dent and Gibson were doubtless delighted by the change. Needless to say, this embarrassing error was not permitted a recurrence! The usual house names returned in the following issues.

This story was reprinted nearly fifty years ago in the 1966 Grosset & Dunlap hardcover collection, *The Weird Adventures of The Shadow*. It was edited down for that occasion, and otherwise has never before been reprinted, so we are bringing it back into print as it was originally presented back in 1944.

One of the scenes that was cut—since the book had been intended for a juvenile audience—was the very subway scene Walter describes above. Maybe he told that story because he was miffed by the cuts.

Modest Stein painted the original cover, and a revised version resurfaced on an Avon paperback edition of Agatha Christie's *A Holiday for Murder* three years later, with The Shadow replaced by a female nude. It's one of his most arresting efforts. But it's strange that he recycled it in 1947. Or perhaps not so strange since Stein had departed Street & Smith by that time.

In any event, here is *Voodoo Death*.... •

Strange drums throbbed through Margo Lane's head as she rode to a rendezvous with destiny—destiny aided by Professor MacAbre and the monsters who served his malignant will. But would the spell of the voodoo tom-toms cloud the plans of The Shadow, master of darkness who ruthlessly righted wrongs?

VOODOO DEATH

by Walter Gibson

CHAPTER I

THERE was a hunted look in the gray eyes that stared from above the upturned collar of the raincoat; eyes as nervous as their owner, whose manner was that of a man lost in a jungle and a prey to all its terrors.

Yet the scene was Manhattan in daylight, a trifle gloomy from the clouds that were pelting rain along the side street where the scared man halted, but with nothing sinister enough to induce such fright. True, the neighborhood was dilapidated, its houses so old that they seemed to stand only because they were built in a solid row; nevertheless the street lacked hiding places where enemies could lurk.

Nor were there any pedestrians except the hunted man himself. The scared eyes took in that detail as they darted from left to right, but they lost none of their fear. There was something rabbity in the man's manner, for when he heard a muffled rumble, he bounded up some steps and into the doorway of the house where he had paused.

The rumble came from the East Side elevated, the last relic of such transportation in Manhattan. The elevated structure followed the avenue at the end of this block, and just as the scared man hopped from sight, an express clattered into view along the central track. At that distance the passengers couldn't have identified the hunted man, but he wasn't taking any chances on being seen. It wasn't until the train had rattled into the distance that he poked his eyes and thin-bridged nose out from the doorway for another quick look; then, as rapidly, he was back into his chosen burrow.

It was actually dark in that doorway, so gloomy that the man had to strike a match with his trembling hands to read the names that were listed on the board. After three attempts, the flame finally flickered and showed a button above a single, pen-printed name:

MacAbre

Steadying his finger, the man in the muffler pressed the button. As instantly as if someone had been waiting for this visit, there came a *clack-clack* from the automatic latch. Thrusting the door open, the hunted man hurried to a flight of stairs and ascended them, unmindful of the creaks that followed him like ghostly footsteps.

At the top was an open door, the entrance to a rear apartment. Within stood a dapper man whose mustached face looked very dark in the dim light. When the visitor hesitated, his eyes showing a worried lack of recognition, the dapper man inquired:

"You have come to see the antiques?"

"No." The visitor's tone was low and forced. "I have come to see Professor MacAbre."

"Ah, oui. *Le professeur* has said that he *expected* someone. And your name?"

"The professor already knows it."

As with the push button, the response was simultaneous. Across a room stocked with rare old furniture and other antiques, a door opened suddenly to reveal a stooped man whose long hair seemed to crowd his shoulders. In the dim light his face wore what could be mistaken for a smile, since his opening lips cackled a chortled welcome. But that smile was a mask, as the visitor knew from previous experience and could see again as he approached the far door.

In contrast to the watery gray of the visitor's hunted eyes, Professor MacAbre had a gaze that carried a searing force. His eyes, black as coals, were

The visitor jumped back as swaying figures appeared on the walls of the room—swaying to the throbbing beat of the devil drums!

hard in their glisten and so deep in their sockets that they seemed to belong in a face beneath his own.

Indeed, there was a change in MacAbre's chortle as he bowed his visitor into a square-walled inner room and closed the door. The tone was harsh, in keeping with those eyes of jet, yet withal it still carried welcome. This customer was a man to MacAbre's liking.

Coincident with the closing of the door, a burst of flame came from the center of the room. The visitor dropped back startled; then forced a laugh, for he had seen this trick before. Though the flame kindled itself into a crackling fire, the whole arrangement was artificial, produced by imitation logs set teepee fashion above an electrical device that combined a heating coil with incandescents set among the logs. How this produced the effect of actual flames was something too complicated for the visitor to analyze; nevertheless, he became more at ease.

It was Professor MacAbre's turn to laugh.

"So simple, is it not?" MacAbre put the question in a chortled purr. "Yet it is a replica of the voodoo fire that inspires spells too great for humans to resist!"

MacAbre was facing his visitor across the artificial flame that provided the only illumination in the room. The professor's black eyes were vivid, for they had enlarged to show the whites around them. In return, gray eyes were frozen as though their watery content had become ice, and their hunted expression had congealed with them.

"I have brought my voodoo magic with me." In the flickering glow, MacAbre's smile was definitely a leer. "Brought it from the jungle where the rite is practiced along with all the atmosphere that gives it power!"

There was a broad, high sweep of the professor's arm, his long-nailed fingers barely missing the hanging pendants of a great glass chandelier that was reflecting the artificial firelight from directly above. As though by magic, there came the thrumm of muffled tom-toms and, of a sudden, the surrounding walls were transformed into a jungle setting where female dancers whirled in voodoo rhythm.

It was still illusion, for these were motion pictures, but the life-size figures and the full-color background transplanted MacAbre's visitor into a state of mental realism. Gray eyes roved these living walls, while the recorded beats of the tom-toms were augmented by the clatter of anklets and bracelets which flashed from the lithe limbs of the mad dancers.

Professor MacAbre had turned the room into a contorted cyclorama brought straight from a Haitian jungle through the man-made magic of the camera.

"This is the spell of voodoo," spoke MacAbre, in a convincing purr. "The longer it lasts, the more you will understand—and believe."

His eyes no longer hunted, the visitor still stared at the dusky shapes that stirred the jungle green. The flash of the gold bangles was capturing him with a hypnotic effect. MacAbre leaned closer across the artificial fire.

"You have spoken of persons who bar your path to wealth," reminded MacAbre. "You have asked if I can dispose of them one by one, through voodoo forces that can never be traced. I have named my price. Are you prepared for the first test?"

With a wrench, the visitor brought his eyes from the captivating walls. Fumbling in his raincoat, he brought out a packet of money and handed it to MacAbre, adding in a hoarse whisper:

"Ten thousand dollars."

"Take this in return." From the robe that he was wearing, Professor MacAbre produced a small figure of hardened wax, dressed in an old fashioned frock coat and striped trousers. He handed it to his visitor who stared amazed at the face above the miniature Piccadilly collar and threadlike necktie.

"Why—why it looks like—"

"Of course," said MacAbre in a tone that was low, but harsh. "You wished it to represent this man. He is your first obstacle."

"But if anything happens to him—"

"It will be through Voodoo," supplied the arch-professor. "But the world will find a more convenient explanation. They will blame it on the Tarn Emerald."

"You mean they will believe the curse exists?"

"Why not?" MacAbre's chuckle was as dry as his gaze. "Only you and I will know what happened here. These witnesses will not see!"

By "witnesses" MacAbre meant the dancers, for he swept his hand around the walls. Gray eyes went fearful as they followed the professor's gesture, but once more the hypnotic effect took hold. Small wonder, for the rhythm had increased to a double beat of tom-toms and the abandon of the dance had reached the fanciful.

Sharp as a rifle came the crackled tone of the man who called himself Professor MacAbre:

"Break it!"

Caught by the madness of the moment, the visitor flung the waxen image to the floor, where it broke in half. The fracture was not visible, because of the doll's garments, but the firelike flickers showed the change of angle between the head and feet of the figurine.

A sweep of MacAbre's hand ended the beat of the drums and as they silenced, the whirling pictures vanished with a final writhe. Taking his visitor by the arm, MacAbre guided him to the door by the flickery light. As the professor opened the door, the artificial fire automatically extinguished itself.

His face muffled in his coat collar, the visitor stumbled out through the antique shop like a man in a trance. Clutching the banister, he descended the stairs and continued out into the street. No longer was his manner furtive; rather, he seemed stunned as he shambled off into the rain like a panhandler seeking the shelter of the elevated.

Professor MacAbre was an interested witness to that departure. The Voodoo maker was watching from between two closed curtains of a front room window. Beside the professor stood the dapper, dark-faced man who had first received the visitor. The dapper man was watching the professor's hands as they thumbed through the stack of bank notes.

"We have made a good start, Fandor," declared MacAbre, as though he knew where his companion's interest lay. "A good start for all of us—and there will be more."

There, MacAbre paused, for the departed visitor was out of sight. Turning, the professor pressed the curtains tightly and added dryly:

"Much more."

From the cryptic tone in which MacAbre spoke, it seemed that the strange professor believed his Voodoo spell would be fulfilled!

CHAPTER II

NOBODY paid any attention to the armored truck that pulled up in front of the International Museum. Whenever the museum received collections of statuary or other bulky exhibits, the stuff always came in armored trucks.

Today, even the truck seemed superfluous, for there was nothing in it except two uniformed guards who stepped out when the driver opened the back door. All three went into the museum, which might have indicated that they intended to bring something out, but that guess was also wrong.

The men from the armored truck were bringing something very important to Doctor Gregg Henniman, curator of the International Museum. At that moment, Henniman was discussing the subject with two visitors in his office.

"I am honestly sorry!" declared Henniman, with a nod of his white haired head. "Honestly sorry that my relatives are not here to congratulate me upon my good fortune. That is"—he faced a visitor and turned the nod into a bow—"with the exception of you, Rex."

A slow smile spread itself across the broad features of Rex Tarn. It was the sort of smile that Margo Lane didn't like, for it carried a "know-it-all" expression. Perhaps Margo exaggerated that point because she knew Rex Tarn and was therefore prejudiced. For Rex, once a wealthy playboy, still considered himself somebody of importance despite the fact that his only ability had been the squandering of a fairly sizeable fortune upon a batch of worthless acquaintances who were already deserting him.

Yet, despite herself, Margo was forced to admit that Rex was rather handsome, for his keen gray eyes carried a friendly flash. Besides, he had his humorous moments.

"Maybe your relatives don't feel like congratulating you, Doctor," said Rex. "There are reasons, you know."

"Reasons?" Henniman's tone was querulous. "What reasons?"

"Approximately half a million," Rex estimated. "You can give the exact number after you count the dollars that you have inherited from the Tarn Estate."

"Money!" exclaimed Henniman. "Bah! All my relatives are wealthy, so why should they want more? Besides, they know that I intend to add the half million to the museum's endowment fund."

"And do you think they care about that? All they want is the cash—and more of it."

"Then you mean my relatives aren't my friends?"

"Did you ever hear of relatives that were?"

"Why, yes." Henniman took off his reading glasses and gave Rex a frank stare. "You appear to be a friend of mine."

"That's because we are very distant relatives," argued Rex. "So distant that we aren't relatives at all."

Margo Lane decided to take advantage of the pause. So far she hadn't managed to put in a word, and the discussion was going further beyond her depth. It wasn't that Margo was dumb, because everyone, including Lamont Cranston, rated her with a high I.Q.—for a member of the brunette bracket. But Margo was beginning to wonder.

"Will you explain this double talk?" she queried. "When is a relative not a relative? When he is or isn't a Tarn?"

"It's very simple," explained Henniman, as he put his reading glasses in a case. "The Tarn Estate was left to the eldest of several possible heirs. I happen to be the eldest, even though my name is not Tarn."

"And the same applies to Numbers Two, and Three," put in Rex. "They are both Tarns on the maternal side, so their names don't happen to be Tarn."

"What about Number Four?" queried Margo. "Is he a Tarn?"

"Very much so," returned Rex, his gray eyes delivering an angry flash. "He happens to be my cousin, Alexander Tarn. Maybe you've heard of him."

Margo didn't recall Alexander Tarn, but Doctor Henniman did. Opening his spectacle case he again put on his tortoise-shell reading glasses and rummaged among a strew of papers that covered his desk.

"I have a letter from your cousin Alexander," Henniman told Rex. "Ah, here it is. He is like you, Rex, because he says that he will be glad to call here at the museum today. Unfortunately he has a luncheon appointment and cannot arrive until afternoon. Nevertheless"—Henniman leaned back with a smile as he removed his glasses—"Alexander is more than anxious to view the celebrated Tarn Emerald."

"The Tarn Emerald!" A hunted look swept Rex's eyes as he came up from his chair. "You mean to say you have it here?"

"It is being delivered," returned Henniman blandly. "I have instructed the chief attendant to place it in the bulletproof display case which contained the dinosaur egg that was here on loan."

"But you know what that emerald means! It has always brought misfortune to its owner! Why, it's—it's a—"

"A hoodoo?" laughed Henniman. "Nonsense. The term 'hoodoo' is as ridiculous as the word that rhymes with it, Voodoo. Indeed, according to their original definition, the two are synonyms." Placing the tortoise-shell glasses in the case, Henniman snapped the latter shut and gestured toward a large bookcase. "Look in the encyclopedia, Miss Lane, under the title 'Obeah' which covers all savage rituals."

Before Margo could comply, Rex Tarn interrupted. His eyes had a watery glisten; his lips were quavering as he spoke to Henniman, whose only response was to sit back with folded hands and smile at Rex's intensity.

"It's more serious than you suppose," insisted Rex. "There's only one way to end that curse, Doctor Henniman. That's for us all to share the burden by dividing it."

"Break up the Tarn Emerald?" ejaculated Henniman. "Impossible! Why it is one of the largest and most magnificent gems of its kind!"

"I mean sell it," explained Rex. "Then divide the proceeds. You won't miss the difference, not with the half million that is coming your way."

Henniman's gaze sharpened to a degree that made Rex's gray eyes waver. Scornfully, the old curator demanded:

"Do you need money badly enough to play upon a superstition that you foolishly think I might believe?"

Rex stiffened at the pointed query.

"Ask Alex what he thinks," retorted Rex, hotly. "There's only one thing he and I agree on, and that's the Tarn Emerald. We're both sure it brings bad luck to the man who owns it. Alex has hung onto all his money, so you'll have to admit that he's in a position to give an honest opinion—if he has one in him."

The addendum didn't help Rex's cause. It expressed his own distrust of his cousin Alex, so Henniman gave a shrug to close the discussion. Before Rex could reopen the argument, a brawny, dark-faced man stepped into the curator's office. Glad of the diversion, Henniman turned and queried:

"What is it, Jeno?"

"I have come for my letter of recommendation;" replied the dark man in a solemn tone. "You said you would have it, sir."

"Of course, of course." Annoyed, Henniman gestured to the muddled desk. "You'll find it among these papers, Jeno. I don't know what I'll do without you around to clear up."

"I am sorry, sir," acknowledged Jeno, soberly. "But the doctor insisted that I go south for my health—"

"I know, I know," interrupted Henniman, drawing back his chair so that Jeno could straighten the papers while looking for the letter. "Well, Jeno, when your health improves, I hope you will return."

Margo was admiring the delicate way in which Jeno tidied the desk. He seemed to know where everything belonged and was putting objects in various drawers as rapidly as he came across them. At last Jeno found the letter and retired with a bow as profound as a Hindu salaam. Then, pausing at the door he stated:

"I might mention, Doctor Henniman, that the Tarn Emerald has arrived and has been placed on display as you instructed."

The effect upon Henniman was electric. Bounding from his chair, he started toward the door, almost blundering into it because he wasn't wearing his glasses. Hopping back to his desk, he pawed around and finally yanked open a drawer to find the spectacle case in its accustomed place. Muttering something about "bifocals" Henniman looked at the glasses before he put them on and ran his fingers along their rimless edges. Then, with a gesture to Margo and Rex, the curator led the way out through the door.

By then, the solemn-faced Jeno had gone. The stairway down to the main floor was deserted when Henniman reached its top. It was a long, steep stairway from the high mezzanine where the curator's office was located, and it led to the center of the main display room. Twenty feet beyond the bottom of the stairs stood a marble pedestal that matched the interior of the museum; built into the pedestal was the burglar proof display case that contained the Tarn Emerald. Flanking it were the armed guards from the armored truck, while the driver stood nearby, speaking with the attendants.

Even from the balcony rail, Margo Lane could see the green glister of the priceless gem that now belonged to Doctor Henniman and was awaiting the inspection of its owner. Pausing, Margo gazed just long enough to draw an astonished breath, and in that interval, she was conscious that Rex Tarn had passed her. Then, before Margo could turn, she witnessed sudden confusion below.

With excited shouts, guards and attendants sprang toward the bottom of the stairway. Hearing a loud clatter, Margo looked in time to see Henniman taking a series of flying somersaults down the steep stairs. There was a call from Rex, who was arriving at the stairtop, a frenzied plea for those below to halt the tragedy that he had been unable to avert.

It was all too late.

So steep were the stairs that Henniman's whirl turned into a final bound that cleared at least a dozen steps and landed him with a half-twist upon the marble floor at the bottom. Striking shoulder first, the old curator's body seemed to cave, finally settling with a contorted sag that left it quite misshapen at the very feet of the rescuers who had failed to halt that flying fall.

In that horrible moment, Margo Lane knew that Gregg Henniman was dead. His motionless figure looked very pitiful and small in its striped trousers and frock coat, with the pointed collar above the shoestring tie. Viewed from Margo's position at the balcony rail, the dead form looked much like a broken doll.

Though she did not know it, Margo Lane was gazing upon the exact reproduction of a scene that had existed only the day before in the voodoo parlor of a certain Professor MacAbre!

CHAPTER III

LAMONT CRANSTON gazed calmly at the blood-stained marble where the body of Gregg Henniman had laid a short while before. He turned

Rex Tarn was too late—the falling figure was already tumbling over in a headlong dive down the steep stairway.

toward the door where the body had been taken and caught a slow shake from the head of the attendant who was standing there. The man came over to where Cranston stood.

"There's no chance, Mr. Cranston," said the attendant. "Doctor Henniman has been pronounced dead. It's the coroner who's looking him over now."

Cranston gave a slow nod; then looked toward the steep stairway. "He fell all the way from the top?" he inquired.

"All the way, from the top," repeated the attendant. "The lot of us were standing down here when it happened. He saw the emerald, that's what Doctor Henniman did, and he just couldn't wait to have a closer look."

The attendant gestured toward the small display case that was set in the marble pedestal. Approaching the tilted box, Cranston looked through the thick unbreakable glass and studied the Tarn Emerald. It was a magnificent stone, so huge that a skeptic would have argued that the glass had magnifying qualities. But Cranston was no skeptic where the Tarn Emerald was concerned.

A connoisseur of gems, Cranston was familiar with the size and shape of every notable jewel, along with the histories of all matchless stones. This was the first time he had ever viewed the Tarn Emerald, for the gem had been buried in a vault for more than twenty years, but to Cranston it seemed an old friend. Strange to regard an object with its history as a friend, but Cranston was a man of strange preferences.

The face of Lamont Cranston was as unfathomable as the great green eye that gazed unblinking from the bullet-proof case. In a sense, those features were as impenetrable as the case itself, for Cranston's countenance was truly a calm mask that hid the thoughts that lay behind it. Whatever the Tarn Emerald had witnessed in the way of death, Cranston could match it.

For in his other self, Lamont Cranston was a personage known as The Shadow.

Deep were the secrets of this famous emerald; deep too were those of The Shadow. Those secrets had much in common, for they involved the greed of men. Perhaps the curse of the Tarn Emerald existed only as a magnetic force that drew the very sort of malefactors whose deeds should rightfully expose them to The Shadow's justice. Such could have been the thoughts behind the inscrutable face of Lamont Cranston, when the train was interrupted.

Rapid footsteps were entering the museum, they approached the spot where Cranston was standing. Looking up, Cranston saw a young man whose features were quite handsome, though not in a rugged way. Perhaps it was the pallor of the face that took away the strength that the strong jaw should have indicated; as for the man's smile, though friendly, it had a tired expression that indicated overwork. Cranston remembered that smile from a few occasional meetings with its owner, Alexander Tarn.

Apparently Alexander recognized Cranston, for his droopy eyes opened a trifle wider, and he gave a nod. Then:

"Doctor Henniman said you would be here," remarked Alex, in an affable tone. "I've heard of your interest in gems, Mr. Cranston, so I should have known that you would find the Tarn Emerald the main attraction."

Turning toward the stand, Alex gazed downward with his tired eyes. He didn't have to ask if this happened to be the famous emerald; the size of the green bauble announced its identity. But he shuddered as he found his hands approaching the case too closely. Turning again to Cranston, he said in a hushed tone:

"You know its history of course. A single word will tell it: Tragedy."

"The plural would be preferable," corrected Cranston. "A whole line of tragedies have followed the Tarn Emerald from its discovery until the present date."

Alex smiled as he added his own amendment.

"Until twenty years ago," he said. "That was when the emerald was buried in a vault, where I hope its curse will remain and be forgotten. Should I say the same to Doctor Henniman, or would it be more tactful to ignore the subject?"

Alex's gaze suddenly narrowed. The expression on his pale face was a cross between awe and horror as he stared beyond Cranston toward a door that had just opened. Out through that door, two attendants were bringing a figure that lay crumpled on a stretcher and Alex Tarn recognized the face that lay tilted half askew.

"Doctor Henniman!" Startled though it was, Alex's exclamation carried a hush. "Tell me"—his hands gripped Cranston's arm and trembled there—"did something happen after the emerald arrived?"

When Cranston gestured toward the stairway, Alex's eyes went to the top and came slowly downward, the horror on his face increasing as he visualized the scene which Cranston did not have to describe. If there was anything of doubt in Alex's mind, it was dispelled by the stain that he saw upon the marble floor. Weakly, his hands relaxed and withdrew from Cranston's arm; then suddenly they tightened into fists.

"Who did it?" Alex spoke coldly, firmly. "Tell me, who killed Doctor Henniman?"

"No one killed him," came a sharp response. "The coroner has heard the details. It was an accident."

The man who spoke was Rex Tarn. He had come from the room with the others, and close behind him was Margo Lane, very pale and very glad to see Lamont Cranston. As Margo's arm reached his own, Cranston drew the girl aside and calmly watched the meeting between the Tarn cousins.

"Why did you come here?" demanded Alex. "You certainly aren't interested in museums nor in emeralds."

"Emeralds perhaps," replied Rex, solemnly.

"Not so unlikely." Alex narrowed his gaze. "What did you do, suggest that Henniman give you the emerald to avoid the curse?"

"In a way, yes," admitted Rex. "Miss Lane will testify to the fact. I said we would all be willing to share it."

"What right had you to speak for me—or any of the others?"

"None, I suppose, but anyway, Henniman wouldn't listen. When we came out from the office, he was so anxious to view the emerald that he rushed ahead of us to the stairs—"

Rex paused; for a moment, his gray eyes showed the hunted waver that Margo had noted before; then, catching himself, he said sharply:

"No, I didn't push him. Miss Lane will testify to that. So will the others who were here at the bottom."

Without a word, Alex marched to the stairs and continued to the top. There he turned and looked down at the group, but his eyes were most interested in the display pedestal. Cranston could see the tightening of Alex's lips when his close-lidded eyes observed the gleam of the emerald, even at that distance. Despite himself, Alex seemed forced to the mental admission that there was something in Rex's story about the emerald's lure.

One step forward; then Alex caught himself. He'd almost done the same as Henniman, and the fact brought a grim smile to Rex's rugged lips, which Margo chanced to notice. Then Alex was coming down the stairs slowly, watching each step, until he paused in deliberate fashion and picked up an object that had just escaped his foot. When Alex reached the bottom, Rex met him and demanded sharply:

"What have you got there, Alex?"

"Only a wire from Henniman's glasses," returned Alex. "I suppose there's another on the stairs if you want to look for it. I suppose they fell and brokc on thc way down."

Rex went up a few steps and found the other wire, pausing as some broken glass crunched beneath his foot. Alex was handing his wire to one of the attendants, so Rex did the same, adding in a rueful tone:

"Poor Doctor Henniman. If I'd thought the jinx was coming after him so soon, I wouldn't have dropped the subject. Well, if the coroner has any further questions, he knows where to reach me."

The cousins departed separately and Margo expected Cranston to follow. Instead, he stood looking at the stairs until finally he undertoned:

"Henniman was wearing the glasses when he came downstairs?"

"Why, yes," replied Margo. "I saw him put them on in the office."

"You mean he wasn't wearing them when you arrived here?"

"He was wearing reading glasses, tortoise-shells with big rims. He kept taking them off and putting them on. That's why I noticed them."

"And did you notice anything else?"

Margo was starting to shake her head, when a recollection struck her, one that seemed a trifle ludicrous despite the tragedy that had occurred since.

"Only that Doctor Henniman couldn't find his regular glasses," said Margo, with a slight laugh, "because they happened to be in the right place, which is where Jeno put them."

"Who is Jeno?"

"One of the museum attendants who was leaving to take another job. He came to get a recommendation from Doctor Henniman."

Cranston's steady eyes turned toward the stairs and followed them upward as though picturing what might lie beyond. Before Margo could begin to form conclusions, Cranston's gaze was back upon the baleful emerald that formed the nucleus of tragedy. Fantastic though the talk of an unknown curse might be, there was a practical side to the emerald question.

"When death strikes," stated Cranston, "certain things are often forgotten during the stress that follows. Sometimes they may prove the real object of a crime. This emerald for instance—"

"You mean someone might try to steal it?"

"Not while I am here," replied Cranston, in a quiet tone that allayed Margo's qualms. "I intend to stay until it is properly returned to the vault where it came from. There are also certain facts that I might learn—meanwhile, and the same applies to you."

"Facts about whom?"

"In your case, about the Tarn cousins. There's more than an ordinary rivalry between those two, and both of thcm gct around quitc a bit. Sec what you can learn about them."

It was the type of assignment in which Margo specialized, and the sooner she began it, the quicker the results. Besides, the atmosphere of the museum was beginning to tell on her, a fact that Cranston had readily discerned. So Margo suddenly found herself out in the sunshine, realizing that the world had something to offer besides death. On her way down the avenue, she decided that if Lamont wanted to worry about the Tarn Emerald, he was welcome to the task.

Lamont Cranston wasn't worrying about the emerald. It was safe enough in its anchored pedestal. Back in the International Museum, Cranston was going up the stairs to the curator's office, the place where tragedy could well have begun.

CHAPTER IV

VOODOO drums were thrumming their muffled mechanical basso, and the walls of MacAbre's lair were alive with their medley of fantastic jungle dancers. Across the artificial firelight, the stooped man with the coal black eyes was watching the effect of his Voodoo magic.

Visitors who thought they could become acclimated to this setting were always wrong. Invariably they learned that they had missed much on previous occasions, for new fascinations were sure to grip them. Sometimes the dull throb of the tom-toms, often the contortions of the dancers, occasionally the weave of the jungle and even the flicker of the curious fire—always something could capture the gaze and hold it in hypnotic fashion.

So it was with the man whose mission involved the Tarn Emerald and the fortune that went with it. Only he believed beyond the capacity of the average visitor and the hunted look in the gray eyes showed it. For this man had received a visible demonstration of Voodoo power. For a price of ten thousand dollars, Professor MacAbre had matched a broken image with a human victim. A mere factor like the law had seen nothing untoward in such an event.

The case of Gregg Henniman was no mystery; it was officially slated as death by misadventure.

"The time has come for another test," reminded MacAbre, in his tone that crackled louder than the mechanical fire. "Have you come prepared?"

Fumbling as badly as he had before, the man who purchased death brought a bundle of currency from his raincoat and placed it in the weird professor's hands. In return, MacAbre supplied another image, stouter than the one that had represented Henniman and differently clad.

This doll had the florid face of a middle-aged man dressed in slacks and sport shirt. Fascinated by the realism of the thing, the gray eyes lost their hunted tremble and stared hard. Then, recalling the part that was his own, the visitor lifted the image to dash it to the floor.

The claw-finger hand of MacAbre stopped the act with a quick, firm reach across the firelight.

"This must be different," chuckled MacAbre. "If the curse of the Tarn Emerald strikes in many ways, so must the power of Voodoo. Take this pin and press it slowly—there."

The long pin that MacAbre supplied was pointed straight toward the doll's heart, but he let his client perform the action. Fingers steadying, the muffled man took the pin and pressed it slowly into the yielding wax until the professor raised one finger and ordered:

"Now! Press hard!"

Home jabbed the pin into the very core of the image. The hand that held it shook and would have dropped the doll if MacAbre had not caught it. With a laugh that chimed with the fire's medley, the professor of Voodoo announced:

"We shall keep this until the charm is complete. Then the wax can be melted and forgotten, like the person the image represents. Go! Your work is done!"

A wave of MacAbre's hand and the whirling cyclorama vanished. Gone was the firelight when the professor opened the door. Once again, a client was stalking from these strange preserves, ten thousand dollars lighter, but this time his departure was simpler. Dusk had already settled, the side street offered little visibility.

As before, Professor MacAbre entered the front room, but this time he did not part the window curtains. Instead, he beckoned to a man who was seated in the dimly lighted room, a person whose face was as dark as Fandor's, but broad instead of dapper.

"Come, Jeno," spoke MacAbre. "It is wise that you should follow."

"But if the man should recognize me," protested Jeno. "Would that be helpful, *mon professeur*?"

"He did not see you often at the museum," reminded MacAbre, "so why should he remember? Besides, it is dark outdoors, Jeno. Dark, like the jungle."

There was a whitened display of Jeno's teeth in a broad, understanding smile. Swiftly, but with the slinky tread of a creature from the jungle that he loved so well, the man who had changed jobs for his health went out to the street.

The darkness was thickened with a drizzle. Jeno, with a glance from left to right, spotted a figure in a drab raincoat turning the corner from the elevated. In panther style, Jeno picked up the trail, confident that his quarry would not elude him.

There was a difference between Manhattan and a jungle. Here there were creatures that even Jeno had come to disregard when he reverted to his stalking ways. They were mechanical things like busses, trucks and taxicabs that belonged to an orbit of their own. One such, a taxicab, was swinging around a corner at this moment, but Jeno gave it no attention, not even when it stopped across the street.

All that Jeno wanted was to trail the man with the upturned raincoat and make sure that he caused no complications. But complications seemed in the making when the man halted at the next corner and began some wary observations of his own. He was stealing Jeno's act when he looked swiftly from left to right, but he went it one better when he suddenly turned and looked behind him.

He didn't see Jeno, for the jungle stalker was sliding into a doorway as easily as he might have sheltered himself beneath a spreading banyan. What the man did see was the halted taxicab. As if he expected it, he turned and cut across the street with long, hurried strides.

Those sharp eyes of Jeno saw something else. In his effort to track MacAbre's recent visitor, Jeno hadn't noticed a girl who had left the cab and moved to the corner on the other side of the street. She was coming back, and from her manner, Jeno was confident that she was bound for the same destination as the man. In matters of rendezvous, Manhattan and the jungle were the same to Jeno, but he had much to learn upon that score. This was one time when Jeno was mistaken. Coincidence, not prearrangement, was at work this evening.

There was one law that governed all followers of Voodoo, jungle or otherwise. Never were they allowed to meet with strangers in the vicinity of their hidden haunt. The lair of Professor MacAbre fulfilled the qualifications of a Voodoo circle, and no believer, even a contributor who paid ten thousand dollars a visit, could break the rule. Death was the penalty for such a violation, but even there a distinction was in order.

Death to a believer could be delivered only by the *papa* of the tribe, in this case Professor MacAbre. The disposal of an outsider was anybody's privilege.

Those factors governed the strange and sudden actions of Jeno, the man with the ways of a panther.

Crossing the street with a long, swift lope, Jeno gave no heed to the man who was entering the cab from the street side. Instead, Jeno rounded the back of the cab and sprang for the girl who was opening the door by the curb. With the same catlike motion, the human jungle killer whipped forth a knife and launched his hand in a long, murderous thrust.

All that stopped the stroke was the door, coming wider than Jeno expected. As the dark-faced man thudded the swinging obstacle, the girl saw him and shrieked. Bouncing up from the sidewalk, Jeno made a slithery sweep around the door intending to thrust the knife as the girl clambered into the car, but either terror or instinct caused her to seek refuge in the open. She started for the front of the cab, half a dozen paces ahead of Jeno.

Before the assassin could overtake the girl, the cab driver came launching, headlong from the front seat. He was wiry and his attack was sudden, for his tackle spilled Jeno to the sidewalk. Wrenching free, the Voodoo henchman displayed another of his rubbery bounds, this time ready to settle either victim, girl or cabby. But by then, a third antagonist was in the fray, the man in the raincoat.

He came right through the cab and out, lunging straight for Jeno. Knife poised, the jungle man halted at the sight of wide gray eyes and square-jawed face. The law of Voodoo was restraining Jeno from the kill, for he felt that decision here belonged to Professor MacAbre. But the man from the cab was freed from such restrictions; however much Voodoo governed his case, he left killings to others.

The man didn't even see Jeno's face, for he blotted it with a fist that punched the jungle stalker clear across the sidewalk. Beckoning to the girl, the man pointed her into the cab and shoved the driver in behind the wheel. Fists ready, he turned to meet Jeno's next attack but none came. True to the way of the jungle, Jeno had bounded off through the darkness fringing the house wall where he landed. Not knowing from where the next attack might come, the man on the curb sprang into the cab and slammed the door behind him. The driver took that thump as an order to get started.

It was fully two blocks before the cab's passengers gained a good look at each other, for not until then did they reach a well-lighted area. Their stares were those of mutual recognition on this their second meeting.

They had witnessed tragedy before; tonight they had almost participated in it.

The man was Rex Tarn, the girl Margo Lane!

CHAPTER V

FORMAL attire was required at the Club Galaxy. That rule, plus the five dollar cover charge, brought the place a wealthy if not exclusive patronage. Among tonight's customers was Lamont Cranston; attired in faultless evening clothes, he was seated languidly at a corner table, watching the doorway.

Slight but significant was the smile that came upon Cranston's lips when he saw two persons enter. Cranston had met one already: Alexander Tarn. The other was a girl who had been described to Cranston and was therefore easily recognized. Her name was Sue Aldrich.

It was Margo Lane who had learned about Sue Aldrich, through inquiry in the various social sets. The girl's name had been mentioned with that of Rex Tarn, but it seemed that they hadn't been seeing much of each other during the past several months. Then, only this very afternoon, Margo had phoned a new development to Cranston. She had been told that Sue Aldrich had been dropping in at the Club Galaxy with Alex Tarn instead of his cousin Rex.

So Alex had stolen Rex's girl. Or maybe he had simply invoked a priority something like the order of inheritance. Whatever the case, Alex hadn't done badly for himself. From Cranston's obscure table, Alex gave the effect of a stuffed owl with his padded evening clothes and droopy, half-closed eyes. But the description didn't apply to Sue.

The girl was worthy of a string of adjectives which added up to rate her as the nicest specimen of blonde nightlife that had wandered into this deluxe clip-joint during Cranston's current term of observation. Nor did other habitues overlook that fact, for Sue Aldrich was conspicuous in what might be termed a double-barreled fashion.

Her evening gown nailed every passing eye. It was blue velvet of a vivid shade, a perfect color for a blonde to wear. It would have been too gaudy had there been too much of it, so the designer had cut down the proportions in Sue's favor. It was difficult to criticize the gown while admiring the lovely shoulders and slender arms that emerged completely from it, and with those as a basis, Sue's shapely figure was more worthy of consideration than the color of the gown.

Nevertheless, blue was this girl's color, and she emphasized it with a necklace and a pair of matched bracelets that were studded with aquamarines against a dazzle of tiny diamonds. If the floor show had been going on, Sue's arrival would have stopped it.

Instead, Sue concentrated on the bar, where heads turned and hands halted with half-raised glasses while the customers watched her order a drink. The veteran bartender accepted Sue as a usual customer, but he was due for astonishment too. Alex was the person who broke down the barkeep's professional nonchalance by calling for a glass of milk.

In the course of things, the serious drinkers began to forget the sample of feminine brilliance that had landed in their midst and Cranston, in his turn, became neglectful of Sue. Cranston found it more interesting to watch Alex, who was distinctly out of place in this assemblage.

Alex was trying to be convivial, as far as milk could help him. This wasn't Sue's coming-out party; the occasion belonged to Alex. It wasn't necessary to watch Sue's reactions to his conversation because they were reflected on Alex's own face. When his tired eyelids gave a slight lift, it meant that Sue was intensely serious. When Alex supplied a weary smile, it was in response to Sue's gay laughter. Indeed, Alex was finding Sue so congenial and vivacious that he forgot himself and ordered a second glass of milk.

Cranston had been watching these proceedings for nearly half an hour when a breathless girl arrived at his table. Rising, he drew back a chair for Margo Lane, at the same time studying her unusual confusion. Sue's arrival must have left the head waiter dazed, otherwise he would hardly have passed Margo into these rarefied surroundings. Margo was wearing a frayed black job adorned with tarnished spangles which showed gaps where some were missing.

"I know I'm a sight," panted Margo, "but I didn't have time to dress. This was the first thing I saw."

"So you grabbed it," completed Cranston. "On the run, I suppose."

"On the run is right," added Margo, "and I've got to be on my way before Rex Tarn gets here."

Cranston's eyebrows raised in silent query. Taking a deep breath, Margo explained.

"When I found out that Alex was bringing Sue here tonight," said Margo, "I decided to go to a cocktail party where both Alex and Rex were supposed to be."

"So Alex is going to cocktail parties," put in Cranston. "On Sue's account, I suppose."

"That's right. Well, anyway"—Margo was eyeing Alex and Sue as she spoke—"Alex wasn't there. I found that out before I got out of Shrevvy's cab. Rex came storming out of the place and started arguing with the doorman; saying that he must have mistaken somebody else for Alex.

"Next thing, Rex was in a cab and scooting away somewhere, so it occurred to me that Shrevvy ought to follow. No, wait!" Margo waived her hand in protest. "It was really my idea, not Shrevvy's. I hadn't told him how important all this might prove to be."

"I'm sure you hadn't," interposed Cranston, dryly. "Otherwise Shrevvy wouldn't have wasted time taking up the trail. He lost it, I suppose."

Margo gave a grim nod.

"But he found it again," she declared. "We had to do a lot of cruising, fifteen minutes of it at least. We'd just swung a corner when I saw Rex sneaking along the other side of the street."

"You're sure it was Rex?"

"Yes, and you'll be sure, too, if you let me finish this story. I saw his face by a streetlamp; he had his raincoat collar bunched around his chin, but those eyes of his gave him away. They had that hunted look."

"I know. Go on."

"Maybe I was foolish," conceded Margo, "but I got out of the car. Next thing, Rex turned around and came across the street, so I hurried back. He'd seen the cab and he wanted it. Before Shrevvy could pick me up instead, a man lunged at me with a knife!"

"Not Rex?"

"No, not Rex, but somebody almost as important in this case. The man was Jeno, the attendant who was leaving the International Museum the day Doctor Henniman died!"

Cranston gave Margo a steady look calculated to crack her strained imagination, but the girl shook her head emphatically.

"You can't talk me out of it," insisted Margo. "I'm sure the man was Jeno. Shrevvy made a dive from the cab and spilled him; then Rex pulled the hero act by punching Jeno in the face before he could make another stab. Rex shoved me in the cab, and Shrevvy got off to a flying start."

"What happened to Jeno?"

"I don't know." Margo frowned. "When Rex found out who I was, he was surprised that I was in that neighborhood. He acted worried, too, but pretended it was on my account. I said I'd lost my way while I was looking for an old antique shop and that I was quite as surprised to run into Rex."

"What did Rex say about Jeno?"

"He either didn't recognize him or pretended that he hadn't. He simply said the fellow must have been some mugger who thought he was smart enough to work alone."

"Did you tell Rex the man was Jeno?"

"Of course not. I said I wished that Rex had caught him, but he claimed he was too worried about me. More important, Rex asked me not to mention what happened to anybody."

"On account of Alex?"

"More on account of Sue." Margo gestured toward the blue vision that was draped across the bar. "He said she'd really pass him up if she heard that he was rescuing damsels in distress. Sue doesn't swallow that type of line."

"And where did Rex leave you?"

"At my apartment. He went on to his own place in Shrevvy's cab, so he could get dressed and come over here. That's why I rushed, because I knew you'd be here, and I wanted to tell you everything first. I thought a chat would be better than a phone call, and I was sure there'd be time before Rex arrived—"

Margo was casting a wary eye toward the doorway as she interrupted herself. But Cranston's gaze was a jump ahead. Across the table, his hand gave Margo's arm a lift and carried her right out of her chair. With a twist, Cranston steered Margo past an ornamental palm tree toward a service door. Catching her footing, Margo heard Cranston's parting words:

"Be outside, in Shrevvy's cab."

This was all in the interval during which Margo had been gasping in surprise because Rex Tarn had arrived so soon. For in her glance toward the doorway, she had seen the very man she wanted to avoid. If it had been left to Margo, she'd probably have sat there gaping until Rex had spotted her, for already he was glaring sharply about the nightclub. But Cranston had whisked the brunette right out of the picture.

When his gaze reached that particular table, Rex saw Cranston seated alone and stiffened. His eyes didn't take on the wide, hunted look that Margo had described; instead, they narrowed somewhat in Alex's style. Then, his lips forming a set smile, Rex gave a nod and came over to join Cranston. Under the table, Cranston's foot drew the opposite chair in his own direction. It was flush with the table when Rex arrived, giving no indication that it had just been vacated.

Cranston was rising with extended hand when Rex arrived. The warm shake that they exchanged gave no indication of the sentiments they felt. If this proved another meeting between the hunter and the hunted, the fact would certainly not reveal itself this soon.

Indeed, if murder really lay behind the recent death of Gregg Henniman, it could raise a question regarding this very meeting. The question was: which was the hunter and which the hunted?

This was one time when The Shadow really wished he knew!

CHAPTER VI

ACCUSTOMED as he was to probing others, Lamont Cranston also could handle the receiving end. He showed his skill when Rex Tarn politely inquired if he happened to be waiting for anyone. Cranston's expression didn't change, but his head gave the slightest of shakes as he remarked:

"I hope not."

To follow that innuendo, Cranston glanced warily toward the door, then let his eye slowly rove the neighboring tables. Rex thought he caught the whole idea, namely that Cranston was "looking them over" in terms of the feminine youth and beauty that flocked the Club Galaxy.

So Cranston wasn't solely interested in Margo Lane. That, at least, was Rex's logical opinion, and a few recollections clinched it. He'd seen Margo several places lately without Cranston in attendance. Maybe their paths just met occasionally over some mutual interest such as museums, though Cranston did seem a little worried that she might be coming here, as indicated by his glance toward the door.

Though Rex didn't know it, that little touch was the clincher. Gradually recalling that he'd mentioned the Club Galaxy to Margo, Rex decided that she couldn't have known Cranston's whereabouts this evening, or she might have insisted that Rex bring her here.

Rex was giving these thoughts away with the

widening and relaxing of his eyes, all noted by Cranston's side glance. Then, letting his gaze rove further, Cranston halted in admiration and remarked:

"Not your cousin Alex! It can't be, not with that dream in blue! And Alex wouldn't be here of all places—"

Alert before Cranston finished, Rex was resuming the real search that had brought him to the Club Galaxy. All he had to do was follow Cranston's gaze to see Sue laughing as she leaned from a stool, slapping away Alex's hands as he tried to stop her from pouring some of her drink into his milk.

"It's Alex, all right," gritted Rex. "He's been getting out of character too often lately."

"Suppose we go over and have him introduce us," suggested Cranston. "Maybe they'll deal a few more hands in the patty-cake game."

"I'll do the introducing!" snapped Rex. "I happen to know that girl a lot longer and a lot better than Alex."

Rex was on his feet, beckoning Cranston across the floor. Alex saw them coming and clapped his hand over the top of the milk glass, saying:

"Easy now, Sue. We're attracting too much attention. Maybe you've taken too many drinks—"

"Too many drinks?" giggled Sue. "Why, I've only had a couple of zombies. Just a couple of zombies! Look!"

Sue was turning toward the approaching men and spreading two slender fingers to indicate them while she tilted her head coyly and closed one eye as if sighting along a gun. Then, as Rex stiffly introduced Cranston, Sue chortled:

"You're zombies, that's what! D'you know what zombies are? They're the walking dead from the Voodoo country."

A wild, wide glare flashed to Rex's eyes. Whether the word "Voodoo" induced it in its own right, or brought up recollections of the curse attributed to the Tarn Emerald, was something for speculation. Indeed, Rex could have been recalling his own adventures this very evening; or contrarily, he might be showing anger over Sue's unruly behavior at the bar. Whatever the case, Rex was too busy curbing his own emotions to make a prompt reply.

Wheeling giddily on the stool, Sue gestured to Alex and said in demanding style:

"Another zombi."

"She means she wants another zombi cocktail," explained Alex. "She's had two already, and I think that's all they're supposed to serve."

"Is that so!" Sue was defiant. "Then we'll go from bar to bar. You've heard of 'Ten Nights in a Barroom'? We'll make it Ten Barrooms in a Night."

Rex grabbed Sue's wrist as she started to leave and twisted her back against the bar to keep her steady while he talked. Trying to wrench her arm away, Sue exclaimed frantically:

"Look out! You'll bend my bracelet!"

"What of it?" snapped Rex. "I bent myself buying that pair of bracelets, bent myself so badly that I finally went broke."

"I didn't ask you for the bracelets," pouted Sue.

"But I'll bet you asked Alex for this dog collar," retorted Rex, snapping his finger against the glittering band that encircled Sue's neck. "He's too much a tightwad to give anybody anything of his own accord. Well, since Alex is going in for aquamarines, I'll find some other preference in gems."

"What, for instance?" queried Alex. "Emeralds?"

Rex swung savagely toward his cousin, resenting the pointed reference to the Tarn Emerald and what it represented. Apparently Alex had schooled himself in the ways of nightclubs before coming back into circulation, for he slid right to his feet and used his arm to ward the first threatening poke of Rex's fist.

Only Cranston could have stopped a fight between the Tarn cousins since he was where he might have stepped between, but he wanted to see how far the feud would carry. It stopped short, however, on Sue's account. Too excited to keep propped against the bar, Sue lost her balance and left the tall stool head first, shrieking as she went. Forgetting their fight, Rex and Alex made frantic grabs to catch the nylon-clad legs that came flying up from the blue gown; missing, they compromised by stooping to detach Sue from the brass rail around which she twined her arms as she flattened to the floor.

Since Sue was a trifle hysterical, Rex turned her over to Alex with the gruff statement: "You brought her, so take her away." This made Sue feel neglected, for as Alex started her to the door, she laid her chin across her shoulder and called back pleadingly: "When will I see you, Rexy? Tomorrow?"

Some retort was on Rex's tongue, but he suddenly withheld it; then gave a polite response.

"I'll call you in the morning, Sue. Good luck and good-night." With that, Rex flashed a glare at Alex, but before his slow-mannered cousin could return the discourtesy either with eye or word, Rex swung to the bar and added loudly: "Give me a drink. Make it anything—except milk."

With Alex and Sue on their way out, and Rex determined on a course of serious drinking, Cranston decided that his own presence was superfluous. Leaving the gaudy nightclub, he reached the fresher air of the dirty street and joined Margo in Shrevvy's waiting cab.

Briefly, Cranston recited his recent experiences as they rode along and the net result disappointed Margo.

"Then you didn't really learn anything," said Margo, "except that the Tarn family is definitely blonde-blind."

"I learned which Tarn has priorities on Sue tomorrow," reminded Cranston. "He happens to be Rex, and he may be taking Sue to the place where we are going."

"Where is that?"

"Out to Long Island to call on a gentleman named Wilfred Walden."

"I've heard of him," nodded Margo. "Big Sugar is what they call him in cafe society. But what has he to do with Rex—or Alex?"

"He happens to be related to them both," explained Cranston. "Walden is second in line for the long disputed Tarn Estate, or I should say first, now that Gregg Henniman has relinquished his rights."

"You mean Big Sugar owns the Tarn Emerald?"

"It will be turned over to him tomorrow, as it was to Henniman. This time"—there was a grim note to Cranston's voice—"I hope to be early enough to prevent another murder."

"Do you really mean murder, Lamont?" inquired Margo, "or just another freak of the strange curse that accompanies the emerald?"

For reply, Cranston brought a spectacle case from his pocket, and Margo saw that it was identical with the one that Henniman had toyed with in his office. When Cranston opened it, he saw a pair of rimless glasses with lower circles indicating them to be trifocals.

"These were in Henniman's desk," stated Cranston. "Do you recognize them?"

"Why, yes," replied Margo. "Only—only—"

"Only what?"

"Only they look like the glasses Doctor Henniman put on before he went downstairs. I expected these to be the tortoise-shells, the big-rimmed glasses that he used for reading."

"Then don't these explain themselves?"

Margo shook her head at Cranston's query. Somehow she couldn't piece the pattern of this riddle. Feeling dumb, Margo risked appearing more so, when she asked:

"Explain what, Lamont?"

Cranston's reply came in a single word, as cryptic as it was ugly. It was the word that he had used before:

"Murder."

CHAPTER VII

IF ANY man didn't need the wealth he was about to inherit, that man was Wilfred Walden.

You knew that the moment you drove into the great grounds of Walden Manor, one of the prize exhibits of Long Island.

Wilfred Walden, or "Big Sugar" as he was known to the trade, was opposed to visitors of nearly all descriptions, for fear that they would pluck some of the ultra-rare flowers from his woods and gardens, carve their initials on specimens of trees that grew nowhere else in America, or frighten away a few coveys of odd and curious birds which had somehow learned that Walden Manor was officially a Bird Sanctuary.

Having been invited to the Manor and happening to be recognized by the gatekeeper, Cranston and Margo were allowed to drive their roadster through the vast estate when they arrived at ten in the morning. However, they were admonished to stop if challenged by any of Walden's private game wardens and were advised to keep under fifteen miles an hour to avoid startling any of the wildlife.

"What kind of wild life could we startle?" asked Margo as they wheeled through woods that formed a veritable forest. "Just flowers, trees and birds?"

"You underestimate Walden," replied Cranston. "He goes in for fauna, too. The place is loaded with unusual species of rabbit, deer and other game. Walden even claims to have a few moose on the premises."

"Does he like snakes?"

"I wouldn't be surprised. Anything may pop out of these woods, Margo."

That brought a slight shudder from Margo. Then:

"And I thought he liked nightlife," she said. "He certainly spends money! No wonder they call him 'Big Sugar' whenever he comes around."

"Wrong again," put in Cranston. "Walden's nickname came from the fact that he imports more sugar from the West Indies than anyone else in the business."

"So that's the reason! Does he own sugar plantations himself?"

"Acres of them. In Cuba mostly, because he goes there often. But I understand he visits Haiti, too."

At that, Margo's eyes went big and wide. For to Margo, the mere mention of Haiti meant something else that she expressed aloud in a tone that was really scared:

"Voodoo!"

Maybe Margo was thinking of Jeno, whose foray of the night before had been a brief demonstration of a jungle prowler's ways. Perhaps she was thinking in terms of the imaginary snakes that Cranston mentioned, fancying them hanging from the boughs of strange, thick-branched trees. Whatever the whirl of impressions that flooded Margo's mind, they were more or less unified by Cranston's next gesture.

The coupé was swinging from the wooded road on to a driveway that led up to Walden's mansion. To the front lay a sweep of rolling lawn, studded with rare bushes and gorgeous flower gardens. The driveway, however, approached the mansion from the side, and Cranston was indicating that portion of the building.

What Margo saw was a huge conservatory that occupied the complete end of the building. Through the glass walls of that huge hothouse, she and Cranston could discern a vast mass of tropical foliage that formed an actual patch of jungle transplanted to this northern clime and preserved through constant heat.

It was just another proof that Wilfred Walden handled more than sugar in a big way. Thinking in such terms, Margo forgot that the indoor jungle was itself associated with Voodoo, because of her increasing interest in meeting Walden on his home grounds and hear him talk about his unusual hobbies.

The wish was soon granted. Cranston pulled the car around by a driveway leading to the rear of the house, and the first man to greet them was Walden. He approached the car wearing slacks and sport shirt representing a golfer's attire. In contrast, Walden was also wearing tennis shoes and swinging an expensive racquet, which he tucked under his left arm while he shook hands.

Walden's face, big, broad and florid, was of a domineering type, but he could be genial in his off-moments. Having too much wealth to work, most of his moments were of the "off" variety, as he proved at present. Nevertheless there was in Walden's tone a constant self-importance that could not be missed.

"Glad you're here, Cranston," boomed Walden in a heavy tone. "Nice of you to bring Miss Lane. That will make four of you in the gallery. Rex Tarn is bringing another girl."

"What gallery?" asked Margo. She looked at the house. "You mean you have an art gallery, too?"

Walden gave an over-hearty laugh.

"I mean the tennis gallery," he explained. "Over by the tennis court." Walden gave a wave with his racquet. "I'm taking Rex on for a match with a stake of five hundred dollars."

Catching Margo's inquiring look, Walden laughed again.

"Don't let my weight deceive you, Miss Lane," assured Walden. "It's all muscle. I'm in trim and Rex isn't. Never is, for that matter. Just wait and you'll see dissipated youth give way to well-preserved experience. That is"—Walden lowered his voice to a confidential tone that couldn't be heard at more than fifty yards—"if Rex puts up the money. It's been a standing offer, but he hasn't taken it to date."

Cranston put in a query:

"Four of us in the gallery? If Rex is playing tennis, who will the other be? Not, Alex, by chance?"

Walden gave a guffaw that echoed with rattles from the walls of the conservatory.

"After last night?" asked Walden. "Didn't you read the columns this morning? The Tarn cousins tried to put the family jinx on each other last night at the Club Galaxy. They won't be in a mood to get together today. The fourth man happens to be a good friend of mine"—Walden added a deep-throated chuckle—"because he's a good customer. He's in the conservatory. Come, and I'll introduce you."

Leading the way into the glass enclosure, Walden picked a path among high entwining branches which made Margo shudder because of their resemblance to snakes. A shiver in these surroundings was quite an achievement, considering that the temperature was at least a moist ninety degrees. They found Walden's friend strolling past some banana trees, and he looked as cool as Margo had felt in the crisp outdoors.

The reason was that Walden's friend was obviously used to tropical climes. He was a dapper man with a decidedly dark face, which formed a striking contrast between gleaming white teeth and jet-black mustache, the moment that he smiled.

"*Señor* Fandor Bianco," introduced Walden. "Just arrived from Havana." Walden gestured to the tropical foliage. "I told him to come in here and feel at home. How do you like it, Fandor?"

"Very good," acknowledged Fandor, maintaining his gleaming smile. "Most very good, Beeg Shooger."

"He even knows my nickname," laughed Walden. "Well, if I'm Big Sugar on the buying end, maybe you'll be Big Sugar on the selling end, Fandor."

"Hardly, *señor*," returned Fandor, his tone serious despite his smile. "I'm just Leetle Shooger. That is what they will call me when I go back home and tell them how big your business is."

The flattery pleased Walden; perhaps that was why he insisted upon showing off some other features of his elaborate hothouse. He led the way to a corner that was boxed off with a smaller glass enclosure, and as they went along, Margo noted that Cranston's gaze was on the mustached gentleman called Fandor. Whatever his opinion of *Señor* Bianco, Cranston was reserving it for later expression; of that Margo was sure.

This was no time for questions, and Margo couldn't have put one anyway, for she found herself panting for breath. The corner room that they had entered seemed twice as hot as the rest of the conservatory, which was of course an exaggeration; nevertheless, its temperature must have been at least a dozen degrees higher.

"You'll get used to it," laughed Walden, as he

closed the door. "This happens to be a very special room. Look around and you'll see why."

He gestured to a semicircle of odd tropical plants, one of which was in bloom. Fandor gave a nod of recognition.

"Ah, the century plants!" he exclaimed. "I have seen them in Mexico."

"Not these," objected Walden. "You have seen the *Agave Americana*. These happen to be an unknown species of flower that I have termed the *Agave Tropicala*."

"And why so, *señor*?"

"Because they are true jungle flowers, sent to me as a special gift. I believe that these bloom regularly each year."

"But, *señor*, such is not possible—"

"I tell you again, these are not century plants," broke in Walden, angrily. "You should listen, Fandor! The name that I heard given them was the Secret Flower."

Margo stepped forward to look at the blooming plant. She noticed that others were on the point of blooming, which bore out Walden's theory.

"Why do they call this the Secret Flower?" queried Margo. "Is it hard to find?"

"That may be the reason," replied Walden. "But I think it is because the flowers bloom secretly. Every day I watch them, hoping to witness the process." He shrugged and gestured at the plant before him. "This is one I missed. If you watch, you may see it fold."

Fandor started to speak; then stopped as he looked at Cranston. With a polite smile Fandor queried:

"You were about to say something, *señor*?"

"Nothing of importance," replied Cranston. "I was only going to ask why the room had to be kept so hot."

"Those were the instructions," stated Walden, as he stepped about, tilting his head from one plant to another. "The Secret Flower is far more delicate than a Century Plant. A touch of even moderate temperature"—he snapped his fingers—"and they would wither like that."

Briskly, Walden glanced at his wristwatch and turned to Fandor.

"How about our warm-up match?" asked Walden. "I want to be in good form when Rex gets here."

Fandor bowed.

"Most certainly, *señor*." With his broad smile, he queried: "If you win from *Señor* Tarn, do I receive—what is it you call it—my 'cut' of the money, is not so?"

"You'll help me spend it at the nightclubs," replied Walden. "Big and Little Sugar will sweeten cafe society. But come along, all of you"—he paused and looked at Margo—"unless Miss Lane would like to watch in case another Secret Flower blooms."

Across Walden's shoulder, Margo saw the slightest of nods from Cranston; she gave an eager nod of her own. Walden opened the door and the men left, Fandor delivering a deep bow. Alone with the century plants that were something else again, Margo took a long, deep breath. Walden was right; it didn't require much time to become accustomed to this humid atmosphere. Indeed, it was rather pleasant when breathed fully. Margo could now detect a heavy fragrance that she hadn't noticed earlier, so she took another breath and caught the scent more plainly.

Voices had faded when the door closed. Looking around, Margo saw that Cranston and the other men were out of sight, gone past the bank of jungle green that gave a curious impression of being heat-frozen. Such didn't seem impossible, in this exotic setting where everything was so unreal.

So calm did Margo Lane feel that her former qualms were all forgotten. Even the word "Voodoo" had faded from her mind, so completely that it didn't occur to her that she might be falling under its very spell!

CHAPTER VIII

WILFRED WALDEN was no mean man at tennis. He gave his serves the vehemence of his golf drives and about the same proportion of hook. Most of his points came when a little cloud of dirt enveloped the white-clad form of Fandor and left the dapper man bewildered.

Nevertheless, Fandor forced Walden into an extra-game set, for his play was smart, particularly following his own serves. Quick as one of the wild rabbits that occasionally poked their whiskers from the shrubbery, Fandor retrieved every stroke that was short on speed. His placements were cunning, keeping Walden on the run from one side of the court to the other and alternating him between the net and the back line.

Seated in a canvas chair near the court, Cranston was close enough to catch the conversation between two other members of the gallery who had arrived to watch the play: Rex Tarn and Sue Aldrich.

"I'm going to take this big baboon," undertoned Rex, referring to Walden. "I'll send him back to his own jungle, five hundred smackers short."

"But Rex," objected Sue, her voice worried. "You know you aren't in form."

"I can stop the fast ones better than that Cuban," Rex argued, "and good old Wilfred isn't going to keep me on the hop, even if he is my third cousin twice removed."

"And why not?"

"Because that little man on the other side of the net is showing up Wilfred's weakness. I'll let Wilf do the hopping, and when I slap through a few of my fast serves, he'll cave. Look, Sue: here comes Chauncey. I wonder what he wants."

Chauncey was Walden's secretary and he looked the part. Frail, stoop shouldered and with a thin face that was mostly glasses, Chauncey stepped timidly toward the court as though expecting a barrage of tennis balls in his direction. Walden saw him and furnished a glare, just long enough for Fandor to place one nicely out of reach.

That point deuced the set again.

"Walden is mad," Rex told Sue. "He'll come through hard."

It was Walden's serve. Waving Chauncey away, he smoked his serves past Fandor for a love game. In receiving, Walden went the limit, outracing Fandor's place shots. They dallied around deuce until Fandor finally fluked a net shot, and it was Walden's set and match.

Hitching up his white flannels, Rex started out to the court, as Sue queried:

"Won't Mr. Walden want to rest a while?"

"Not if I know Wilfred," replied Rex. "When he's hot, he wants to keep on going, which is swell."

Sue wasn't wearing her aquamarines, and though it was hardly likely that she would have included them with her present sport ensemble, even though it was blue, Cranston held the notion that at least one bracelet might be reposing in a pawn shop. Sue was the sort who never liked to lose a man, if only to hold him as competition for another.

On such opinions, Cranston liked to check with Margo, but she hadn't yet arrived from her vigil with the Secret Flowers. Looking toward the conservatory, Cranston saw Fandor going in that direction, after shaking hands with Walden. Cranston was coming to his feet, when the door of the conservatory opened and Margo emerged in hesitating style.

Pausing where he was, Cranston watched Fandor bow to Margo and exchange a few words. Then Fandor went indoors while Margo came toward the tennis court. Her stride looked wobbly, so Cranston went to meet her, but with a secondary purpose. Walden had finished looking at some letters shown him by Chauncey and was thrusting something in the breast pocket of his sport shirt, while Rex was coming over toward them. Cranston wanted to hear what Rex might say to Walden.

Heady perfume from the Secret Flowers was wafted toward Margo, inducing a strange calm in the exotic setting of the conservatory.

There wasn't any interruption from Margo. She was catching her breath as Cranston supported her arm. It was as if the cool outdoor air had taken an opposite effect upon her, for normally Margo should have been breathing more easily after coming from the oppressive atmosphere of the inner hothouse.

"Here's the five hundred," Rex was saying to Walden, displaying the money. "Want Chauncey to hold the stakes?"

"That won't be necessary," boomed Walden, "unless you think I ought to put up my cash, too."

"You ought to be good for five hundred," returned Rex, "unless the mortgage has caught up with this big place of yours. Only we ought to start our match right away."

"Why do you think so?"

"Because I want you to have a sporting chance. You see"—Rex adopted a tone that suited his canny air—"I don't think I need a jinx to help me beat you. Let's finish this match before they deliver the Tarn Emerald."

Walden's lips curled in a broad sneer.

"Your cousin Alex spoke about the hoodoo," said Walden. "He said you tried to relieve Gregg Henniman of the family curse."

"That's right."

"But since it involved relieving him of the emerald too, Henniman didn't fall."

"You're wrong there," put in Rex, bluntly. "Henniman *did* fall, but not in the way you meant."

Curbed anger flushed Walden's face. He looked ready to boom a loud indictment of Rex for his more than casual treatment of Henniman's death, but Walden finally compromised with sarcasm.

"Would you like to know how much that bunk about the Tarn Emerald counts with me?" demanded Walden. "Would you like proof that the jinx is a joke?"

"Very much," assured Rex. "I'll make you the same offer that I gave Henniman. Let me sell the emerald for you and divide the proceeds among the family. That's a fair way of sharing the possible misfortune."

"Generous, aren't you?" sneered Walden. "You follow the rule of never giving a sucker an even break."

"You'll have a better break than Henniman," insisted Rex, seriously. "There's one less person to divide the money, now that he's dead. I think I can convince you that the curse is real, Wilfred. Of course, I don't want to hold up our tennis match, even though it's only for five hundred dollars—"

"Then why hold it up?" interjected Walden. "Let's start and talk about the emerald later!"

With a triumphant wave to Sue, Rex took the far court and volleyed a few with Walden while Cranston was piloting Margo around to a comfortable chair. Sitting down with a sigh, Margo pressed her hand against her breast and took a long breath.

"I—I guess I was frightened in there," admitted Margo. "I forgot all about the flowers and began thinking of Jeno."

"Of Jeno? Why?"

"I seemed to remember him, not from last night, but when I saw him leave Henniman's office. It was the way he bowed, I suppose."

"The way Jeno bowed?"

"Why, of course. Who else would I remember? But it began to worry me, Lamont. When I came out of the conservatory, I thought I saw Jeno again. Only when I looked, you were coming toward me."

Cranston glanced toward the conservatory; then studied the silent house. His meditation was interrupted by the thwacky thud of a tennis ball. The match was under way in earnest.

Rex Tarn had overrated his ability, condition or both. His serves were fast, but they didn't swamp Wilfred Walden. Though he was able to return Walden's serves, Rex couldn't press the advantage. He was using Fandor's system of racing Walden all over the court, but Rex either lacked the necessary inches or Walden was pushing himself to greater effort.

Taking four games in a row, Walden was ready to receive, his face flushed with the triumphant prospect of a love set. If he could take this game that Rex was about to serve, Walden was confident he could smoke his opponent under for the sixth. Overanxious, Rex planked two in the net. Controlling his next serve, he took Walden's return and began a determined volley.

Walden wanted that point more than any other, on the theory that if Rex lost it, he would be through. Back and forth across the court, Walden was playing like a fish on a line, getting the ball back every time with Rex too desperate to poke a stroke too far from reach, for fear it would miss the court. Judged on the basis of his annual income, Walden was doing five hundred dollars worth of work right there.

The break came when Rex laid one just within the sideline. Walden took a long, loping stride and lashed a backhand scoop from the dirt. The ball flipped over the net to Rex's total astonishment; caught flatfooted, Rex could only stare in absolute chagrin. He didn't look toward Walden until he heard Sue shriek.

Margo looked up suddenly to see Cranston coming to his feet. With that diving backstroke, Walden had flattened on the clay and was rolling on to his back. His hand was clutching at his heart, scooping the cloth of the sport shirt, pocket and all. So frantically did he claw that the pocket ripped, but Walden's hand stayed fisted.

Just as Cranston reached the prostrate man, Rex leaped the net. Both were too late, for Cranston heard the gargly sigh that choked from Walden's throat as his body sagged back. Rex was near enough to see that death slump, and he stopped with a horrified pose.

Then, a strange thing happened. As though actuated by the invisible hand of Fate, Walden's left fist came open finger by finger, to reveal a thing that he had tugged from his pocket with that final rip. Whatever the cause of Walden's death, it could be charged to the jinx that he had boasted he could beat.

Like the green eye of some evil monster, the Tarn Emerald was glowing from the center of Wilfred Walden's outspread palm!

CHAPTER IX

PROFESSOR MACABRE turned from the curtained windows of his quiet front room and gave a nod to Jeno who was sitting morosely in a corner chair. The gleam in MacAbre's coal-black gaze was pleased, but Jeno's eyes did not reflect it.

"Fandor is coming along the street," announced MacAbre. "He will be glad to know of our success. Let us welcome him, Jeno."

The mode of welcome was the usual sort. When Fandor came up the stairs, he found Jeno in the antique shop acting as though in charge, a job which Fandor had personally handled on occasion. Their meeting was simply a blind in case of followers: Fandor, the arrival, was acting as a customer, while Jeno passed as a seller of antiques.

After a reasonable interval, Professor MacAbre appeared from the rear room. Nodding to indicate that he regarded all as safe, the Voodoo leader gestured for Jeno to lock the outer door; then beckoned both Jeno and Fandor into the rear chamber where weird rites were held for the benefit of paying customers.

These men being partners in his crimes, MacAbre ignored the usual theatricals, except for the artificial fire which ignited itself automatically. Gesturing his companions to folding chairs that were standing against the bare white walls of the windowless room, MacAbre gave a demoniac leer at Fandor, which brought a broad gleam of the latter's white teeth.

"Yes, Fandor, you have guessed," spoke MacAbre. "Walden died as effectively as Henniman, shortly after you left. I might say"—those coal-hued eyes showed sharply from their sockets as they turned toward Jeno—"that Walden's death was handled better than Henniman's."

Whatever his awe of MacAbre, Jeno still was stout in his own defense.

"I did all that I was told, *mon professeur*," Jeno argued. "It was not my fault that *le docteur* should be forgetful in a different way. Never before did he make that mistake with his glasses—"

"We must be prepared for all mistakes," interposed MacAbre, "including our own. You nearly made a serious mistake again last night, Jeno."

"When I saw the girl? It was my duty to follow the law of our jungle—"

"But this is not our jungle. You must remember that, Jeno. Her coming to this neighborhood may have been a pure mistake. That is why I do not blame the man. You did well to restrain your knife in his case, and he was equally justified in attacking you. I do not intend to deal him Voodoo vengeance, as you wish."

"*Mais, professeur!* In our jungle—"

This time MacAbre's interruption was a furious snarl that utterly silenced Jeno. Then, turning his outburst into a low, hissed tone, MacAbre waved his hand and declared:

"Fandor understands the difference between jungle life and civilized. You would do well to follow his example, Jeno. And now, Fandor"—MacAbre's tone reverted to its purr—"it will please you to learn that Walden died within a half hour after your departure."

There was satisfaction in Fandor's gleaming smile.

"I was very careful, *mon professeur*," Fandor declaimed. "I pressed Walden hard, but stopped when I felt the limit was close. It was very easy to leave, for I simply went to the telephone in the great house and called the city. I told the secretary, the one called Chauncey, that an appointment was taking me back to town."

"It must have been an hour later that I phoned," acknowledged MacAbre. "I talked to Chauncey, too, and told him I had business with his master. He was telling me of Walden's sudden death when another man took the telephone, a man of very calm speech."

Fandor narrowed his eyes and nodded.

"Cranston, probably," said Fandor. "He was there with the girl."

"With what girl?"

"The one that Jeno mentions. The Lane girl, who was at the museum with Rex Tarn."

"So? Why should she have come with Cranston?"

"Because she is his friend and not the friend of Rex. Another girl, a blonde called Sue Aldrich, came with Rex Tarn today."

MacAbre's black eyes seemed to sink back in their sockets as he weighed these facts.

"Perhaps it would have been better had I talked to Cranston," mused the professor, "rather than cut off the call the way I did. But tell me, Fandor"—the eyes opened and glistened sharply—"did you remember to destroy the evidence?"

"Of course, *mon professeur*." Fandor's tone was shrewd. "And I did even more. I placed the blame upon someone else."

"Upon whom?"

"Upon Margo Lane. She remained in the room with the Zombi Plants. They will believe that she found the air too oppressive and therefore opened the windows."

MacAbre's long claws scraped his chin with a light stroke that Fandor recognized as the Voodoo professor's only symptom of worry.

"Walden was used to the tropics," reminded MacAbre, "for he made many trips to Cuba. This Margo girl is not. Therefore what happened to Walden slowly, but in large degree, would affect her rapidly but in small degree."

"Which is very good," put in Fandor. "*Tres bon!*"

In return for his enthusiasm, Fandor received the sharp glare that MacAbre had previously awarded Jeno.

"It is for me to decide what is best!" hissed MacAbre. "As you say, Fandor, the girl will be blamed for something apart from Walden's death, but it may be that you have left a dangerous clue, as Jeno did!"

"But the girl will remember nothing," reminded Fandor. "When I met her coming from the conservatory, she stared at me like something from a dream. Why, my face is handsome"—Fandor smiled to prove it—"but she was afraid of it. She acted as though she saw someone like Jeno."

Fandor's gesture toward Jeno was polite, and the broad man took it as a compliment. Indeed, the leer that spread on Jeno's face signified that he preferred to be regarded ugly. But when it came to sinister quality, Fandor's smile could rival Jeno's sullen glare. These henchmen of Professor MacAbre were shaped much to their insidious master's pattern, despite their pride in what they thought was individuality.

"Someone like Jeno," repeated MacAbre, smoothly. "You are right, Fandor; the girl could have thought so. She saw Jeno last night and would remember him so well that his face will creep into her imagination at the slightest suggestion. Perhaps it is well that she stayed among the Zombi Plants. It will be a few days before the stimulus wears off."

Going to a corner, MacAbre unfolded a portable stand that was lying flat against the wall. Upon it he placed a small cauldron, closely resembling a chafing dish, and lighted a burner beneath it. From his robe, MacAbre brought the effigy in sporting togs that represented Wilfred Walden. He carefully removed the pin from the figure's heart, removed the miniature attire and tossed the doll into the metal bowl where a quantity of wax had already begun to boil.

"There will be a few days' wait," purred MacAbre, "before we need another image for which our client will pay the usual price. Meanwhile, we shall prepare an effigy for our own purposes according to the description that you two can give me.

"It is well that others should believe in Voodoo power, even when we use hidden methods to invoke it. But there are times when the Voodoo influence is real, as all of us can testify. You have seen it in the jungle; it can be witnessed here"—MacAbre indicated the whole room with a broad sweep—"because through mechanical art I can bring the jungle to this room."

MacAbre was stirring the waxen broth with a long spoon that had an insulated handle. In his other hand, he held an object that looked like a miniature coffin, its outer layer a rubbery material. The interior of that little casket was a mold, shaped to human form. Into it MacAbre began to ladle molten wax while Fandor and Jeno watched with eager eyes.

They were like the Witches of Macbeth, these three; perhaps it was from that legend that MacAbre had chosen his peculiar but significant name, as thin disguise for the thing the term "macabre" represented: Death.

Though Professor MacAbre was the instigator of the heinous scheme he now intended, it was difficult to mark him as the ringleader. The handsome face of Fandor was as livid as the ugly countenance of Jeno, those other members of the Evil Three, and

Carefully the voodoo master withdrew the pin from the heart of the weird little effigy.

both looked capable of serving in MacAbre's place, should occasion so require.

Voodoo magic was again upon the march!

CHAPTER X

DUSK was streaking the long lawns of Walden Manor like a belated portent of death already done. But whatever the mystery such gloom might signify, all doubt regarding Wilfred Walden had been officially dispelled. The living room of the great mansion was fringed by a cordon of physicians all summoned from New York, and to a man these specialists agreed upon the cause of Walden's death.

It was a very common thing, an unsuspected heart ailment which Walden had not only ignored but challenged.

When a man of advancing age and increasing weight disported on the tennis court, he was running an undue risk. One specialist put it in the form of a brief analogy that brought approving nods from the rest.

"I've often told men like Walden," said the doctor, "that if I gave them a rare but fragile crystal and said that so long as they carried it unbroken their lives and health would continue, they would act with due accord. Always, they would hesitate before risking that priceless possession.

"Excitement, exertion, anything wherein their charge would be neglected would be something that they would strictly avoid. Simply picture such a crystal as a heart that has seen long service and must therefore have been subject to the wear that a man recognizes in the rest of his physique. You then have the case in terms that a layman should understand."

The terms applied to Walden's case. He had been careless with the precious crystal. However, the analogy could be interpreted in another way, for Walden had actually been carrying something on his person which might be likened to a priceless crystal.

That something was the matchless Tarn Emerald.

The green gem had been sent back to the lawyers who represented the Tarn Estate, and in due course it would be offered along with half a million dollars to the next inheritor. But though the physicians had omitted the emerald from their verdict, it wasn't totally forgotten.

Rex Tarn was mentioning it in rueful tones to Sue Aldrich and Margo Lane as they stood near the passage that led to the conservatory.

"I saw Chauncey give something to Walden," expressed Rex, "but I hadn't an idea it was the emerald. Honestly, I wouldn't have thought of starting that game if I knew that Wilf was defying the curse. I've gone into the history of the thing, and it's been bad news for everybody who tackled it. Why, the original Tarn who brought the emerald from Colombia was washed overboard from the schooner that was taking him to New York. Within a few months, the man who inherited it was also dead, which showed how fast the jinx could work."

"That wasn't very fast," put in another man's voice. "The curse seems to be working in days instead of months, ever since you took an interest in it, Rex."

Turning indignantly, Rex saw his cousin Alex standing in the passage. During that moment, Margo caught the wild, hunted look in Rex's gray eyes, a thing she'd noticed earlier when he had stopped short at sight of Walden lying dead.

In contrast, Alex was eyeing Rex narrowly and firmly. There was a purpose in Alex's manner, which he had acquired since last night. That run-in with Rex at Club Galaxy had turned him into a decided extrovert. No more of the quiet life for Alex, not if there was any reason to assert himself, as there seemed to be right now.

"And speaking of fast workers, Rex," Alex's words carried punch instead of a drawl, "you may think you belong in that category yourself—"

"I had nothing to do with what happened to Walden," broke in Rex. "I was in the other court when he dropped dead, further away than I was from Henniman when he tumbled down the museum stairs. I've had enough of these accusations, Alex! Nobody can prove a thing against me!"

"Who was making accusations?" demanded Alex. "Not I, that's certain. I called you a fast worker because of the way you ran off with Sue today, before I had a chance to see her." Swinging to Sue, Alex added reprovingly: "I told you I was going to a bank directors' luncheon and that I'd call for you afterward."

"But I couldn't leave here," protested Sue. "Not until the doctors settled the question of Walden's death."

"And you shouldn't bother with directors' meetings," Rex told Alex, "not if you expect to get along with Sue. She isn't the sort to stand by and be neglected."

Alex gave Rex a cold, narrow stare.

"Sue's future isn't being neglected," declared Alex. "Not when I attend directors' meetings. I regard financial interests as important on her account, because someday I expect to marry Sue."

In an indirect way, this must have been Alex's first proposal of marriage, for Sue's surprise was so sudden that she couldn't speak when she tried. Noticing it, Rex spoke for her.

"Perhaps Sue has other ideas, Alex. She might be just independent enough not to marry you."

"She won't be independent long," Alex retorted,

"if she keeps lending you money to replace the fortune you squandered."

"How do you know I squandered it?" asked Rex. "Maybe I've invested it, Alex. There are ways of making bigger money than through bank stocks, even though it means tying up cash until the payoff comes."

"If you mean through roulette wheels," scoffed Alex, "I hope you're a man who owns one. That's the only way to make those playthings pay. Come along, Sue, we have a dinner date this evening. Remember?"

Taking Sue's arm, Alex started out through the hallway with Rex following as though hoping to renew the argument. Margo would have gone along just because she felt it was her duty to witness any trouble, but a hand suddenly grasped her and she turned with a startled gasp, clamping her hand below her throat to keep her heart where it belonged.

It was Cranston who halted Margo.

He had stepped from the doorway of the conservatory after listening unnoticed to the dispute between the Tarn cousins.

"Frighten you, Margo?"

"A bit, Lamont." Margo felt easier as she heard Cranston's calm voice. "I—I feel jumpy inside. I guess it's because of what happened to Walden."

"You felt the same after Henniman died?"

"Well, no. Only that was the first time—"

"And a worse experience," put in Cranston. "That's when your heart should have begun the thumps."

"I suppose you're right, Lamont. In a way I know you're right, because I'm sure this was beginning when I reached the tennis court. I felt tense as though something was to happen."

"Not as if something had happened?"

Slowly, Margo shook her head, not grasping Cranston's question fully. By way of explanation, Cranston led her through the silent jungle of the tropical conservatory until they reached the door of the small corner room which was kept in a superheated condition. There, Margo gave an involuntary shudder as Cranston gestured her across the threshold, but his smile reassured her.

"You won't have to worry, Margo. The room is different now."

It *was* different. It was cooler than the main conservatory; indeed, the chill of evening was penetrating it with air that had the tang of wine. Closing the door to protect the flora in the main conservatory, Cranston gestured to a pair of wide open windows.

"Did you open them, Margo?"

"Why, no, Lamont."

"You're sure?"

"I—I think I'm sure. Only it was so strange in here, with the scent of the flowers so oppressive."

"Chauncey says you were in here when he came through the conservatory. He thinks you must have opened the windows."

"But I passed someone when I was going out, Lamont!" exclaimed Margo. "I passed Jeno!"

"Jeno—or Fandor?"

"I suppose it was Fandor," recalled Margo, hazily. "Funny that I should have them mixed. Maybe it's because they are both dark and bow so profoundly. But Jeno looked almost like a Hindu while Fandor is a Cuban."

"No, Margo. Cubans speak Spanish, but Fandor had a habit of dropping into another language, French. It happens to be the language spoken in Haiti."

Margo's eyes opened as they had before; she could feel herself seized by one of those hunted fits that Rex Tarn was always trying to fight off. To Margo, Haiti spelled Voodoo, the word that prompted fear.

Again, Cranston's calm took hold; he turned Margo's mind to other matters as he gestured to the plants that Walden had admired so greatly. Margo's gasp was one of sorrow when she saw that those precious specimens had wilted, flowers and all, from the cool air through the open windows.

"Why, they're dead," expressed Margo. "I—I suppose I'm partly to blame. But I supposed century plants would be more hardy."

"They are," acknowledged Cranston. "A single treatment shouldn't have killed them, which proves that these weren't century plants. I'll tell you more about them later, Margo."

Going out by the rear door, Cranston and Margo entered the coupé and drove back to Manhattan. During the ride, Margo came under Cranston's keen-eyed scrutiny more often than she realized, for at the moments when he watched her, she was staring straight ahead. Cranston drove across a bridge instead of using the East River tunnel because he felt the open air was doing Margo good; at least she was quite relaxed when the car reached the familiar city streets.

It was then that Cranston said:

"I spoke to Chauncey about Fandor. It seems that the handsome *Señor* Bianco may have much less background than we supposed."

"But Walden said he was a sugar planter," reminded Margo. "They did business, didn't they?"

"Walden expected to do business," replied Cranston, "purely on Fandor's say-so. The chap came here with an offer of sugar in huge tonnage at the lowest wholesale figure that Walden could expect. Of course, Walden treated him like a long-lost friend. That's business."

"You mean they'd just met for the first time?"

"That's right. Chauncey corroborated it. I doubt that Fandor could deliver a hundred pounds of sugar, let alone a thousand tons."

"Then what was Fandor's game?" Margo was experiencing new palpitations. "Tell me, Lamont—"

"Tomorrow," interposed Cranston, as he swung the coupé to the curb. "You're tired and here's your apartment. Why don't you nap a while and then go out to dinner? But forget all that happened today—until tomorrow."

After leaving Margo, Cranston drove the car to a garage where a cab was waiting outside on the darkened street. It was natural for Cranston to choose that cab in order to ride to his club, but what happened during the cab trip savored of the unexpected. From a hidden drawer beneath the rear seat of the cab, Cranston brought black garments in the shape of a cloak and hat, with which he enveloped himself so rapidly that he seemed to literally disappear within the cab.

This was Shrevvy's cab, the one that Cranston used on many missions, particularly when he became his other self, The Shadow!

CHAPTER XI

FROM beneath the structure of the old-fashioned elevated, a furtive figure detached itself and started rapidly along the street toward MacAbre's house. A huge tumult was raging overhead for a northbound express on the central track was overtaking a local on its right, while another local was coming southward on the left.

In fact, the avenue trembled as if from a man-made earthquake transmitted down the el pillars, and the furtive man shuddered in his turn. Just away from the corner, he dived into the security of a doorway and cringed there in the darkness. It wasn't just because the vibration of the paving reminded him of Voodoo drums; the thought of faces at the windows of those el cars frightened him.

This habitual visitor to MacAbre's preserves could not afford to be spotted in the neighborhood. He had been seen once, the night when Margo Lane had come here and another such episode could spell the end to all his plans for wealth. That was why gray eyes were wide when they peered from the doorway after the trains had rumbled away; wide with the hunted stare that had become indelibly identified with Rex Tarn.

But it would have been impossible to mark the man as Rex when he started along the street again, for he was huddled with his face deep in his raincoat, and his eyes, when they gave darting glances, were too hurried to be noted in the light.

All doorways looked suspicious on this dark night. A fog that was weaving in from the river produced fantastic shapes. Lampposts, fireplugs, even house steps seemed to cast their own reflection as if against a misty mirror, producing the effect of lurkers everywhere. Sometimes those figures actually moved, but that could have been charged to the swirl of the fog.

Nevertheless, these things didn't please MacAbre's visitor. He was glad for once when he found himself in the Voodoo professor's preserves. Tonight, MacAbre met him personally in the antique shop and bowed a deep greeting to this black sheep of the Tarn family. Ushering his visitor into the Voodoo chamber, MacAbre closed the door that produced the simulated fire blaze and announced with his most cheerful cackle:

"I have summoned you to complete a pleasant duty; one you will enjoy because it requires no payment of the usual fee, yet will prove to your advantage."

Hunted gray eyes didn't understand.

"This does not concern the Tarn Emerald," explained MacAbre. "It can wait for the next heir apparent. But meanwhile, there is a certain person whose account must be closed. She has been concerned in matters much too often."

"You—you don't mean Sue?"

"You mean the girl your cousin would like to steal from you?" MacAbre cackled a laugh. "Of course not. Here, identify her for yourself from the face of this image. I would like to know how accurately Fandor and Jeno described her."

Across the flickery artificial logs, MacAbre thrust a shapely waxen effigy into his visitor's hand. Gray eyes reflected horror in the changing light as the lips below them gasped:

"Margo Lane!"

"Excellent!" With a wave of his hand, MacAbre started the thrum of tom-toms and brought the walls to life with a whirl of pictured Voodoo dancers. "And now to choose a suitable garb for this image, which will properly represent its fate."

Stooping beside the fire, MacAbre raised the metal bowl that an hour before had boiled with molten wax. At present, the miniature cauldron contained a more potent substance. Its contents consisted of melted bronze, glistening and seething as it bubbled. Pointing to the image, MacAbre lowered his claw-tipped finger to the bowl and stated:

"Drop it!"

A hand trembled, then moved forward. Opening mechanically, fingers let the wax image slide into the bubbling metal which swallowed it with a hiss. Taking a pair of odd-shaped tongs, MacAbre dipped them into the bronze stew and brought out the effigy with the pincers. In that brief bath, the Voodoo doll had become a bronze statuette!

"You wonder at this?" clucked MacAbre. "It is

really very simple. Why do you suppose I deal in antiques? Only to dispose of life-sized statues such as this"—he leaned across the fire and his tone changed to a hiss that tuned with the music of the simmering bowl—"statues that represent the bodies of victims who have defied my power."

"I export statuary." Carefully, MacAbre set the bronze image on the floor to let its coating harden. "There is little difficulty in shipping it to certain points; the complications come when customs officials examine it at the receiving ports. But for some strange reason"—MacAbre reverted to his chuckle—"these shipments never arrive."

Abruptly, MacAbre cut off the pictured whirl that swept the walls, and the beat of drums stopped also. He ushered his best customer out through the antique shop, and on the stairs MacAbre paused, to put the invitation:

"Would you like to stay and witness the working of a Voodoo charm? After all, you received very little entertainment from the deaths you purchased. You are welcome to remain—"

The reply that interrupted MacAbre's offer was the slam of the front door, so fast did his horrified visitor scurry down the stairs. With a chortle, MacAbre went into the front room, where Fandor and Jeno were peering through the slits of the front curtains.

"They are too commercial, these people who call themselves civilized," commented MacAbre. "They are willing to buy death, as any other investment, but its beauty does not appeal to them, any more than the other commodities from which they profit."

"Shall we follow him?" asked Jeno, thumbing toward the window curtain. "I shall be careful tonight, *mon professeur*."

"No, Jeno," returned MacAbre. "I shall need you here. Besides, I have arranged with others to make sure our client does not behave unwisely as he did the other night. I am leaving it to the men who will handle our shipment. Crooks, they call them in this country. Come. Let us go below."

Outdoors, two sweatered men were meeting near the corner by the elevated. One gave a gesture through the thickening fog.

"Say, did that bloke hustle," said the man who gestured. "You wouldn't have knowed him for the fellow who came sneaking up so cautious like. Or was he the same, Griff?"

"He was the same all right, Johnny," returned Griff. "Only that don't mean he won't be coming back. Maybe he wants to see somebody and tip them off to something. I don't like it. So keep your sea-eye peeled."

"Righto," agreed Johnny. "How soon do we ship the cargo?"

"As soon as they have it ready." Griff stepped to the curb and waved to a truck that came rumbling from beneath the elevated. Griff's gesture was a sweep that ended in a half circle. "The boys will park in back and leave the truck. I'll use them as lookouts, too."

"What a lot of trouble over one statue!"

"It's important, that statue, and your job is important, too. Remember, the statue goes overboard before you reach port."

"Agreed. But what will I tell my matey when he helps me bring the crate up from the hold?"

"Tell him it's an insurance gag," suggested Griff. "The statue is being sold for more dough than it's worth, so it's got to turn up missing in order to collect."

"And Lloyd's will stand the difference, as they can blooming well afford. That will suit my matey."

Griff was gesturing Johnny along the avenue so they could meet the truckers and deploy. Professor MacAbre had chosen good helpers for this occasion; except for Johnny, Griff's men constituted an experienced highjack crew who had specialized in anything the black market wanted.

No blacker market could exist than Professor MacAbre's deals in statuary. In the windowless cellar of his house, the Voodoo specialist was completing his preparations for another masterpiece in death. Fandor and Jeno were stirring a bronze broth in a full-sized cauldron that loomed shoulder high beside a half door that looked like a large wicket, set at head level in the wall. The arch-professor was at the telephone, which oddly was in the cellar, speaking in a smooth, persuasive tone that copied the soft, snakelike simmer of the steaming bronze.

It was a night of madness, this, indoors and out. By now, the side street was shrouded in a whitish pall as ominous as blackest night. Through the thick, ugly fog came basso blares of river whistles, singularly like tones of doom. Amid the thick swirl, Griff and his expert crew had spread to patrol the district, with the fog as perfect cover.

Strangest of all was the ghostly shape that glided through the neighboring streets like the stalking figure of death itself. It seemed a human shape plucked from night's own blackness, visible only where it stirred the whitened mist, disappearing in the grimy background beyond the swirls of its own making.

The Shadow was seeking an arch foe whom he had never seen nor heard of, but whose existence was a matter beyond all doubt: Professor MacAbre, the brain of Voodoo crime!

CHAPTER XII

WHY Margo Lane believed the voice, she could not tell.

It was a voice that she had never before heard,

persuasive in its purr yet pointed in its statements. It simply told her where she was to go, not why.

There was no use putting questions to that voice; it wouldn't have answered them. Somehow it caught the tempo of Margo's excited heartbeats and brought from her a breathless "Yes" each time it paused.

So Margo was riding to her destination in a cab that wasn't Shrevvy's, and through her brain there throbbed a peculiar rhythm that was an aftermath of the strange coma which had gripped her when she breathed the fragrance of the Secret Flowers in Walden's oppressive conservatory.

The doorman at Margo's apartment house had watched the girl get in the cab and had noted a fixed expression in her eyes. He was still thinking about it when another cab wheeled up and a young man sprang from it, much excited.

The doorman saw the full, square jaw of Rex Tarn, before the latter bundled his raincoat collar about his chin. All that remained visible of his features were gray eyes above a thin, aristocratic nose, but his disguise was by no means complete. Those eyes were the sort to be remembered, by their wide, excited expression.

"Miss Margo Lane." Rex glanced upward at the building. "Has she gone out?"

"About five minutes ago," replied the doorman. "She took a cab."

"Didn't she say where she was going?"

"No, sir."

"But you must have heard her tell the driver."

"Sorry, but I didn't. She hadn't told him when the cab started. She seemed to be thinking about something else."

It wasn't exactly a hunted look that flashed from Rex's eyes; rather, their gray glint expressed guilt because of his belated arrival. Certain it was that Rex wanted to make amends for his delay, for he sprang back into his cab and told the driver to get going without stating where.

Apparently he had a general idea where Margo had gone.

In her own cab, Margo was sitting silent with half-closed eyes. Somehow the throbbing in her head was taking on the beat of drums. It seemed that such an obligato had come with the voice across the telephone, and now Margo could remember a curious effect at the finish of that talk. The voice had given a crackle, like that of fire. Mentally, Margo could picture the flicker of flame accompanying it.

The cab stopped suddenly and the driver leaned back to state the fare. It was eighty cents and Margo pushed a dollar bill through the window, wondering how she could have come so far in what seemed only a few minutes. Then she was standing on the sidewalk, staring at a house she'd never seen before, and shivering as the cold fog crept about her.

Oddly, Margo was wearing the same rejected evening gown that she'd put on the other night. Why she'd picked it again, she couldn't understand, except that the voice had told her to hurry, and therefore she'd let her thoughts revert to the last occasion when she'd been in haste. At any rate, the flimsy gown was a good argument for getting indoors, so Margo went up the steps of the house where the cab had stopped.

Pressing a button, Margo heard the click-clack of the automatic latch so suddenly that the thing must have been geared to the button itself. Going upstairs, she saw an open door and entered a room well-crammed with antiques. A far door was open, so Margo went there, following instructions that the crackly voice had given.

Beyond the door was a blank-walled room. Its sheer whiteness gave the effect of a motion picture screen on every side. Even the inside of the door was a smooth white that matched the slight glisten of the walls, another feature that made them resemble picture screens. As Margo crossed the threshold, the door closed behind her, and she was startled by a crackle accompanied by a blaze of light.

Staring at a fire in the middle of the floor, Margo was amazed by its apparent reality. Her eyes went upward to study the scintillating effect of the artificial firelight upon a crystal chandelier above. That was when she

Outside there was more than darkness—there was a ghostly shape that glided through the neighboring streets like the stalking figure of death itself—The Shadow!

noted curious beams spread from above the chandelier, like the glare of movie projectors focused on the walls.

Margo felt quite herself, for the hypnotic effect of the voice no longer bothered her. She was simply experiencing a state of simple posthypnosis, wherein a subject has a craving to complete a given duty, which in Margo's case was to come to this place. The effect of her sojourn in the glass room where Walden kept the Secret Flowers was practically gone by this time, remaining only as the faintest recollection unless something stirred it strongly.

Something did.

Turning around to leave the room, Margo noticed something, resting on the fire. She could tell by now that the fire was artificial, so she stopped to examine the object. It was a little statuette of bronze, simply shaped in the set form of a doll. Even when she picked it up, Margo didn't realize that its face was formed to represent her own.

By then, Margo had forgotten the doll.

The mere action of picking up the statuette had cut the photoelectric beam that controlled the mechanical effects of this strange room. Drums began to throb, bringing back the maddening note that had gone through Margo's brain. She dropped the statuette, which didn't break like a wax doll would have, because its coating of bronze kept it intact.

Then the room became alive.

To Margo, the effect of jungle scenery in full color was more than startling, for it took her back to that setting at Walden's. When the figures of the Voodoo dancers whirled into sight, Margo was gripped with momentary terror, which caused her to turn from wall to wall. Everywhere those mad dancers, brown like the bronze statuette, were flinging themselves into abandoned gyrations, with the furious scintillation of golden bangles clanging a tempo to the drums.

Professor MacAbre had added another effect tonight, in addition to sight and sound.

Wispy smoke strayed up from the electrically heated fire, like the trail of perfume. It carried the scent of the strange plants that had withered at Walden's that afternoon. As Margo sensed the aroma, she stiffened, for the fragrance brought her mind to a state of seeming reality.

Her eyes closed, Margo recalled a rapid series of events: the death of Henniman, her encounter with Jeno, the sudden fate that had overtaken Walden. All seemed to be happening in the broad light of day, and when she opened her eyes again, her present surroundings, though those of night, seemed to savor of complete reality.

Literally, Margo was in the center of a Voodoo jungle, for to her distant gaze, the dancing figures had gained a three-dimensional effect. They seemed to loom forward from the screen and crowd around the firelight where Margo stood, but always they receded in tantalizing style. They were beckoning with clanging bracelets, madly inviting this newcomer to join their circle, and Margo found herself swaying to the beat of the drums. Her mind was actually moving ahead of itself, for as she swayed around the firelight, she seemed to be among the dancers, sharing their happy hysteria.

The reels that MacAbre had brought from Haiti provided for that response to the increasing Voodoo spell. In their dance, the dusky maidens weaved their hands with snakelike undulation toward one spot in the circle, indicating it from both directions. Her eyes attracted, Margo saw an opening in the far side, a gap that the dancers wanted her to fill.

It was subtle, that serpentine weave. Upon Margo, it produced the same effect as the hypnotic power of a snake directed toward a helpless bird. She was moving forward, slowly, under an irresistible spell, while the dancers at the opening in the circle were waving extra bangles, inviting her to accept these tokens of the dance.

A dance macabre, had Margo known it!

Ignorance, however, was the theme of Voodoo, and all rational ideas were gone from Margo's mind. Her civilized intelligence gave way to the lure of primitive savagery as she approached the wall, hoping to receive the glinting bangles. Margo was on the very verge of going berserk, when there was a sudden wobble in the dancing circle behind her.

That wobble came when the door swung inward. Through the gap came the cloaked figure of The Shadow. Only briefly did the firelight disappear, for the door went shut again, restoring the weird flicker. But the colored pictures did not waver, not at the spot where Margo was about to cast aside all civilized restraint and fling herself into the ring of jungle dancers.

With a long leap past the fire, The Shadow caught Margo by her shoulders above the slipping straps of the evening gown. He tried to wheel her away from the spot that lured her, but in her eyes he saw a mad determination that challenged his own.

Margo herself would never have believed that she could fight so hard. To her wide-eyed gaze, stimulated by the drugged perfume, The Shadow was a clouded blur that lay between herself and mad desire. She became a jungle wildcat, clawing, kicking at this hated shape that intervened, her strength increasing with each frenzied moment that she was thwarted from joining the circle in which she insanely believed she now belonged.

Hurling her whole weight against The Shadow, screaming wildly above the beat of drums, Margo was actually driving her cloaked friend back against the screen, when he took the only course that could terminate this folly. Slashing Margo's clawing hands aside, The Shadow drove a thin-gloved fist straight to the jaw below her crazed face.

It was an expert punch, well placed. It had to be, to counteract Margo's maddened mood. It was meant to score instantaneous knockout and it did, but it would have given Margo a broken jaw as a souvenir, if The Shadow hadn't pulled the punch at the proper instant.

The Shadow's forearm gave the punch, his body provided the pull, and he was unstinting with the recoil. As Margo slumped to the floor, The Shadow wheeled back and away, expecting the wall to stop him.

It didn't, because there wasn't any wall.

Striking the exact spot where Margo had hoped to fling herself into the circle and take her place among the bangled tribe, The Shadow crashed a paper-thin barrier. The spot was an open doorway that had been papered over with the white, glistening wallpaper that MacAbre had chosen for a surrounding screen.

The doorway led directly to a rear stairway that had also been altered to suit the machinations of MacAbre. It was a steep stairway, and it was provided with a ramp as smooth and polished as a bowling alley.

Before he could catch the sides of the doorway, The Shadow was skidding headlong down that slide, bound for the reception that Professor MacAbre had provided for his Voodoo victim, Margo Lane!

CHAPTER XIII

PROFESSOR MACABRE turned with chin in hand to watch what happened at the half-door above the cauldron. He knew that the trap had sprung, because an automatic cut-off had stopped proceedings in the Voodoo chamber and flashed a signal light below.

It would mean a new statue in MacAbre's unlisted collection. A flash, a plop in the cauldron beside which Fandor and Jeno waited; then all would be over. Death from boiling bronze was practically instantaneous and it would simply be a case of fishing out the human statue, the way MacAbre had done with the wax figure when it gained its coating of bronze.

With a clatter, the half-door cracked open.

In a mere split-second, MacAbre and his patient henchmen were overwhelmed with a complete surprise. Instead of a live Voodoo dancer with arms waving in quest of imaginary bangles, a black-cloaked shape came lunging forth. As for the surprise that greeted The Shadow, it was equally forceful.

However, The Shadow expected a surprise.

If Margo had come skidding down that chute, her mind would still have been upon the Voodoo dance. The most that she could have done would be to try stop herself, and the cauldron was perfectly placed for anyone who made that despairing effort.

But The Shadow was thinking in terms of what he found. He wasn't wondering why he wasn't wearing the clanging costume of a Voodoo dancer in exchange for cast-off civilized attire. He was expecting anything from a bed of spikes to a battery of machine guns and whatever it was, he planned to rush it.

So The Shadow rushed the cauldron.

It was just a matter of turning a slide into a dive. Doubling his knees as his arms spread the half-door, The Shadow turned his plunge into a spring. His hands, jabbing as far as they could reach, went beyond the seething brew of deadly bronze and struck the far side of the cauldron. If the thing had been anchored hard and fast, The Shadow would have plopped back into it, but it wasn't fixed in place.

Over went the cauldron and The Shadow with it, in a somersault that carried him ahead of the pouring bronze. His fate at that moment was really in the balance, for unless the flip landed him on his feet, he couldn't hope to escape the flood that followed. The concrete floor was hard, and a flat landing would have been a stunning blow, so The Shadow did his utmost to avoid it.

His grip on the cauldron edge helped. The massive iron vat was firm, even when it tilted, and The Shadow added the necessary hoist to his flying turnover. Hitting on his feet, he reached the far wall with a run, caught himself with one hand and wheeled around with the other producing the latest specimen of a .45 automatic from a holster comfortably situated beneath his cloak.

If The Shadow was fast, so were his challengers. In fact they were no longer challengers at all.

The moment that the cauldron tipped, MacAbre set the precedent for safety. The arrival of a fighting foeman instead of a helpless victim was trifling compared to the menace of the cauldron. Close to the edge from which the molten metal poured, MacAbre did a rapid dive for the nearest doorway, and both Fandor and Jeno followed with quick leaps past the flood of bronze.

When The Shadow turned, he saw figures disappearing in a steam as thick as the fog outdoors. Rolling towards him like a trailing surf was the bronze bath meant for Margo, and it was spreading wide. Instead of trying to dodge it completely, The Shadow cut across its thinning mass, without pausing in a single stride. Using the door that the fugitives had taken, The Shadow found his way upstairs. A quick slam from a rear passage announced that MacAbre and Company had taken the back way out.

Where they went, it was The Shadow's job to follow, for the simple reason that Margo was still upstairs enjoying the sweet coma of a knockout punch. If MacAbre doubled the trail in that direction, it wouldn't be pleasant for Margo, considering that these Voodoo artists could be quick with knives when cauldrons failed.

So The Shadow kept to the trail, and in the course of it, he could have chopped the Voodoo villains one by one, if it hadn't been for the fog. Ducking around corners, they were just ahead of gunfire, thanks to the grimy haze that so promptly swallowed them. But their fear of The Shadow kept them in full flight, as was evidenced when they finally dashed beneath the elevated and took to a side street toward the river, which was the opposite direction from the headquarters that they had abandoned.

The Shadow fired three shots through the fog to spur the flight. That volley brought him trouble.

Instantly, guns opened from all sides. Griff and his gang were converging on the scene, and in the light from the corner, they made out a cloaked shape that they recognized. Perhaps the perpetrators of Voodoo terrorism were unacquainted with the prowess of The Shadow, but these men of common crime knew all about their superfoe. If gangdom ever gained a dictator, that post could be claimed by the man who settled crime's great scourge, The Shadow.

Plenty of candidates had gunned for The Shadow and failed, but never had better opportunity been at hand. Here was a chance to stay within close and open range, firing potshots for The Shadow who was somewhere in the middle, yet avoid his return fire by trusting to the thickness of the fog, which in terms of the gang's courtesy member, Johnny, was as much like suet as any London pea-souper.

Tongues of flame were spurting through the fog, their location difficult to trace in that illusive atmosphere. As many as six assailants were surrounding The Shadow, shooting for anything that looked like blackness. To cleave a path among them would be foolhardy, the way stray shots were flying.

Amid those deadly gun coughs, The Shadow laughed. His tone came strident through the thickness, inviting enemies to do their utmost. Maybe

With a last violent effort, The Shadow threw his muscles into play and overleaped the boiling cauldron.

they took it as a bluff, for with one accord they charged, shouting to each other to "get The Shadow," embellishing his title with various unnecessary adjectives.

Shots from thrusting guns stabbed at a common target, looming blackness that could only represent The Shadow since there was no one else about. Instead of collapsing, that shape loomed higher and grew huge, as though magnified by the fog. The Shadow seemed to be gaining a gigantic stature, his taunting laugh rising with him.

The burst of guns was drowning the metallic clang of bullets, otherwise Griff's marksmen might have realized what their target was before they reached it. Coming together at the focal spot, they saw the thing they had mistaken for The Shadow take its rightful shape. The bulking monstrosity was the steep, covered stairway leading up to the elevated line!

It was one of those stairways with several turns, which accounted for its massive appearance. It was made of metal; steps, rails and all, a zigzag pillbox towering up into the foggy night. Already well up the steps, The Shadow was laughing down at the foemen from whose very midst he had escaped.

Two could play that game; namely, two in terms of factions. Griff snarled the order for attack and with a mad surge, six mobbies stormed the stairs, blasting shots upward at every turn. Either The Shadow was out of shots or saving them, for his laugh was the only response. Always it was a full turn ahead, and the gun bursts did not drown it.

What did drown the laugh was the heavy rumble of an elevated train, stopping at the station. During the brief pause, The Shadow halted somewhere to jab a few delaying shots below, then as the train pulled out again, his strident laugh was lost in its increasing clatter.

This was an express station, where the central track mounted to a superstructure above the local platform. Until noon, that track was used by downtown trains; after that hour it became a path for rapid uptown traffic. The train that had just pulled out was a local, but from down the line, approaching lights were twinkling upward through the mist, announcing that an express was taking the rise toward the double platform of the superstructure.

The Shadow was at the local level when he saw those lights. Griff's maddened mob was very close, taking the final turn of the steps. Instead of making for the turnstiles that led to the local platform, The Shadow whirled toward a flight of steps that marked an exit from the upper level. The first of his pursuers glimpsed him and shouted to the rest. With a massed drive they followed The Shadow, all guns blazing, expecting to box him at an exit gate.

There wasn't any gate at the upper platform. This was an oddity of elevated lines that practically everyone had overlooked, except The Shadow. What he reached was a short passage of a dozen feet, with about the same width of platform just beyond it. Then came the deep-set single track in a space wide enough to accommodate an el train; beyond it the far platform.

This was at the south end of the station, and as The Shadow started along the short passage, three of Griff's thugs made the turn behind him. Charging full tilt, they saw The Shadow dash ahead of them, in a brilliant light that suddenly sliced the fog. It was the headlight of the elevated express, coming fast.

Crooks raised triumphant shouts, confident that The Shadow would be blocked. They were hurling themselves after him, intent upon slugging him with their empty guns, the moment that he turned about, because of the intervening train. But The Shadow didn't turn; he had timed his coming exploit almost to the exact second.

Reaching the edge of the platform at full speed, The Shadow launched himself in air. His was the action of a broad jumper, perfectly performed. A capable jumper can cover twenty feet with a running broad, and the width of the track pit was considerably under that distance. But few athletes would have taken the chance in circumstances such as this.

The Shadow's leap carried him right across the path of the inrushing train, the gleaming headlight growing as if to swallow him. His flight through air seemed painfully slow compared to the metal juggernaut that was roaring at him, but his timing wasn't wrong. The Shadow struck the far platform and reeled onward, half a second ahead of the mighty mass that threatened to doom him.

His pursuers weren't so lucky. The first man reached the brink just as The Shadow landed on the far side; making an effort to halt, the thug couldn't. His shriek was louder than the grind of brakes as he toppled from the platform's edge and was slapped by the full tonnage of the el train. The clattering express knocked the puny thug half the length of the platform and before the motorman could stop the train, the wheels were slicing the body of the victim who had landed dead when he struck the tracks.

The second mobbie met the passing train head on and was ricocheted like a dummy made of straw. He went whirling along the platform, crashing a bench against which he struck, while the third crook halted and stared aghast. Then Griff arrived and shouted at the man who was standing stupefied. Together they grabbed the stunned thug who had crashed the bench and rushed him back down the steps.

Above the groan of the halting train, a weird laugh floated back from the stairs beyond the opposite platform. The Shadow hadn't waited to witness the fate of his pursuers; having let the train cut them off, he was on his way elsewhere, taking advantage of the dozen seconds or more that would elapse before the doors could open and let Griff's tribe through.

Only they weren't coming through. Flinging themselves madly to the street, they wanted flight, knowing that The Shadow was somewhere at large in the dank fog, probably prepared to chop them down at leisure, if they crossed his deadly path. They weren't even going back to get their truck.

They were lucky, those scattering gunners who had dared The Shadow. He was letting them go their way—for The Shadow had another person to consider: Margo Lane.

Turning in the misty gloom, The Shadow gave a brief departing laugh as he started back along the avenue to cover the few blocks to the abandoned lair of Professor MacAbre.

CHAPTER XIV

MUCH had happened in a short time at MacAbre's house. In a few brief minutes, the tide of excitement had swept in another direction, and during that interval, Margo Lane had retrieved her senses.

Sitting on the floor beside an artificial firelight, Margo was holding her chin and wondering what had kicked it, along with other things that puzzled her. For The Shadow's punch had obliterated Margo's recollections of the vanished Voodoo dance.

Looking toward one wall, Margo saw a jagged gap with a peculiar slide beyond and recognized that it couldn't be the right way out. Coming to her feet, she rearranged her draping gown, found a shoe that she had kicked off during her struggle with The Shadow, and looked for a door. Since the walls were no longer alive with fantastic pictures, the crack that represented the corner door was very evident. Opening the door, Margo went out through the antique shop, staring as though she had never seen it before, and so down to the street.

Once in the fog, Margo experienced her former chill. This neighborhood seemed ghostly, if for no other reason than that she couldn't remember how she had arrived here. The clatter of Margo's high heels was music to her own ears, for it offset the silent creep of the fog while she was walking toward the nearest corner. Margo didn't like the stillness of that shrouded atmosphere.

At least not until the rumble came. High overhead, something roared past with a gush of light, sending Margo back in a wild stampede, until she realized it was only an elevated train. By then, Margo was tripping into a basement entry, or would have, if firm hands hadn't caught her.

In the hazy light from the corner streetlamp, Margo saw Rex Tarn. In his eagerness to find her, Rex had let his coat collar fall, but that wasn't necessary to identify him. His wide, excited eyes were enough.

As the rumble of the southbound local faded, Rex began to pour quick explanations.

"I thought you'd be around here," he said. "I was afraid it would be dangerous after the other night, you know."

"Around where?" queried Margo. "What other night?"

"The time that knife just missed us," returned Rex. "I've felt as though someone was after me ever since. I guess seeing Walden die upset me, because I was worried all the way into town.

"Then when I got here—into town I mean—I began thinking that whoever was after me would be after you, too. So I went around to your apartment and found you'd just left. I was afraid you'd come to this neighborhood, so I came to overtake you."

Rex was speaking in an earnest tone that made his story plausible, though why he'd so suddenly become troubled over Margo's welfare, and how he had guessed her moves so promptly, was something he didn't explain. In fact, Rex was quick to change the subject, once he had stated it briefly.

"You're shivering!" exclaimed Rex. Tightening his grip on Margo's arms, he darted a hunted look across his shoulder. "Something must have terrified you."

"I'm only cold," returned Margo. "I didn't notice the fog when I started out, or I'd have put on my cape."

Noticing that Margo's arms were bare, Rex hesitated, then whipped off his raincoat, to drape it over the girl's shoulders. In a quick undertone, he asked:

"Did you just get here?"

"Why, no," replied Margo, slowly. "At least I don't think so."

"Then where have you been all the while that I've been looking for you among these streets?"

Margo's memory was back again, beginning with the other night and working toward the present.

"Why, I found the antique shop I was looking for," she stated. "Don't you remember? That's why I was in this neighborhood."

"Where is the shop?"

"In a house several doors along the street. Don't ask me which one, because I lost count when I came out through the fog. Somehow I can't recall the address either."

"Did you go into the place?"

Margo nodded; then added truthfully:

"But there was no one in there. When I saw I couldn't buy antiques, I came out again, that's all."

Although Margo still couldn't recall the Voodoo ceremony that had nearly lured her to oblivion, she was realizing that the less she said about the strange house, the better. Its menace must have been powerful to obliterate all recollection of it. Usually canny, Margo had returned enough toward normal to recognize that Rex's sharp probe might be intended to make her betray herself. So she just shook her head.

Doubt mingled with impatience on Rex's hard but handsome features. Noting something looming through the fog, he put his fingers to his lips and gave a sharp whistle. A cab nudged warily toward the curb and Rex pushed Margo toward it; momentarily resisting, the girl yielded when she recognized Shrevvy as the driver.

"No word of this to anybody," undertoned Rex, as he put Margo in the cab. "Some people might not approve of it."

"You mean people like Sue?"

"Yes, or my cousin Alex, who likes to make trouble for everybody." Not sure that the argument would stand, Rex added another: "And then there's Cranston. Maybe he wouldn't like it."

"Lamont would understand," insisted Margo, closing the cab door; then, with a note of reassurance, she said: "Nevertheless, I won't tell him."

The cab was on its way, and Rex had become a crouched figure, skirting the corner toward MacAbre's house. Having no raincoat to disguise himself, he was working from doorway to doorway, pausing intermittently in each. Still short of MacAbre's, Rex was making another foray through the fog when he sighted blackness that literally filtered toward him. Only briefly did it take a human shape, but that was enough.

Launching himself upon the evasive figure, Rex was amazed when it vanished from his driving clutch. He didn't realize the illusive effect of the fog; how it could make objects seem closer than they were, when the eye tried to gauge in terms of normal visibility. The Shadow had wheeled before Rex reached him and, by angling sharply into the fog, was circling his attacker, when Rex suddenly halted.

What stopped Rex was another human figure that suddenly replaced The Shadow. Thinking that the cloaked specter was back, Rex looked furiously, to find himself eye to eye with the glaring face of Jeno!

Apparently the Voodoo law was off, where Jeno was concerned. On a previous night, Jeno had failed to knife Rex Tarn, classing him as a man who accepted Voodoo rule. All such were answerable only to MacAbre—or had been. But now, with Voodoo schemes gone wrong, Jeno showed lust for vengeance on a man whose very presence here was indication that he might have aided Margo Lane. With a wide sweep of his arm, Jeno produced a knife that looked immense as he drew it, catching the handle to direct the blade.

Rex's warding swing was unnecessary. Though he thought the knife was meant for him, it wasn't. Hand halting, Jeno scaled the dirk across Rex's shoulder toward a figure that was lunging in from the fog: The Shadow!

A whirling shift of shoulders, the weave of a flying cloak as the knife slashed through it, and the missile rammed its point upon a brick building front. Jeno needed a trifle more accuracy, plus a dash of speed, to clip The Shadow on the whirl. He managed, though, to trip Rex against the curb, and fling him into The Shadow's path.

Then Jeno was bounding up the steps into the house, waving two figures ahead of him. MacAbre and Fandor were back, having doubled their trail with Jeno while The Shadow was shaking off Griff's crew with the assistance of an elevated express.

Spilling Rex into the sprawl which Jeno had started, The Shadow took after the Voodoo trio. His path was barred by doors which they bolted in closing, but The Shadow made short work of such barriers. The front door was mostly plate glass, which The Shadow shattered with a swing of a big gun. When he reached the door of the antique shop, he blew its lock apart with a single bullet; then rammed a few more shots that gnawed the wood around a bolt. But there was to be trouble before The Shadow reached the third door.

Professor MacAbre was diving through to the Voodoo chamber carrying an armful of odd items from his antique shop. Fandor and Jeno were standing ready with heavier exhibits; they began flinging them in a fast barrage: chairs, taborets and brassware. Warding off the flying objects, The Shadow kept on his way, forcing Jeno and Fandor to follow MacAbre and slam the final door. One crash of The Shadow's shoulder wrecked that barrier, but he was too late to overtake his prey.

Having gathered his prized projectors and other devices of the Voodoo chamber, MacAbre was sliding down the chute to the cellar with his helpers close after them. By now the molten bronze had hardened, and they would be ready, this time with bullets, if The Shadow took that route.

Speeding down the front way again, The Shadow saw that the street was deserted when he arrived, Rex having decided on flight as his own best course. That MacAbre and his partners in Voodoo believed the same was evidenced when The Shadow reached the avenue, intending to follow it to the rear street. A fading rumble greeted The Shadow, and it wasn't from the elevated line.

The sound represented the truck that Griff had

brought. MacAbre and his two lieutenants had commandeered it for their own departure. Alone, The Shadow stood in the swirling fog, master of a situation which no longer existed!

CHAPTER XV

MARGO LANE still didn't believe it until Lamont Cranston made her read the newspaper.

The discovery of an antique shop, with a polished slide down to a cellar filled with molten bronze, in a house not far from where a mob battle had ended in a death upon the el track, was indeed a riddle.

Of course, the police had the answer and curiously they were partly right. The shop was a blind for the peddling of "ancient" statuary that was faked and aged down in the basement. This tallied with some reports that had reached the law, regarding statuary shipped from certain East River piers. But that was as far as the investigation went.

A budding racket had simply exploded itself, due to friction among the men who operated it. The police were willing to question a certain racketeer named Griff Torrock, on the chance that he was acquainted with the mobbie who had perished under the wheels of the el train, but there wasn't a link with anything resembling Voodoo.

Not to the law there wasn't, but there was to Margo Lane. After reading of the unique setup in MacAbre's house, she was ready to credit the details that Cranston added. Gradually, it all came back like a dream.

"You're right, Lamont," declared Margo, her eyes half closed as they rode in Shrevvy's cab. "Why, it's horribly vivid, that maddening dance! Only the whole thing was so real that I imagined I'd joined it, gold bangles and all!"

"It's lucky you didn't keep up with your imagination," asserted Cranston, "or instead of gold bangles you'd be wearing a bronze kimono of a permanent pattern."

"That strange perfume!" recalled Margo. "Like the odor of the Secret Flowers!" She took a long sniff of the evening air. "I've lost the impression, though, since last night."

"Which is logical," agreed Cranston. "Twenty-four hours should be sufficient to offset the treatment. How's your heart?"

"No more pitty-pats."

"That's logical, too. The effect of that flower grows on people in proportion to the time they are exposed to it. After a while, it creeps into the system and stays."

"But why did it influence me so fast?"

"Largely because you weren't used to the tropical humidity of the greenhouse. Moreover the place was loaded with specimens of the Obi Weed."

The term puzzled Margo.

"The Obi Weed? What does Obi mean?"

"It means Voodoo," defined Cranston, "especially the West Indian sort."

The dread word gave Margo shudders, even though she was wearing a wrap over the new evening gown that she had picked for another visit to the Club Galaxy. Cranston noticed her quiver, and added calmly:

"If you can stifle those creeps, I'll tell you more about the Obi Weed, now that I've checked the facts."

Stiffening, Margo said to "go ahead."

"In certain inner circles," declared Cranston, "particularly in Haiti, the Obi Weed is affectionately termed the Zombi Plant. Perhaps you get the connection."

Margo got it. She didn't shudder, but simply froze. Her own experience in mechanical behavior convinced her that the term was literally true. She'd heard of "zombies"—otherwise termed "walking dead"—and knew that they were supposed to thrive in Haiti. Margo was willing to believe that such creatures could perambulate in New York as well, for she realized that she'd come very close to becoming one of them.

"Some scientists ridicule the Obi Weed," remarked Cranston. "They class it purely as a plant used in witchcraft, its virtues—or should we call them vices?—exaggerated as in the case of the famous Mandrake. They even claim that it lacks potency as a drug."

Margo was in a mood to disagree with science, but didn't say so. She decided to leave that to Lamont.

"What they have overlooked," continued Cranston, "are the combined properties of the various species. The Obi Weed is usually found singly; a cluster, in bloom and properly confined, could readily provide a heart stimulus to anyone who imbibed their odor."

Unconsciously, Margo's hand went to her throat, to learn if her heart was creeping there.

"As for the extract of such weeds," concluded Cranston, "it might conceivably live up to the reputation of the Zombi Plant if mixed in due proportions. The stories of zombies seen in Haiti are not myths. The only doubt is whether they are actually walking dead."

The lights of the Club Galaxy terminated Cranston's grisly theme, much to Margo's relief. They left the cab and entered the club where Margo shed her cape to display an olive evening gown decorated with a topaz pendant, a combination that attracted the eye as readily as Sue's familiar blue and aquamarine.

Sue was there, again sporting her favorite regalia. She was the first to envy Margo's get-up, even though it was strictly suited to a brunette. About the only advantage Sue's creation could claim was brevity, but the envious blonde soon found a better point of satisfaction. Sue had bracelets to match her necklace, while Margo hadn't. Sue didn't know that Margo had sworn off bracelets—with good reason.

Flanked by the Tarn cousins, Sue gave a very pretty smile when Cranston and Margo approached. The smile was Sue's self-compliment at her ability to keep two rivals in line, but she was taking undeserved credit. Alex and Rex had their own reasons for being on friendly terms tonight.

"Hello, Cranston," greeted Alex, "and Margo, too! We looked for you last night, after we came in from Long Island. Thought you might have enjoyed a drink or two."

"Two zombies," added Sue, very seriously. "That's the limit. This is only my second."

Sue held up a tall glass containing a dark concoction. Rex turned to the barkeeper and ordered:

"Make mine another zombi."

"You've had two already, Rexy!" warned Sue. "Better look out! They do things to you!"

"And I do things to zombies," retorted Rex. His eyes, looking past Sue, met Margo's, and for the first time she saw them narrow, the way Alex's did. "Have a drink, Margo. I'm sorry, too, that I didn't see you last night."

Alex was watching Rex suspiciously, with the tight gaze that his cousin had begun to copy. Cranston's manner was totally indifferent, the best of poses if it hadn't been for Sue. The blonde liked the stare that Alex gave to Rex, for she felt that it might be on her own account. But to see Rex giving Margo the eye meant that he might be slipping toward brunettes, a particularly serious thing when Sue noted Cranston's indifference.

Revolving on the stool, Sue made an off-balance twist, her cute way of gathering complete attention. Both Rex and Alex grabbed to save her from decorating the brass rail, and with murmured thanks, Sue added:

"That's better. Now we can be chummy again."

"It suits me," said Rex, easing his gaze and reaching for his drink as it arrived. "Maybe Alex won't be so cryptic about Lee Selfkirk."

"Why shouldn't I be?" demanded Alex. "Since he's next in line for the Tarn Emerald, why should I help you play him for a sucker?"

"I only want to warn him about the curse—"

"Like you warned Henniman and Walden? I don't think Selfkirk would thank you, even if he lived long enough."

Rex started forward from his stool, to be slapped back by Sue, who was providing excellent insulation whenever sparks began to fly between the cousins.

"Both of those deaths were accidents," snarled Rex. "You can't prove otherwise, Alex."

"Funny to hear you say that," returned Alex, candidly. "You yourself claim that the curse was working. Do you call it an accident?"

"Yes, because it could be avoided."

"By giving you a cut on the price of the emerald," laughed Alex. "Of course you'd argue it that way."

"You'd come in for the same amount, Alex. I asked both Henniman and Walden to divide the proceeds among all the family."

"And the split is getting bigger," put in Alex, "like those eyes of yours, Rex." Over his zombi, Rex was resuming his wide-eyed glare, which he promptly stifled. "It would be three ways according to your present calculation, since we're all the family that's left, except for Selfkirk.

"But I don't want any part of the Tarn Emerald." Alex became emphatic. "Whoever gets it is welcome to it and at present that means Lee Selfkirk. So I wouldn't help you find him even if I did know where he was. Maybe you're the jinx and not the emerald. You were right with Henniman and Walden before the emerald was delivered to either."

Rex brushed Sue off the stool when she tried to stop him this time, but Cranston was there to catch her so promptly that Margo experienced a surprising flare of jealousy. Fortunately, Rex had finished his third zombi, and the rule of two proved true. He wobbled as he tried to shove a punch through the space where Sue had been, and his other elbow missed the bar when he tried to catch himself.

A couple of waiters were coming up before Rex could renew hostilities. Alex gave them a weary nod along with his gesture toward Rex.

"Better start him home," suggested Alex. "He's feeling those swift ones."

Slipping a bill to one of the waiters, Alex received quick cooperation toward the removal of his unruly cousin and from then on the party quieted. Margo found herself chatting very pleasantly with Sue while Lamont and Alex went into a serious huddle.

It was an hour before the couples parted and Margo was able to ask Lamont the question that bothered her.

"What about Lee Selfkirk?" Margo queried. "I know he's in line for the Tarn Emerald, but what does he do and where is he?"

"He's an artist," replied Cranston, "and he has an income. Other artists like to borrow from him, so Selfkirk never lets anyone know where he is."

"Then how will he receive the Tarn Emerald?"

"I suppose he'll arrange it privately through the lawyers," stated Cranston. "Alex says it's due to be delivered tomorrow night, but he didn't like to tell Rex."

"But what if Rex finds out?"

"If he does, it will be our job to learn it," asserted Cranston. "I know that Alex hasn't guessed all that lies behind the so-called jinx, but he called one turn correctly. Death won't follow the delivery of that emerald unless Rex Tarn knows how to reach the man who receives it."

Margo's shudder was very noticeable despite the warmth of Shrevvy's cab, which was taking them from the Club Galaxy. Twice having met Rex Tarn in the vicinity of the Voodoo lair, Margo Lane felt that her information was complete. Nevertheless, she rallied when Cranston declared:

"It will be our job to watch Rex Tarn."

Family curse or Voodoo spell, Margo was willing to do her part in stopping the next impending stroke of death.

CHAPTER XVI

HUNTED eyes were rapid in their glance outside the rear door of the old and obscure hotel. Quite as quick was the dart of the man himself, as he slid indoors and bolted the door to produce complete darkness. Soon there was a rumble from a service elevator in which a flashlight blinked. Stopping on the third floor, the visitor muffled himself in his drab raincoat and approached the door of a corner suite.

A rapped signal admitted him. He crossed to an inner room, where artificial firelight flickered as soon as he closed the door. Muffled drums began to throb, and fantastic dancers writhed in picture form upon the walls. But this was no time to stand on Voodoo ceremony. Across the imitation fire, an eager hand thrust a bundle of currency.

The cash was taken by a clawed fist, above which was another that held a deep-buried chin. From lips that were muffled, as suited the guarded drum-beats, there came a cackled tone:

"You are fearful even here at this new meeting place."

"Why not?" was the reply. "I was seen outside the other. So whatever happens—"

"Will be blamed upon Professor MacAbre!" With that pronouncement, MacAbre lowered his hand to reveal his face. "Unless you would rather have it blamed upon Rex Tarn!"

"No, no! If I defy the curse and live, after the emerald is mine, the world will know that I am guilty! You must take the blame, MacAbre! It is part of our bargain!"

"Agreed." MacAbre chuckled as though he relished the prospect. "So let us proceed with this night's business. Take this doll and place it on the stand."

The effigy was an odd one. It represented a bearded man, wearing an artist's smock and beret; so lifelike was the image representing Lee Selfkirk that it brought wavers from the gray eyes that viewed it. As for the stand, it was significant, too. It was built in little tiers, ten in all, a fact that made MacAbre's visitor recoil.

Nevertheless, the proxy murderer placed the waxen image on the top tier of the standard; then, at MacAbre's command, he tipped it over the edge. Falling headlong, the effigy crashed upon the floor. With a wave toward a ceiling fixture, MacAbre stopped the tom-toms and the kaleidoscopic dance; rolling a screen upward, he revealed a window leading across an adjoining roof.

"Out that way," ordered MacAbre. "If you were followed here, the trail will be lost."

OTHER persons were speaking of lost trails. In her apartment, Margo Lane was answering an urgent phone call from Lamont Cranston. Though the situation offered serious angles, Cranston's tone was very calm.

"Rex has left the Cobalt Club," declared Cranston. "I had to let him go alone."

"But why, Lamont?" asked Margo, anxiously. "I thought we weren't going to let him out of sight."

"I said more than that, Margo," came Cranston's voice. "I said not out of sight or earshot."

"What has earshot to do with it?"

"Too much, Margo. Where has your ear been for the last fifteen minutes?"

"On the telephone," admitted Margo. "I've been listening to Sue, the pest. She's full of weeps over the Rex and Alex question. She prefers love over money but thinks that the two ought to mix. Why don't they repeal a lot of silly laws and allow bigamy for girls like Sue?"

"It wouldn't be bigamy," objected Cranston. "When a woman marries two men, it's called biandry. But let's stop being technical. I'm turning Rex over to you."

"How do you mean?"

"He tried to make a phone call just ten minutes ago, after we finished dinner. He was in a booth here at the club."

"And you kept him in sight?"

"No, in earshot." Cranston was precise about it. "Remember that trick of catching the clicks from a dial and naming the number from it?"

"Yes, I've tried it," replied Margo. "But it won't work with me. Anyway, I give up. What number did Rex call?"

"He called yours, but the line was busy. At least that told him you were home. So when he came from the booth and said he had an appointment, I knew where he was going. But I didn't press the question, because after all, you're supposed to be my girl."

"Supposed is right!" snapped Margo. "If Voodoo wizards didn't try to sling me into cauldrons, we wouldn't be meeting up except once in every leap year. All right, how soon will Rex be here?"

"In about ten minutes. Keep me posted."

IT wasn't ten minutes. It was more than twenty, with a yearning to be called a half-hour. When Margo opened the door of her apartment, Rex came in with a legitimate stagger, which was something that Lamont would have mentioned if Rex had owned it when he started.

"H'lo, Margo," greeted Rex. "Glad to see you. Just stopped at the Galaxy for a couple of zombies."

"You look better than a couple," retorted Margo. She was standing by the window and caught the blinks of a taxicab's lights below. Those blinks were from Shrevvy's cab, meaning that he'd be on call, whenever Margo needed him. "Sure you didn't have a head start?"

"They were double zombies," laughed Rex. "New invention of my own, so's to avoid arguments with barkeeps. By th' way, I just left your boyfriend."

"You mean Lamont?"

"Thass right. Went from Lamont to Galaxy; then here. Got a cab waiting, so's to go some other place next. Let me use your phone, will you?"

Margo nodded. She watched Rex go to the phone, where he fumbled a few moments with the dial. Then:

"Wait a minute," said Rex. "Don't tell Lamont I stopped here, will you?"

"And why not?" demanded Margo.

"Because I came to get my coat," replied Rex. "You borrowed it—remember? Guess you wouldn't want Lamont to know you'd been looking at antiques when a lot of trouble started. Would you?"

Margo shook her head and went to get the coat, while Rex resumed operation with the dial. This time he made it and his fumbly pauses enabled Margo to count the clicks fairly well. She heard Rex's voice, abrupt and thick, while she was marking down her version of the number.

"H'lo. Yeah, I got your message..." Rex straightened his tuxedo tie with one hand. "Sure, at the Galaxy... Glad to hear from you... Thought maybe you didn't want to see me on account of what's happened... Thass nice... Glad you don't blame me... Sure, I'll be right over..."

Rex was scribbling something on a pad that was attached to Margo's telephone. He tore off the sheet, poked it in his pocket and let Margo help him into his raincoat. Margo watched him navigate the stairway in steadier fashion; then closed the door and grabbed the telephone book.

What Margo wanted was Sue's number, which she didn't have because the call had come from Sue tonight, instead of Margo making it. But Sue's number proved to be Gotham 4-3856 instead of Alcott 2-3266 which Margo had written after listening to the dial clicks. Much annoyed by her error, Margo called the Cobalt Club and asked for Mr. Cranston, who was promptly on the wire.

"They don't work," declared Margo, after describing Rex's brief visit. "The dial clicks I mean. I missed completely on Sue's number."

Over the phone, Margo described the difference in the tally. Cranston's reply was pointed:

"Are you sure that Rex called Sue?"

"Why, no!" exclaimed Margo. "Come to think of it, he didn't mention her by name. Of course, she might have been somewhere else, because he wrote down an address. Still, Sue called me from her own apartment—"

"Take a pencil," interrupted Cranston's voice, "and rub it lightly over the telephone pad. Right away, Margo!"

Margo obliged. Cranston's guess was correct; Rex's heavy hand had pressed the impression to the second sheet. Under the graphite treatment, words appeared, as if from a sheet of carbon. Margo read them over the telephone:

"Quentin Apartments. 1O-A. 33O River Avenue."

"Phone the number that you checked," ordered Cranston. "You may have it correct, Margo, but I'm sure it's unlisted. Tell him not to admit anyone."

"You mean tell Rex?"

"No," Cranston's word came sharply. "Tell Lee Selfkirk! He's the man that Rex Tarn wants to see, and death is riding with him!"

CHAPTER XVII

THE telephone bell in the top floor studio was ringing at full blast. Lee Selfkirk gave it an annoyed glance and shrugged; he was busy on a painting and couldn't be disturbed. So he let the phone keep right on ringing until he heard a sharp knock at the door. Stepping over to the telephone, Selfkirk took it off the hook, thus silencing it.

Unbolting the door, Selfkirk admitted Rex Tarn. From deep in his beard, the artist furnished a smile, and gestured his visitor to a chair beside the telephone table. The first thing that Rex noted was the lifted receiver. In an undertone he inquired:

"Who are you talking to—Alex?"

Selfkirk shook his head.

"I don't know," he replied. "I just didn't want to be disturbed. But you're wrong about Alex. He's really a good friend of yours. He might stop up before the evening is over."

"And before the Tarn Emerald gets here?"

In reply, Selfkirk reached in a pocket of his smock

and smilingly produced a jewel case. Opening it, he laid it where Rex could view the magnificent contents. There, glowing in its full brilliance, was the mighty emerald!

"Just what was your proposition, Rex?"

Selfkirk smiled with the question, and Rex's eyes came wide open, but without their hunted stare.

"You mean—"

"I mean I'd like to hear it," completed Selfkirk. "If this gem carries a curse, the best thing is to avoid it."

"You can!" Rex's eyes were hungry. "Sell it, Lee! Split the proceeds—and why not? You're getting half a million from the Tarn Estate. Why worry about the emerald?"

Selfkirk's eyes were as dark as his beard. They fixed on Rex with a deep, significant stare.

"You are hard up, aren't you?" queried the artist. "To let Alex have his share, despite the way you hate him."

Rex came to his feet, indignant.

"I'm square with the world!" he began. "That includes Alex—"

Funny sounds were coming from the telephone receiver. Noting Selfkirk's annoyance, Rex paused. The next interruption was from the door, in the form of another knock. Having bolted the door, Selfkirk gestured for Rex to open it.

"I think it's Alex," declared Selfkirk. "Let's have this out, Rex."

"Gladly," stormed Rex, as he strode to the door. "If I'm hard up, Lee, I'm still willing to be honest. This curse is a thing that bothers me."

"How badly, Rex?"

As he spoke, Selfkirk reached beside his canvas. The thing that he picked up did not remotely resemble any item in an artist's paraphernalia. It was an iron rod, about the length of an average crowbar. Holding the rod upright, Selfkirk turned his back toward the open window of his studio. Again, the artist smiled.

Often, Selfkirk had practiced this pose in the hope of lulling an unwelcome visitor. He waited until Rex had drawn the bolt; then, coolly, Selfkirk asked:

"Badly enough to help the curse along? For instance, by aiding it with murder?"

Angrily, Rex wheeled about. His hands lunged toward the easel, to stop when he saw that Selfkirk had retired toward the window. That glare in Rex's eyes convinced Selfkirk that his guess was right. With a nod toward the door, he called:

"All right, Alex. Come in."

THE man who entered wasn't Alex Tarn. Turning along with Selfkirk's gaze, Rex Tarn stared at the sweatered figure of Griff Torrock. In his hands, Griff was balancing a pair of revolvers, nicely determining their individual weight.

"I've come for the emerald," said Griff, coolly. "Kind of surprised to see me, aren't you—both of you?"

"So that's the game!" stormed Selfkirk, savagely. "A fake robbery. This stooge of yours is playing it too strong, Rex. Chase him out of here!"

Rex's hands were creeping upward as he gave his head a shake. But before Rex could speak, Griff was prodding him playfully with the muzzle of a revolver.

"Over there," ordered Griff. "By the telephone. As for you"—Griff was approaching Selfkirk—"if you don't get those mitts up quick, I'm going to show you curtains"—he gestured with the gun—"and they won't be fancy curtains like those you've got hanging around this joint!"

Backing away from the threatening gun, Selfkirk was tightening as he neared the window. His back was almost against the balcony rail when Griff made the gun gesture. It was a low rail, of iron, with the wire from a radio aerial attached to it, but Selfkirk wasn't thinking of such details. His thoughts were on the crowbar, which he was shifting backward, preparatory to a lunging swing.

Then the incredible happened.

As the crowbar grazed the rail, Selfkirk gave a backward stagger and tightened his grip on his pet weapon. There was a clang of metal meeting metal as the crowbar clamped the rail in horizontal style. Over went Selfkirk, shrieking; flung by some strange force, he lost both grip and balance, as he disappeared with a plunge that was measured by the trailing cry that followed it.

On the balcony rail, planted as if glued, remained the iron rod that had figured so curiously in Selfkirk's doom!

With a grin, Griff Torrock gestured both guns toward Rex Tarn.

"All right, double-crosser," sneered Griff. "You've been double-crossed yourself. The prof has told me all about you and what's to be done about it. For first, I'm taking that emerald."

Fists clenched tight, Rex backed against the telephone table as though to protect the priceless gem. Griff made Rex's hands rise again, with a two-gun gesture.

"Pick up the phone," ordered Griff. "Call the cops and tell them to come here. They can figure what happened to Selfkirk and the Tarn Emerald. Move."

Rex moved, but couldn't find the telephone receiver. For the first time, Griff noticed that it was off the hook. With an indulgent shrug, he shoved one gun to his hip, then followed with the other. Seating himself in a chair, Griff kept his arms akimbo, his hands ready to draw the revolvers on an instant's notice.

"Jiggle the hook," suggested Griff. "You'll get an answer. I'm not here to croak you, unless you act foolish."

Reluctantly, Rex complied. His eyes were wide, as often, but their glare was angry rather than hunted. He kept thumbing the hook until the operator finally responded; then, in a forced tone, Rex asked for police headquarters. At last his call was put through, but Rex's tone was still forced when he stated:

"There's trouble up in Selfkirk's studio. Quentin Apartments, tenth floor front."

"Tell them what you did to Selfkirk," growled Griff, coming up from his chair and shoving his hands to his hips. "What's more, make it natural."

"Selfkirk just fell out the window," explained Rex, his tone still forced. "It was an accident, of course—"

"Lay off that guff!"

With his interruption, Griff was coming forward, only to halt rigid. The guns that he hadn't drawn were outmatched by a single weapon that loomed through the half-opened doorway, a mighty automatic, held by a gloved fist as black as the cloaked form behind it.

"The Shadow!"

Griff coughed the name as Rex turned. Standing idle with the telephone, Rex showed the same rigidity as Griff. If ever a scene was indicative of double-crossing doubly dealt, this scene portrayed that picture. Too late to prevent the death of Lee Selfkirk, The Shadow had arrived to settle the affairs of the men responsible.

The first to welch was Griff Torrock.

"There's the guy!" Hands trembling, Griff was backing toward the window, but his nod was in Rex's direction. "He's the champion double-crosser, he is. You can't blame MacAbre for slipping a fast one past him, or me for working the way the prof asked. Look"—Griff thought he had an inspiration—"there's the emerald he's been after all along!"

Turning as he passed Rex, The Shadow looked and saw the giant emerald. Perhaps Griff thought that the great green eye would capture the full attention of The Shadow. At least it appeared that way, for Griff suddenly halted his back-step and sped both hands to his hips. It was then that The Shadow gave a rapid twist, bringing his automatic full about with a forward lunge that cowed the startled mob leader.

Griff Torrock took one more backward step.

There was the clang of metal as Griff's hips thwacked the rail and the crowbar that was clamped along it. With a howl wilder than Selfkirk's, Griff teetered backward, waving his hands wildly. Over he went, and in his fall, he caught the straggly aerial wire, ripping it with his plunge.

Again, a screech was wailing up from below. It ended in a solid crash that was accompanied by a metallic clang, for in Griff's headlong drop, the hanging crowbar had gone with him. As those echoes died, The Shadow turned to look for the stupefied figure of Rex Tarn.

The man in the tuxedo was gone. Always an opportunist, Rex hadn't missed his chance. He had fled from this studio of death, the moment that Griff Torrock had begun his duplication of the plunge that had carried Lee Selfkirk to a sudden death. Nevertheless, The Shadow's laugh came in a sinister whisper as he viewed the spot where Rex had stood.

From the telephone table gleamed a great green stone, like a huge, unblinking eye. In flight, Rex Tarn had forgotten the object that he coveted most, the mighty emerald whose famous curse was backed by Voodoo spells!

CHAPTER XVIII

A WAXEN image stood upon a plate that was resting on the upright logs of MacAbre's artificial fire. A circle of light shone on the effigy, for tonight there was no thrum of Voodoo drums, nor any dance along the walls.

This was the final transaction in the chain of death, a deal in which no money was involved.

Into the light crept a shaky hand, carrying a miniature pistol only a few inches long. Small though it was, the gun was real, and at last it steadied between this bearer's thumb and fingers.

The crackly voice of Professor MacAbre commanded:

"Fire!"

The trigger clicked; the pistol spurted. A tiny slug, smaller than a piece of lead from a mechanical pencil, was embedded in the body of the waxen image, which promptly toppled on the plate. There was silence; then MacAbre's tone:

"And now the award for this priceless deed. I promise that the Voodoo spell shall work. In return I claim the Tarn Emerald!"

"No, no—"

The protest came fiercely from the darkness, to be interrupted by MacAbre's purr:

"But you cannot keep the emerald. It would lead to suspicion of your guilt. I told you I would take full blame. Unless I have the emerald, I cannot."

"But if I give you the emerald—"

"Who said that it was to be a gift?" MacAbre's query was velvety, yet firm. "Suppose the emerald should be stolen, despite the greatest of precautions. Take this"—a paper crinkled from MacAbre's steady claw into the hand that trembled in receiving it—"and follow all instructions!"

Out went the circle of light. There was the scrape

of an opening window. Again, a Voodoo deal had been completed, with the croaking laugh of Professor MacAbre the final note that certified it.

WHEN Rex Tarn entered the sumptuous apartment belonging to his cousin Alex, a courteous secretary bowed him to a lounge and provided him with an evening newspaper. If ever Rex's eyes had flinched, it was when he scanned the headlines.

The death of Lee Selfkirk was big news. A wealthy artist wouldn't pitch himself ten stories down after receiving an added legacy. It was murder, that death, unlike the sudden fates of Gregg Henniman and Wilfred Walden. Of course, the murderer was known; he happened to be Griff Torrock, already wanted by the law. The fact that Griff had perished with his victim, probably in a death grapple, was at least some solace.

Even robbery had failed, for the Tarn Emerald had been found on Selfkirk's premises and had been passed along to the next heir, Alex Tarn. But this smooth settlement of the situation did not allay Rex's worries. As a witness to the actual crime, he was fearful that the law would question him, and the source of his worry was the fact that he had not been the only witness to the actual death scene.

Through Rex's harrowed brain kept pounding the name that Griff had gasped before his surprising death plunge:

"The Shadow!"

Many a man of hidden crime had quaked at mere recollection of that name. But Rex Tarn had failed to hide his part in the death scene that involved Lee Selfkirk. In The Shadow, Rex pictured a master of unquenchable vengeance who would never stop until he had dealt with all concerned.

When the door opened, Rex nearly sprang from his chair, expecting to see the cloaked invader who had been at Selfkirk's studio. Instead, it was only Alex's secretary, coming to tell Rex that his cousin would see him.

On the desk in Alex's sumptuous study, Rex saw the great Tarn Emerald gleaming from its open case. Beside it was an old-fashioned revolver, a family heirloom that belonged to Alex. With a mild smile, Alex drew the gun away.

"Sorry, Rex," said Alex. "Just a precaution, you know. After what happened to Lee Selfkirk, well—"

Finishing with a shrug, Alex dropped the revolver in the desk drawer; then leaned forward and queried:

"You didn't go up to see Lee, did you, Rex?"

Stolidly, Rex shook his head.

"I hoped not." Alex leaned back, relieved. "There seems to be some talk about a visitor other than the murderer. I'm glad you didn't go there, because I now appreciate the advice that you have been giving all along. I am going to sell the Tarn Emerald."

Rex's eyes popped wide; then narrowed in a doubtful stare, which brought another smile from Alex.

"On a fifty-fifty basis," added Alex. "Half yours and half mine. The jewelers are coming to appraise it very shortly. I have arranged a display stand in the reception room. What bothers me"—Alex hesitated as his hand moved forward—"is whether I should touch the gem. The curse is now mine, you know."

"I'm still free from it," returned Rex. "I'll put it there if you want. But maybe you'd better follow with the gun, just to see that I don't skip."

Rex's tone carried its old challenge, as though he expected a resumption of the bitter feud with Alex. In return, Alex thrust his hand across the desk, offering a clasp that Rex accepted with only a slight show of reluctance.

When the privileged guests arrived, they were treated to the novel sight of the Tarn cousins playing the part of friends. Sue Aldrich was among the invited and she looked very happy and handsome, all done up in blue polka dots. When Lamont Cranston arrived with Margo Lane, the party seemed complete. Sue immediately corralled Margo to ask her advice regarding which Tarn cousin to accept. While Rex was taking to the other guests, Alex beckoned Cranston to the room where the emerald was on display.

Through half-drawn curtains, they looked into an old-fashioned reception room where the Tarn Emerald rested on a table not far beyond the curtains. Past the table was a high cabinet to which Alex pointed with pride.

"Can you see it, Cranston?"

"See what?"

"All right," chuckled Alex, "you can't, so that answers my question. I've planted a special movie camera in that cabinet, focused straight down on the lighted table. It contains a color film, by the way."

"To show the emerald in full tints?"

"And more. It's a thief trap, Cranston. You've heard of gems disappearing in circumstances such as this. If anything should happen this evening, there would be no trouble picking out the culprit, for the camera would register the deed. It has a shortwave control, similar to the instrument they call the theremin. If anything approaches the table, the camera will begin to operate."

Alex was raising his tone for the benefit of two new arrivals. One was Cranston's friend, Police Commissioner Weston, a brusque man with a military mustache. The other was Inspector Joe Cardona, ace of the Manhattan force. They nodded their approval of Alex's theft detector.

"After what happened to Selfkirk, I felt we

ought to be here," announced Weston. "As for this precaution of yours, I hope you haven't mentioned it to anyone else?"

"To no one," replied Alex. "Not even to my cousin Rex. That may amuse you, Cranston"—Alex turned about with a smile—"but I think you must have noticed that Rex and I are now upon good terms."

BOWING the group back to the main reception hall, Alex introduced them to the jewelers, and drinks were promptly served. It was apparent that Rex had gained a head start on the beverages, for he was imbibing the second round of his latest favorite, the double zombi, which he had specially ordered. Rex's daring was really troubling Sue, who had decided to forego zombies altogether, and the blonde's apprehensions were promptly realized.

While Alex was still talking to the guests, the drinks began to take effect on Rex. Brushing Sue aside, he said he was going to the study to lie down, and when last seen Rex was reeling through the hallway, past the little reception room. Alex gave an indulgent shrug over his cousin's condition.

"Rex is celebrating his luck," said Alex. "I've promised him a half share in the sale of the emerald. Which reminds me"—Alex rubbed his hands warmly—"since all the bidders are present, suppose we view the gem."

Proudly, Alex led the way to the display room, and drew aside the curtain. He stepped back as he saw the lighted table. Where the emerald had glistened from its casket, there no longer was a gleam, not even the casket.

The Tarn Emerald was gone!

Before anyone could stop him, Alex wheeled from the curtain and strode down the hallway, taking the turn to the rear study. Hardly had he passed that bend before a gunshot blasted. Cranston was first to dash in the direction of the sound, with Weston and Cardona close behind him.

A slumped figure blocked the study door, motionless in death. The man was Alex, and pointed down toward his heart was the smoking muzzle of an old-fashioned revolver, clutched in the hand of Rex Tarn. If ever a man had shown open pride in murder, Rex was that person.

As he saw the arrivals, Rex tilted back his head and laughed in maddened glee. Then, savagely, he thrust the death weapon toward the intruders, only to have it knocked from his grasp by a lunging stroke of Cranston's hand.

Another tragedy had marred the history of the ill-fated Tarn Emerald, and with it, murder no longer lay hidden. The curse of the Tarns had reached its fulfillment, with the guilt placed full upon Rex Tarn, the last member of the line.

The Tarn curse, backed by a secret Voodoo spell!

CHAPTER XIX

THE brilliant light of the study lamp was gleaming full upon Rex Tarn's sweat-stained face. His eyes wide in the stare of a fanatic, Rex was insanely shifting his plea from innocence to guilt.

Under the blunt questioning of Inspector Cardona, whose favorite catchphrase was "Why did you do it?"—Rex kept chortling that he hadn't. When Commissioner Weston snapped, "You know you're guilty, Tarn—" Rex nodded and gesticulated like a happy madman.

This variance of testimony produced a huddle that included Cranston, who was seated at the desk.

"If he keeps this up," argued Weston, "he'll get by on an insanity plea if he gets a lawyer who isn't crazier than himself."

"Why question him further?" demanded Cardona. "We have the gun; that's evidence enough."

"Except that no one saw Rex fire it," reminded Cranston. "It's a long hallway and the back door is very close."

"But you saw how Rex was hanging onto the gun," argued Cardona. "Do you think somebody handed it to him? Alex for instance?"

"It wouldn't have been impossible," replied Cranston, "and when you speak of hanging onto things, why didn't Rex keep the Tarn Emerald? You haven't found it on his person; in fact, you can't prove he even stole it."

In answer, Cardona turned and called to the door. In came two headquarters men with a movie projector and a film that had been rapidly developed. Cardona thrust Rex into a chair and let him sit there chattering to himself, while the film had its run.

That movie was the clincher. It showed the curtains of the room where the Tarn Emerald had been on display. The curtains parted and the face of Rex Tarn came into sight, his eyes wide in their gleam, but sane. Rex's hand came forward and closed on the casket; then drew it away, closing it between his hands, as though nursing the precious prize.

Only a few steps forward and back; but they were enough. In that brief action, the theft of the Tarn Emerald stood proven. What had become of the priceless gem might still be a mystery, but the guilt of Rex Tarn was not.

Sue was sobbing on Margo's shoulder as they took Rex out through the hall. The blonde's hope of happy romance had been dealt a double blow. One of her suitors was dead; the other was the murderer. No wonder Sue's sobs reached the distant study, where Lamont Cranston still sat at the desk, going through scrap papers that consisted largely of penciled notations.

At last Cranston reached for the telephone book

and checked a number. Picking up the phone, he called headquarters and gave a message to be delivered to Joe Cardona as soon as the inspector arrived. With that, Cranston left Alex's study, opened the back door and went down a convenient fire tower that led to a rear alley.

ABOVE the imitation flames of an artificial fire, a man with long clawed fingers was completing a curious effigy of wax that was dressed entirely in black. It was lifelike, that puppet shaped by the skilled hands of Professor MacAbre, for it represented a figure which even when motionless, produced a pronounced effect.

The black-clad doll was attired in miniature cloak and hat to represent The Shadow!

Over the shoulders of MacAbre gleamed the dark, insidious faces of his henchmen, Fandor and Jeno. They watched the lift of MacAbre's head; saw it go toward a weapon that hung upon the wall of the otherwise undecorated room. That weapon was a long bladed machete, a great knife that had the size and weight of a saber.

In front of MacAbre glistened a great green trophy, the Tarn Emerald. Viewing the stolen gem, the arch professor laid the puppet in his hand and sneered his contempt.

"It was so simple," spoke MacAbre. "You should have been there, Fandor, and you, too, Jeno. Of course the path was open, because I had ordered that it should be. The drug worked perfectly as it always does when properly administered. But the timing was perfection; a single shot where it was least expected; the simple placement of the gun—"

Pausing, MacAbre drew a strange pin from the lapel of his robe. It was shaped like a machete, but in miniature. Detail for detail it was a tiny replica of the great blade that hung on the far wall.

"All very easy," added MacAbre. "As simple as this!"

With a thrust he stabbed the tiny machete straight through the image of The Shadow!

"This will be our final mission," affirmed MacAbre, "to rid ourselves of the only enemy who has even suspected our game. We shall set the trap and await The Shadow. I do not doubt that he will come!"

There was something heinous in MacAbre's cackly laugh, the tone that drowned all nearby sounds. Even the slight scraping of the window sash could not be heard, for it had ended when the Voodoo's wizard's laugh began to dwindle. Amazing, though, were the echoes of MacAbre's laugh.

The tone seemed to rise again, though MacAbre's lips no longer moved. Instead of coming from the walls, the echo issued through the window. That is, if it could be termed an echo, for its tone was changing now to a sardonic mirth that even MacAbre could never copy!

Swinging about, Professor MacAbre saw the guest he had promised to invite, but not on so early an occasion. Within the window stood the foe of everything that MacAbre represented, the avenger who styled himself The Shadow!

Cowering at their cloaked visitor's approach, MacAbre and his partners watched The Shadow place a gun beneath his cloak, a single automatic being all he needed, with its muzzle practically in reach of three cringing heads. Then, on the plate that topped the fire logs, The Shadow tossed the evidence that stood for Voodoo crimes.

"This was your mistake, Jeno," gibed The Shadow, as he brought a spectacle case from his cloak. "You switched Henniman's glasses, giving him a pair so badly focused that he pitched himself down the museum stairs.

"But you overlooked the fact that Henniman's reading glasses, not his bifocals, were in the case you took. I found these—his own bifocals—in his desk; rimless glasses instead of the tortoise shells that should have been there."

Next of the exhibits were letters of reference bearing the name of Fandor Bianco, who winced when he saw them. Steadily, The Shadow said:

"You shouldn't have left these with Chauncey. I have checked them as forgeries, proving you an impostor. You were clumsy, Fandor. Margo was too weak to have opened those windows; or had she been strong enough to open them, she would not have weakened."

The simple logic caused MacAbre to switch his glare from Jeno to Fandor. The Shadow's response to MacAbre's action was another laugh during which a coil of wire dropped from the gloved hand to the plate.

"Your error, MacAbre," stated The Shadow. "I didn't overlook the radio wire that Griff pulled from Selfkirk's balcony. I checked its real hookup, to the electromagnet underneath. That was the force that clamped Selfkirk's crowbar and toppled him back before he could let go. The same applied in a way you didn't expect; to the guns in Griff's hip pockets. He broke the current when he snatched the wire, but he was too late."

Picking up his own effigy, The Shadow studied it along with the miniature machete that transfixed it.

"A childish notion, these," remarked The Shadow, "but they influenced the man they were meant for, making him believe that Voodoo charms were really responsible for death. I refer to your steady customer, Alex Tarn."

An angry hiss accompanied the vicious glare that MacAbre furnished. The calm way in which

The Shadow bared MacAbre's deepest secret was a final humiliation for the mad Voodoo genius. To make it worse, MacAbre had no choice but to listen as The Shadow tallied off the count:

"It was obvious that Rex was checking on his cousin Alex, or he would not have shown himself openly in your neighborhood. Rex was following Alex, the night that Jeno picked up the second trail by mistake.

"If Rex had been your client and had weakened the night you doomed Margo, Rex could have reached her with a phone call. Instead, he went to her apartment; he gave his real reason later, his fear that she might be in danger of the threat that he felt hovering over himself.

"Alex knew where Selfkirk could be found. He persuaded Selfkirk to communicate with Rex. It wouldn't have been possible for Rex to come here that evening, for he was with me earlier and with Margo later. Between times he was riding in a cab that I provided, except for a short stop at the Club Galaxy.

"Besides"—The Shadow stressed the final point—"Rex no longer had the raincoat that Alex had copied to be mistaken for his cousin. It was at Margo's apartment, because Rex had given it to her the time I raided your old headquarters."

Pausing, The Shadow flung the cloaked effigy upon the plate with the other exhibits.

"Alex couldn't afford to blame Rex openly for crimes," added The Shadow. "Unless he too became a victim of the emerald's curse, Alex would have appeared its instigator, once he gained the gem. So he gave you the right to steal the emerald, with the guilt to be pinned on Rex. Your promise to make Rex appear a suicide also pleased Alex."

The Shadow was practically repeating MacAbre's own instruction sheet, even though Alex had destroyed it. The Voodoo fiend was coming up with his claws trembling forcibly, but he was afraid to thrust them toward The Shadow's throat.

"You loaded Rex's so-called zombi drink with the real zombi drug," described The Shadow. "Alex did the act that you had planned and you murdered him at the finish, simply planting the gun on Rex. In death, however, Alex gave himself away, as he hadn't in life.

"His eyes are wide open now, MacAbre. They are hunted eyes, like those of your regular visitor. Another of Alex's imitations when he came to see you, although I have an idea that on those occasions his fear was real."

Before MacAbre could reply, a door flung open, and Inspector Cardona lunged in from the threshold, followed by a trio of detectives. Fandor and Jeno tried to spring away, despite The Shadow's gun, and in their scramble, they screened Professor MacAbre.

Madly, the Voodoo killer kicked the artificial logs at The Shadow and dodged past him toward the wall. With a wild wrench he hurled the full-length machete point-first toward The Shadow. Even as the blade was leaving MacAbre's claw, a gunshot responded.

MacAbre's hurl became a jolting lunge that sent the machete high and wide, pinning it above the door. Striking the floor, the evil genius of hidden crime rolled dead, a bullet in his heart. Not a silver bullet, the only sort that could supposedly kill a master of Voodoo wizardry, but an ordinary leaden slug. The Shadow had dispelled that myth along with MacAbre's own fantastic claims to Voodoo power.

The Shadow was gone through the blackened window while Cardona's men were subduing Fandor and Jeno. By the time they were brought to headquarters, Lamont Cranston was waiting there with Margo Lane and Sue Aldrich, to hear the confessions that the prisoners would repeat since MacAbre could no longer speak them. But Cranston was due for congratulations first.

"It was a swell tip-off, Mr. Cranston," declared the ace inspector, "sending us to that old hotel. I ought to have gotten there sooner, but I had to wait to try the thing you suggested with the movie. It clears Rex Tarn, all right. Watch."

The picture flicked on the wall of Cardona's office. It showed curtains parting; then Rex Tarn's hands came through as he stepped forward. Those hands were opening a jewel case to display the great Tarn Emerald as Rex placed it on the table. Stepping backward, Rex withdrew his empty hands and closed the curtains.

"Alex must have told Rex to put the emerald on display," declared Cardona. "That's when you figured the picture was taken, didn't you, Mr. Cranston?"

"That's right," agreed Cranston, "and the camera was specially geared so when you developed it, you naturally ran it backward."

"Maybe Rex will remember it," said Cardona. "He's coming out of that zombi trance."

"He won't remember," declared Cranston. "Professor MacAbre intended to clinch a case that could never be disproven."

Disproven it had been, despite the cunning of MacAbre. A greater brain than that of the Voodoo genius had cracked the case well apart. With murder placed where it belonged, all other evidence was nullified. Such was The Shadow's method.

Death was the commodity in which MacAbre dealt, and The Shadow had rewarded him in terms of his own product!

THE END

A TALE OF TWO SHADOWS *by Anthony Tollin*

Radio listeners experienced two very different Shadows during the quarter-century history of the famous radio series. The early 1930s CBS and NBC broadcasts featured The Shadow as a sinister storyteller. Frank Readick's mocking laugh and sibilant tones helped make The Shadow a national sensation on *Street & Smith's Detective Story Hour*, and in 1931 he became the first actor to portray the mystery man on the silver screen when he reprised his famous radio role in *Burglar to the Rescue,* the first of six "Shadow Detective" two-reel "filmettes" released by Universal Pictures.

The classic 1937-54 Mutual series was inspired by Walter Gibson's pulp novels, and featured Lamont Cranston as an invisible crimebuster. Orson Welles starred as The Shadow during the first year of the revamped series, and was succeeded in 1938 by Bill Johnstone who quickly made the role his own.

Having played supporting roles on *The Shadow* opposite Readick and Welles, Bill was familiar with both of The Shadow's radio incarnations. "The Shadow was originally the voice of conscience and it was through the fear which he aroused in the minds of criminals that they exposed their own villainy or destroyed themselves," he told the *New York Times* in 1941. "Ten years ago, when the show was first presented, The Shadow was only a sound effect, a nasty, snarly voice that would burst in with a blood-curdling laugh, and sneer, 'The Shadow knows.' Now the part has been expanded into that of a dual personality—Cranston, the educated society man, and The Shadow, the name he affects when employing his unusual talents to a good cause."

However, the invisible superhero from the Mutual broadcasts finally encountered the sinister Shadow of the early seasons in a single landmark adventure. In *The Shadow Challenged* (January 19, 1941), an archeologist discovers the arcane secret of hypnotic invisibility from ancient Hindu manuscripts, and uses his newfound powers to murder his rivals as The Shadow. The murderer lures Cranston into a deadly trap, determined to be the only Shadow and continue using the secret of invisibility for evil!

In an ingenious piece of casting, Frank Readick returned to voice The Shadow's evil impersonator. The radio veteran had departed the series at the conclusion of the 1934-35 CBS season, though his sibilant opening and closing signatures were rerun throughout Orson Welles' 1937-38 broadcasts. Readick may have been recruited by Johnstone and *Shadow*-regular Dwight Weist (Commissioner Weston), who shared an apartment with Frank near the broadcast studios where they pursued their respective hobbies (woodworking, photography and model railroading) between broadcasts.

Johnstone quit *The Shadow* in the spring of 1943 to follow *The Cavalcade of America* to the West Coast, but was drafted almost immediately after arriving in California. Returning to civilian life in January of 1946, Bill soon became a fixture on such top series as *Suspense* and *The Lux Radio Theatre*, and later starred in Blake Edwards' *The Lineup.*

Bringing things full circle, during the summer of 1948 Johnstone enacted the title role in CBS' "intercontinental" production of *The Whistler*, a series patterned after the mysterious narrator of the early 1930s *Shadow* broadcasts. The program featured an opening echoing *The Shadow's* famous signature: "I am The Whistler, and I know many things for I walk by night. I know many strange tales hidden in the hearts of men and women who have stepped into the shadows. Yes, I know the nameless terrors of which they dare not speak!"

Though Frank Readick was heard as The Shadow through four early radio seasons, only his onscreen appearance from *Burglar to the Rescue* and his opening and closing signatures are known to survive, so his performance in "The Shadow Challenged" is an important historical record of the actor whose mocking laugh set the standard for his successors. •

Frank Readick reprised his shadowy radio role onscreen in *Burglar to the Rescue*, a 1931 Universal two-reeler.

Bill Johnstone (left) and Frank Readick

THE SHADOW

"THE SHADOW CHALLENGED"

by Jerry Devine

as broadcast January 19, 1941 over MBS

(MUSIC: "GLOOMS OF FATE" … FADE UNDER)

SHADOW: Who knows what evil lurks in the hearts of men? The Shadow knows! (LAUGHS)

(MUSIC UP … SEGUE BRIGHT THEME)

ANNR: The thrilling adventures of The Shadow are on the air .. brought to you each week by the 'blue coal' dealers of America. These dramatizations are designed to demonstrate forcibly to old and young alike that *crime does not pay!*

(MUSIC UP… SEGUE INTO NEUTRAL BACKGROUND)

ANNR: The SHADOW, mysterious character who aids the forces of law and order, is, in reality, Lamont Cranston, wealthy young man-about-town. As The Shadow, Cranston is gifted with hypnotic power to cloud men's minds so that they cannot see him. Cranston's friend and companion, the lovely Margot Lane, is the only person who knows to whom the voice of the invisible SHADOW belongs. Today's story—"The Shadow Challenged."

(PHONE RINGS… RECEIVER UP)

RICE: Hello… no… no, I can't speak to him! And please don't put more calls through, operator… I'm busy working and I don't wish to be disturbed! Thank you…

(RECEIVER DOWN, SCRATCHING OF PEN…)

RICE: (TO HIMSELF) Now..let me see..where was I… oh, yes…

VOICE: (ON FILTER..AN IMITATION OF THE SHADOW… LAUGHS)

RICE: What was that?

VOICE: I'm sorry to interrupt your work, Professor Rice…

RICE: Who is that? Who is speaking? I see no one.

VOICE: I am called… The Shadow…

RICE: The Shadow! I've heard of you… what are you doing here?

VOICE: That manuscript you're translating, Professor Rice… it is of great value, is it not?

RICE: Yes, of course..

VOICE: I want you to give it to me, Professor…

RICE: Give you this manuscript? Why, that's impossible! It's not mine… it belongs to the museum… it's a direct key to ancient Hindu culture!

VOICE: I know..that's why I have come here… I want that manuscript!

RICE: Now see here, I've always had a great respect for you, Shadow… you've worked for the forces of good against the forces of evil… but now you-you're behaving like a common thief!

VOICE: Give me that manuscript!

RICE: No… *No!*

VOICE: Very well, I see that I must use other methods…

RICE: What do you mean? What are you going to do?!

VOICE: This is what I'm going to do, Professor Rice!

(SEVERAL SHOTS)

RICE: (GROANS)

(BODY FALLING)

RICE (WEAKLY) Shadow… Shadow… why did you do this?

VOICE: (LAUGHS)

(MUSIC)

(FOOTSTEPS ON GRAVEL…)

MARGOT: (LAUGHING) To think that I have believed you all these years, Lamont Cranston, when you told me what a golfer you were!

CRANSTON: I just had an off day, that's all, Margot… I'm not used to playing in the sun!

MARGOT: You weren't in the sun… you were in the nice shady woods… you never saw the fairway.

CRANSTON: All right, you win.

MARGOT: Do we have time for a swim?

CRANSTON: I think so.

NEWSBOY: (OFF MIKE… FADING IN) Extra… read about the blizzards in the north… big snow storms… extra.

CRANSTON: (TALKING OVER THE NEWSY) I've got to vindicate my athletic ability in some fashion.

NEWSBOY: Paper, mister. Read all about the snowstorms in the north…

CRANSTON: Don't they ever change that headline down here?

NEWSBOY: Not 'til they think of a better one… paper, mister?

CRANSTON: All right… here you are…

NEWSBOY: Thanks… (FADING) Extra, entire northern states buried by snowstorm… read all about it here… extra!

MARGOT: Well, how bad was the storm… how many feet of snow?

CRANSTON: Margot… you're talking like a tourist… all they need is a flurry up north to cause a headline like this..

MARGOT: Really?

CRANSTON: Sure… you get used to those headlines after you're… (SHARPLY) Margot! *Margot!* Look at this!

MARGOT: What is it?

CRANSTON: This story on the front page! (READING) Museum Professor murdered by… The Shadow!

MARGOT: The Shadow?!

CRANSTON: That's what it says! (READING) Professor Rice of the Cosmopolitan Museum was found dying in his apartment late this evening by the police… in a deathbed statement to Commissioner Weston he described his assailant as an invisible man who called himself The Shadow!

MARGOT: Lamont, that's impossible… How do you explain it?

CRANSTON: I have no explanation… but one thing is certain… we're catching the next plane north!

(MUSIC)

CRANSTON: And you say, Commissioner Weston, that the dying man swore that his assailant was The Shadow?

WESTON: That's right…

MARGOT: I don't believe it!

WESTON: Now, look, Miss Lane, facts are facts!

CRANSTON: What Margot means, Commissioner, is that she cannot believe that The Shadow would do such a thing…

WESTON: Well, that's her opinion… me, I think different…

MARGOT: What do you mean?

WESTON: I've always suspected that The Shadow was a criminal at heart...

MARGOT: That's not true!

WESTON: Then why has he always remained invisible... no, I tell you he's a bad egg..and this murder confirms it!

CRANSTON: This manuscript... the one that the killer stole from Professor Rice... what do you know about it?

WESTON: Well, it's something that the professor was working on..Rice and three other scholars are employed by the Cosmopolitan Museum, specializing in the restoration and recreation of ancient Hindu culture...

CRANSTON: Yes, I'm acquainted with all of them, and their work..

WESTON: Well, you probably know more about it than I do then... anyway, this manuscript was very valuable to them.

MARGOT: But what value would it have to anyone else?

WESTON: That's out of the department, Miss Lane... my job is who put it to the corpus delecti, in other words, who killed Professor Rice... and the answer to that is The Shadow.

CRANSTON: And the motive?

WESTON: Larceny, my friend... gold old-fashioned larceny... The Shadow wanted that manuscript, and he killed the guy to get it.

CRANSTON: Commissioner... I don't think The Shadow had anything to do with it.

WESTON: Look... I heard the accusation with my own ears just before the erstwhile Professor Rice gave up the ghost.

CRANSTON: Nevertheless, I believe The Shadow is innocent, and I intend to prove my point...

WESTON: How?

CRANSTON: Well, with your permission, I would like to go to the museum and talk to Professor Rice's associates... see what I can learn...

WESTON: (LAUGHS) Go ahead...

(MUSIC)

(CAR SLOWING DOWN AND STOPPING)

CRANSTON: We'll leave the car here, Margot... I believe that the night entrance to the museum is in this wing...

(CAR DOOR OPENING)

MARGOT: Lamont... Do you suppose that someone has discovered your secret and is misusing it in The Shadow's name?

CRANSTON: That's possible, Margot.

MARGOT: What else could it be?

CRANSTON: Well, perhaps Weston is putting the blame of the crime on The Shadow to excuse his department's inability to solve the murder.

MARGOT: What a horrible thing to do!

CRANSTON: That's just supposition, Margot... well, here we are... we'll have to ring for the watchman...

(BELL RINGING OFF MIKE)

MARGOT: What do you expect to learn here, Lamont?

Marjorie Anderson and Bill Johnstone starred as Margot Lane and Lamont Cranston in "The Shadow Challenged."

CRANSTON: I want to talk to the other professors… find out more about the missing manuscript.

(DOOR OPENS)

WATCHMAN: (WEIRD-VOICED OLD GENT) Yea, what is it?

CRANSTON: Good evening… we wish to see either Professor Carter or Hagen or Professor Amud… I know they are working here this evening…

WATCHMAN: Are you expected?

CRANSTON: Yes, we are…

WATCHMAN: Come in…

(DOOR CLOSES… FOOTSTEPS)

WATCHMAN: (AFTER PAUSE… ECHO CHAMBER EFFECT) We seldom have visitors at this late hour…

CRANSTON: I… I guess not…

WATCHMAN: I must ask you to walk quietly please… "they" do not like to be disturbed…

MARGOT: You mean the professors?

WATCHMAN: Oh, no… not the professors… I mean those who live here…

MARGOT: Oh, are there people liv—

WATCHMAN: Shhhh! This is their time to rest…

CRANSTON: Who?

WATCHMAN: Those that you see about you… the statues… the paintings… it tires them, you know….people staring at them through the day…

CRANSTON: Oh, yes… yes… I can understand that…

MARGOT: Lamont, does he mean—

CRANSTON: (QUICKLY) Margot! The… the statues must appreciate your consideration for them, sir…

WATCHMAN: Oh, yes… they do…they know that I watch over them…through the night. There is the door to the offices… I must leave you here…

CRANSTON: Oh, well thank you…

MARGOT: Yes, yes… it was… nice of you to show us the way…

WATCHMAN: Not at all… good night…

(FOOTSTEPS RECEDE…)

MARGOT: Cheerful fellow… makes you feel right at home….

CRANSTON: (CHUCKLING) Yes… well, let's get into the—

(DOOR OPENS AND CLOSES)

CARTER: (STARTLED) Oh… I… oh, it's you, Mr. Cranston… I didn't expect to see anyone…

CRANSTON: Sorry… this is Miss Lane, Professor Carter…

(AD LIB GREETINGS)

CARTER: Won't you go into the office…Professor Amud is there… I have to consult a file… I'll be right back…

CRANSTON: Yes, thanks, Professor Carter… come along, Margot…

(FOOTSTEPS… DOOR OPENS)

CRANSTON: May we come in?

AMUD: (A VERY CULTURED HINDU WHO SPEAKS WITH A TRACE OF AN ENGLISH ACCENT… BUT HIS DELIVERY MUST SUGGEST A HINDU) Oh, yes… yes, of course, Mr. Cranston, do come in…

CRANSTON: Thank you… I don't believe you know Miss Lane.

AMUD: No. I have never had the pleasure…

CRANSTON: This is Professor Amud, Margot…

MARGOT: How do you do, Professor…

AMUD: I am most delighted to make your acquaintance… won't you both be seated…

MARGOT: Thank you…

CRANSTON: I spoke to Professor Hagen this afternoon; did he explain to you the purpose of my visit?

AMUD: Yes, he did. You are interested, I believe, in solving the murder of our most worthy colleague, Professor Rice?

CRANSTON: Yes.

AMUD: A very noble endeavor.

CRANSTON: I thought I might begin by learning more about the manuscript that Professor Rice was working on when he was killed.

AMUD: An excellent beginning…

CRANSTON: What was its value, Professor Amud?

AMUD: The missing manuscript was quite priceless in rarity… but its monetary value was slight indeed because any attempt to resell it would bring immediate arrest.

MARGOT: What was in the manuscript, Professor?

AMUD: I must confess that I do not know. You see, it was one section of a single volume that the four of us were translating… each of us took one quarter of the work.

CRANSTON: The work deals with ancient Hindu culture, does it not?

AMUD: Yes.

CRANSTON: Would it by any chance contain any secrets… secrets of that civilization which could be of value to someone today?

AMUD: I fear that I am not at liberty to answer that question, Mr. Cranston… perhaps… perhaps Professor Hagen might be of greater service to you… He is our superior, you know.

CRANSTON: Where is the professor?

AMUD: He's working in the laboratory upstairs… I shall be most willing to go up and get him for you…

CRANSTON: But can't you—

AMUD: (INTERRUPTING) I shall return in a moment with Professor Hagen… you will excuse me… Miss Lane… Mr. Cranston… thank you…

(FOOTSTEPS… DOOR OPENS AND CLOSES)

MARGOT: Well, our Hindu friend didn't appear to be too willing to talk…

CRANSTON: No… I believe that he knows much more than he cared to tell.

MARGOT: Lamont, I wonder if—

(PHONE RINGS)

MARGOT: Should we answer it?

CRANSTON: Well, I…

(PHONE RINGS AGAIN)

CRANSTON: I suppose I'd better…

(RECEIVER OFF HOOK)

CRANSTON: Hello?

VOICE: (ON FILTER) To whom am I speaking?

CRANSTON: This is Lamont Cranston….

VOICE: Oh… then I can leave my message with you.

CRANSTON: What is it?

VOICE: Of the three men who once were four… one more is about to die!

CRANSTON: (ALARMED) Who is this? Who is speaking?

VOICE:	(LAUGHS) The Shadow!
	(RECEIVER CLICKS… JIGGLING OF HOOK ON MIKE)
CRANSTON:	The Shadow!!! Hello! Hello! Hello!
MARGOT:	What's the matter, Lamont?
CRANSTON:	That person on the phone called himself… The Shadow!
MARGOT:	Then there is an impersonator!
CRANSTON:	Yes!
	(DOOR OPENS)
CARTER:	Sorry to be so long, I—
CRANSTON:	Professor Carter… someone just called on the phone..he said that one of you three professors is about to die!
CARTER:	What?!
CRANSTON:	It might be a crank, but we can't take any chances!
CARTER:	Where are the others?
CRANSTON:	Upstairs in the laboratory… you'd better take us up there at once!
CARTER:	Yes! Yes! Follow me!
	(RUNNING FOOTSTEPS)
CARTER:	Up these stairs!
	(FOOTSTEPS)
	(MIDWAY UP STAIRS WE HEAR A MAN SCREAM…)
CRANSTON:	There's trouble up there… hurry, Carter!
CARTER:	That sounded like Amud's voice! Right in here!
	(DOOR OPENS…)
CRANSTON:	What's wrong in—ehhhh…
MARGOT:	(SMALL SCREAM)
CRANSTON:	You'd better stay out of here, Margot… it's not a pleasant sight.
CARTER:	Amud… what happened? What happened to Professor Hagen?
AMUD:	I found him so… on the floor… dying…
CRANSTON:	Was he still alive when you got here?
AMUD:	Yes… barely alive…
CRANSTON:	Could he talk to you? Did you learn anything?
AMUD:	Yes… yes… he told me that his attacker was an invisible man who called himself… The Shadow!
	(MUSIC)
CRANSTON:	Well, Margot… we now have definite proof that someone is impersonating The Shadow!
MARGOT:	Yes..what can you do about it?
CRANSTON:	(ANGRILY) Don't worry, Margot… I have always used the power of The Shadow to aid the forces of law and order… to help good conquer evil…
MARGOT:	Yes, I know…
CRANSTON:	And now that someone else has discovered my secret of invisibility, and is misusing this power, I shall travel to the ends of the earth to conquer him! This, Margot, is The Shadow's greatest challenge, but I'm sure that I can meet it and come out… on top!
	(MUSIC) (MIDDLE COMMERCIAL)
MARGOT:	Lamont, have you uncovered any clues… any leads as to the identity of the person who is masquerading as The Shadow?

CRANSTON: Nothing important... no... But in the past twelve hours I have received two mysterious, unsigned messages...

MARGOT: What about?

CRANSTON: I'll read you one of them... it says, "Why don't you inquire into the jealousy of the four who now are two?"

MARGOT: Does that refer to the four professors?

CRANSTON: Yes... and I learned that it's quite true. A great jealousy existed. All four men, although they worked together, were constantly vying with one another for individual glory.

MARGOT: Then that's why the original manuscript was divided among the four of them.

CRANSTON: Yes...

MARGOT: You mentioned that you received two messages, Lamont... What was the other one?

CRANSTON: I have it here... listen to this... "What were the secrets to be found in the manuscript that was being translated by the four who now are two?

MARGOT: And did you learn the answer to that question?

CRANSTON: Not very satisfactorily... I can only guess that these secrets were of an occult nature... secrets of the ancient Orient.

MARGOT: I see...

CRANSTON: And it was in the Orient, Margot, that The Shadow learned his secret of invisibility.

MARGOT: Yes, of course... Lamont, who could have sent those messages?

CRANSTON: I don't know his identity, but judging by the phrases he used, they were written by the same man that I spoke to on the telephone... the man who called himself The Shadow.

MARGOT: But why should he be helping you?

CRANSTON: I wish I knew...in any case, Margot... his messages bear further investigation... so I think I shall begin by paying a call on Professors Carter and Amud as... The Shadow!

(MUSIC)

AMUD: Do you by any chance have a feeling of uneasiness, my dear Professor Carter?

CARTER: How do you mean?

AMUD: We still have in our trusted possession the remaining parts of the manuscript... that would make us, shall I say, logical victims...

CARTER: Then you believe, Professor Amud, that we too are marked for death?

AMUD: That was not my statement... I merely point to the past as a warning of the future.

CARTER: Well, that's a pleasant picture... if you don't mind, Professor, I'd rather not hear any more of you prophecies tonight...

SHADOW: (LAUGHS)

CARTER: What was that?

SHADOW: You'll pardon my intrusion, gentlemen...

AMUD: Who speaks... I see no one...

SHADOW: Allow me to introduce myself... I am called... The Shadow!

CARTER: The Shadow! He's come! He's here to—

SHADOW: Now, now, don't be alarmed, Professor Carter... I shan't harm you... I have merely come here seeking information...

Everett Sloane voiced Amud in "The Shadow Challenged."

AMUD: It is true… it is true… just as we have heard… you are invisible, Mr. Shadow…

SHADOW: Yes…

AMUD: How do you achieve this invisibility?

SHADOW: By hypnotizing your minds, gentlemen…

CARTER: Are you here to kill us as you did the others?

SHADOW: I did not kill the others, Professor Carter… that was done by an imposter who used my name… and you both can help me trap this murdering masquerader.

AMUD: Help you? How?

SHADOW: By telling me what I wish to know… by answering my questions.

CARTER: What… what are your questions?

SHADOW: What precious secrets were contained in the manuscripts that were stolen?

AMUD: Secrets? I do not understand…

SHADOW: No evasions, please, Professor Amud… you are both working on sections of that book… what is it about? What mysteries of the ancient Orient does it reveal?

AMUD: I am afraid you have been misinformed, my dear Shadow… hasn't he, Professor Carter?

CARTER: Yes… yes… there are no secrets…

SHADOW: You're lying, both of you!

AMUD: Lying?

SHADOW: Yes… and your lies are most incriminating… you see, gentlemen, I happen to know the circumstances surrounding the death of Professor Hagen… and based on these circumstances, either of you could have been his murderer!

CARTER: That's not true!

AMUD: You don't know what you're saying, Shadow.

SHADOW: Ah… but I do… so let me warn you, gentlemen… you are both under suspicion… and every move you make will be watched closely… very closely by… The Shadow!

(MUSIC)

MARGOT: Did you learn anything from Amud or Carter, Lamont?

CRANSTON: Nothing definite… they wouldn't talk… either one of them…

MARGOT: Well, what's to be done now?

CRANSTON: I'm not sure… I think that I'll—

(PHONE RINGS.)

CRANSTON: I'll take it…

(RECEIVER UP)

CRANSTON: Hello?

VOICE: Is this Lamont Cranston?

CRANSTON: Yes…

VOICE: I just want to tell you that of the four who now are two… one more is about to go…

CRANSTON: Who is this?

VOICE: You know who this is, Mr. Cranston… I am… The Shadow. (LAUGH)

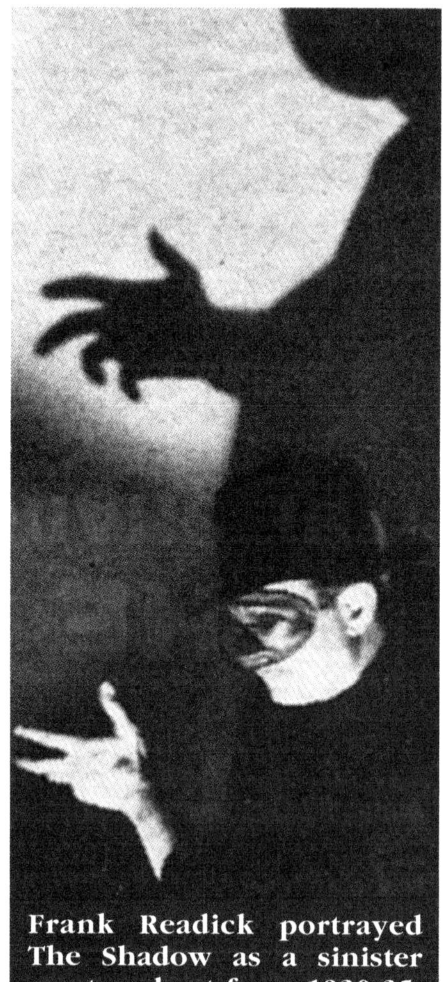

Frank Readick portrayed The Shadow as a sinister mystery host from 1930-35, and returned to the series as an evil doppelganger in "The Shadow Challenged."

(RECEIVER ON FILTER CLICKS...)

CRANSTON: Hello... hello...!!

MARGOT: Lamont... was that the imposter?

CRANSTON: Yes. He's delivered another warning...

MARGOT: What is it?

CRANSTON: Another one of the professors is marked for death!

MARGOT: Which one?

CRANSTON: He didn't say... we must warn them both at once!!! Come on, Margot... Carter lives right down the street... we'll go to his place... if he's all right, we'll call Amud from there... but come quickly... we must hurry!

(MUSIC)

(POUNDING ON DOOR...)

CRANSTON: (CALLING OUT) Professor Carter! Professor Carter!

MARGOT: Lamont, do you suppose something has happened to him already?

CRANSTON: We'll soon find out... I'll use this skeleton key...

(KEY IN LOCK...)

CRANSTON: I hate to do this, but...

(DOOR OPENS...)

CRANSTON: (CALLING OUT) Professor Carter...

MARGOT: Lamont! Look! The living room! There's been a fight!

CRANSTON: Yes... furniture overturned... lamps broken...

MARGOT: But where is Carter?

CRANSTON: I'll look in the bedroom... (FADING) Carter... Carter... are you in there?

MARGOT: Any sign of him, Lamont?

CRANSTON: (OFF MIKE) No... and this is the only other room in the apartment...

MARGOT: What could have happened to him?

CRANSTON: (FADING IN) I don't know... it's quite obvious though that he was the one selected as the next victim...

MARGOT: This whole thing becomes more baffling every minute...

CRANSTON: Quite the contrary, Margot... I think it becomes increasingly clear...

MARGOT: What do you mean, Lamont?

CRANSTON: Before we came here, Margot, I was practically convinced that either Carter or Amud was the one who murdered Hagen and Rice.

MARGOT: Lamont! Are you serious?

CRANSTON: Yes, Margot... I felt that one of them had learned something from their share of the manuscript that made them kill to obtain the other men's copies...

MARGOT: I see... But how was The Shadow impersonated?

CRANSTON: That fits into it too, Margot, very neatly... I learned the secret of invisibility in the Orient... it came from an ancient source... and one of those men could have learned this secret form his manuscript...

MARGOT: Yes... yes... that's very logical... but now that Carter is missing...

CRANSTON: That leaves only Amud... and I think we should pay a call on that gentleman at once!

(MUSIC... HOLD TO B.G.)

CRANSTON: We'd like to see Professor Amud, please...

MAN: I'm sorry, sir... he's not in his apartment...

CRANSTON: When do you expect him?

MAN: Not for some time, sir... he's been called out of town unexpectedly...

CRANSTON: When did he leave?

MAN: A short time ago...

CRANSTON: Did he say where he was going?

MAN: No, sir... he just said he'd be gone for an indefinite period.

(MUSIC UP AND OUT)

(FOOTSTEPS WALKING DOWN HALL)

MARGOT: I guess that just proves Amud's guilt, doesn't it, Lamont?

CRANSTON: I don't know, Margot... I've been reviewing the entire case in my mind, and several new factors have occurred to me...

MARGOT: What are they?

CRANSTON: Well, let's wait till we get into the apartment... we'll talk about it over a cup of tea...

(KEY IN LOCK... DOOR OPENS)

CRANSTON: Won't you go in, Margot?

MARGOT: Thank you—Lamont! There seems to be a note here right under the door...

CRANSTON: A note? Let me have it...

MARGOT: Here...

(RATTLE OF PAPER)

CRANSTON: Well... listen to this, Margot... (READING) Tonight at the hour of midnight, in the storage room in the basement of the museum, the one whom you seek can be found.

MARGOT: Does that mean the person who is masquerading as The Shadow?

CRANSTON: I think it does... what time is it, Margot?

MARGOT: Let's see....about twenty of twelve...

CRANSTON: Well, if I don't want to keep our friend waiting... I'd better be getting over to the museum...

MARGOT: Lamont, suppose this is a trap of the killers... a scheme to do away with you as he did the others...

CRANSTON: I'll chance that, Margot, but I want you to get word to Commissioner Weston... have him at the museum with his men at twelve-fifteen... tell him that there he will find the murderer who has pretended to be...The Shadow!

(MUSIC)

(FOOTSTEPS....ECHO CHAMBER EFFECT)

CRANSTON: (CALLING OUT) Is there anyone here?!

VOICE: (ON FILTER) (LAUGHS)

CRANSTON: Who is it?

VOICE: Don't let me frighten you, Mr. Cranston... I am your old friend... The Shadow.

CRANSTON: You are *not* The Shadow!

VOICE: No? How would you know that? Answer me!

CRANSTON: I repeat, you are *not* The Shadow!

VOICE: I see... and would your knowledge be based on the fact that you yourself are The Shadow... would it, Mr. Cranston? (NO ANSWER) You don't have to answer... I know... I have known for sometime now... you *are* The Shadow.

CRANSTON: What makes you think so?

VOICE: I have followed the activities of The Shadow for many years... I was most curious to learn his real identity... I began keeping track of the people who were present before and after all of his appearances...

CRANSTON: And after discarding many suspects, your search narrowed down to me, is that it?

VOICE: Exactly...

CRANSTON: Well, I must compliment you on your cleverness... I admit to you...I am The Shadow.

VOICE: Ah, but a very powerless Shadow at this point..Having learned your secret of invisibility, I have hypnotized your mind before you were aware of me… this time, the real Shadow is visible… and I am the one unseen.

CRANSTON: How did you learn my secret?

VOICE: From the ancient Hindu manuscript…

CRANSTON: Then you admit the murder of Professor Hagen and Professor Rice?

VOICE: Yes… yes… unfortunately they were in the way…

CRANSTON: Why did you commit these crimes in my name?

VOICE: Because I wanted to attract the attention of you… the real Shadow… and I succeeded! I led you on, Lamont Cranston, with my phone calls and anonymous notes..

CRANSTON: Why? What was your purpose?

VOICE: My purpose was and is to put an end to your activities. After tonight, Mr. Cranston, I alone will be the Shadow… and I shall capitalize on this power. You were a fool!

CRANSTON: Why do you say that?

VOICE: Always working for the powers of good… I shall take real advantage of the name… with the trick of invisibility the world will be mine!

CRANSTON: I gather that I am to be the next victim in your chain of murders…

VOICE: To put it bluntly… yes.

CRANSTON: I should think that you would make sure of your talents for invisibility before you attempted that…

VOICE: What do you mean?

CRANSTON: Unlike your other victims, my mind is not receptive to your hypnosis…

VOICE: What are you saying?

CRANSTON: I mean that you have been perfectly visible to me ever since you entered the room… Professor Carter!

VOICE: You… you see me?!!!

CRANSTON: Most clearly… and now, if you will observe closely, I shall instruct you in the true art of hypnosis… look at me, Professor Carter… look at me!!!

VOICE: No….no!

CRANSTON: I am disappearing before your very eyes… you see… YOU SEE!

VOICE: (VOICE CHANGES TO NORMAL MIKE SETTING) Wait… wait… you can't do this… you are destroying my power… do you hear… you're clouding my mind. Cranston!

SHADOW: (VOICE CHANGES TO FILTER SETTING) I am no longer Cranston, Professor Carter… I am… *The Shadow*…

(LAUGHS)

VOICE: You think you've tricked me, don't you… you think you've gained the upper hand… but you're wrong…you're wrong!

SHADOW: That revolver won't be of much use… how will you ever find your target?

VOICE: (CRAZED WITH ANGER) I'll find you… I'll find you!

(SEVERAL SHOTS)

SHADOW: (LAUGHS) Try again, Carter…

Bill Johnstone as The Shadow

(SEVERAL MORE SHOTS..POUNDING ON DOOR)

WESTON: (OFF MIKE) Open up in there!!!

SHADOW: I believe that is the police, Carter… you'd better put down that gun!

CARTER: Let them come and get me… and they'd better come shooting!

SHADOW: (CALLING OUT) You'll have to break open the door, Commissioner… and beware, this man in here is armed!

(CRACKING OF DOOR UNDER POUNDING)

CARTER: Keep out of here… I'm warning you… keep out!
(DOOR BREAKS OPEN…VOLLEY OF SHOTS)

CARTER: (GROANS…)

SHADOW: He's been hit, Commissioner, come ahead…

WESTON: Shadow! So you're here too!

SHADOW: I came here to apprehend that man on the floor… he is the one who used my name in killing Hagen and Rice…

WESTON: What… what are you saying?

SHADOW: Look…he's still conscious… ask him… ask him…

WESTON: All right… I'll—why it's Professor Carter!

SHADOW: Yes… he was my impersonator…

WESTON: Carter?... Professor Carter… is this true?

CARTER: (WEAKLY) Yes… yes… it's true…

WESTON: How did you make yourself invisible…

CARTER: I learned the secret… from the manuscript which I've destroyed… (GROANS)

WESTON: Carter... Carter… listen to me… you must know the identity of the real Shadow… don't you?

CARTER: Yes…

WESTON: Who is he? Tell me?!!!

CARTER: The…the real Shadow is… is… (GROANS) (DIES)

SHADOW: (AFTER PAUSE) You'll never learn now, Commissioner… but I think you should know this… in the future you must always believe one thing about me… The Shadow at all times will be working on the side of right… and justice…

(MUSIC… CURTAIN)

(STANDARD CLOSING)

ANNR: Today's program is based on a story copyrighted by *The Shadow Magazine.* The characters, names, places and plot are fictitious. Any similarity to persons living or dead is purely coincidental.

(MUSIC: "GLOOMS OF FATE" UP AND UNDER)

SHADOW: (LAUGH) The weed of crime bears bitter fruit. Crime does *not* pay. The SHADOW knows. (LAUGH)

(MUSIC UP… SEGUE BRIGHT)

ANNR: Next week… same time… same station... the 'blue coal' dealers of America bring you an adventure of The Shadow that will amaze you with its breath-taking thrills. So be sure to listen. And be sure to phone your friendly 'blue coal' dealer for *greater* heating comfort at *less* cost. This is Jean Paul King saying… "keep the home fires burning with '*blue coal*'."

(MUSIC UP…) •